D1559212

THE PIPER'S SONG

The Piper's Song

SESYLE JOSLIN

Harcourt Brace Jovanovich, *Publishers*

San Diego　　　*New York*　　　*London*

Requests for permission to make copies of any part of the work
should be mailed to: Permissions, Harcourt Brace Jovanovich,
Publishers, Orlando, Florida 32887

Library of Congress Cataloging-in-Publication Data

Joslin, Sesyle.
  The piper's song.

  I. Title.
PS3560.0816P5   1986   813'.54   86-9846
ISBN 0-15-171977-2

Designed by Jackie Schuman

Printed in the United States of America

First edition

B C D E

For Phoebe

"Good evening, I'm Sister Clotilde."

The nun in charge of the third floor at Villa Monte Sacre was waiting for us by the elevator.

"We've been expecting you." With a cordial smile she took in everything—the bloodied green robe of the emergency room nurse accompanying us, Simon's eyes shut smooth in their deep hollows and him so pale and still he might have been carved out of the white cot; me, hanging onto its spindly staff in a muskrat cape and Gina's dusting slippers.

"Mr. West is going into Room 305," Sister Clotilde told the orderly, and taking a chart from the nun in green, read it in a glance. Her serene expression unchanged, she passed it on with a whisper to a third nurse who had materialized by the potted palm.

She was a small rosy nun, that one, not much bigger than her medication cart. "*Bonsoir, madame,*" she said, sending me a little beam, and I was struck by the comforting thought that this demure hospital, this peaceful Roman hilltop so discreetly tended by a religious order from Normandy was as unreal as the accident that brought us there.

"If you'll come this way, please." Sister Clotilde now bent a kindly veil toward me. "Mr. West has a corner room," she said as we started down the hall. "They're not quite as large as the others, but they get more sunshine, and that's always so pleasant."

"Yes, isn't it," I replied, my eyes fixed on the wheels of Simon's cot. Despite the calm English the head nurse spoke and the quiet stir of her long skirts, our procession was rolling down the corridor at a surprising clip.

"Dr. Pagello has been notified, and I'm sure he'll be coming in soon."

I thanked her, aggrieved to hear that Simon and I were not yet to be left alone. By the time I thought to ask who Dr. Pagello was and where he was coming from, we had turned the corner and I glimpsed him, a short-legged man in a dinner jacket scuttling across the threshold of Room 305.

"Good, he's here already," Sister Clotilde said. "I'm sorry, we shall need some time, an hour, perhaps, to get Mr. West settled." Her gentle smile barred my way into the room. "There's a lounge for visitors down the hall and to the left. I think you'll be comfortable there."

Haughty with fear, I drew my musty cape around me. "I prefer to wait here."

"Of course, as you wish."

Yet once confronted with the blank look of that door I did go to the lounge, empty but for Our Lady of Lourdes standing holy and shy among a gift of gladiolus. I sat first in a soft, deep chair, left it for a plush couch, and sprang up from the latter just as quickly, my nerves rebelling against such comfort.

An hour, perhaps, Sister Clotilde had said, and confusing motion with time, I began to walk the halls of the ward. Corners filled with flowering plants, dim lights, patients tucked out of sight; even the television sets were turned down to an impassioned Italian whisper in this tactful, sweet-smelling hospital. At the end of one corridor I let myself out on a balcony high above the city, hoping, I suppose, for the reassuring glitter of a metropolitan night. But Rome had drawn in her exuberant breath and closed the shutters, and all I could see below me was a vast domed shadow, oriental, unfamiliar, and darker than the sky.

Twice I rushed back to Simon's room, certain I'd find the door open and him awake, watching for me, his eyes their most dazzling blue. "Tell me what happened, Anna. I bet I won't believe a word of it," he'd say, ready to be amused by tales of his own eccentricity. And twice, stealthy as an insomniac houseguest, I returned to my prowling, exchanging startled nods with the occasional nursing sister who passed by close to the wall, moving toward the light on a patient's door with the swift flutter of a great moth.

It occurred to me after a while that I should try to repair my face before Simon saw me, and I slipped into a room marked Patients Baths. I could imagine only too well how disheveled I must look.

That evening, when the doorbell had started its clamor, Gina had been shut away in the kitchen pounding the veal we were to have for dinner should it survive her assault. I was in my bedroom at the back of the apartment, getting dressed after a bath. Thinking it was Simon at the door, that he had forgotten his keys, I ran barefoot to let him in.

"*Buona sera, signora.*" The little *portiera* stood at the door with a face as black and crumpled as her dress and a tiny furtive claw still pressed on the bell that, clearly, I was answering.

"Are you crazy, ringing like that? Who is it?" Gina shouted, slamming out of the kitchen and marching into the hallway. "Oh, Francesca, it's you." She stopped short, her hand clasping one breast. "What is it? *O Dio.* What's the matter? What's happened?"

"It's Signor West," the *portiera* whimpered with a pitying glance at me. "Such an accident, Madonna, such a disaster." Distressed, thrilled, frightened, she rattled off her message not to me but to Gina. "The signore was hit by a car in Piazza del Popolo, only it wasn't just one car, it was two, maybe even three. Nobody's sure yet, but Pina, the fat redhead who sells flowers on the corner of Via Ripetta, says it was three at least."

I had gone shopping the day before with my friend Margot. "I want to buy something marvelous, something a bit mad," she said, but at her frivolous secondhand shop it was I who fell upon an old fur cape with a giddy lust. Simon, when I got home, summed up its charm in a teasing sniff. "A Beardsley look and a barnyard smell," he said.

Designated for the cleaners, the cape lay on a vestibule chair, and I flung it over my blouse and skirt, leaped into the felt slippers Gina had been polishing the floor with, fled down the marble stairs, across the courtyard, and into the evening crowd, racing the ambulance siren, flying to Simon through a storm so violent my hair, the very features of my face were blown awry.

Ah, well. It was, of course, no more than my wild breath and thundering heart, that raging storm. Yet, standing between two tubs in the Patients' Baths room, staring into the small chaste mirror placed high above them, I was astonished to find my reflection so intact. Black hair that fell to the shoulder in as straight and precise a line as ever, gray eyes gazing at me in their usual steady, sober way—and a mouth whose full lower lip Simon had caught between his teeth early that morning, had tasted, bitten, and sleepily pronounced ripe. I turned away from the mirror, dismayed by an image who yielded only this inscrutable intimacy, who refused to show even me what she was feeling.

Eventually I gained entrance to, and possession of, Simon's room. As I approached his hall on one of my many laps around the third floor, I saw Sister Clotilde flowing toward me in her white habit, smiling.

"I was coming to look for you. You may go into Mr. West's room now," she said, and mistaking her luminous grace for good news, I made a dash to Simon's bedside.

"Simon? It's me, darling," I said, taking his hand in mine. Those long elegant hands, they were like an extravagant but ill-chosen gift that didn't quite fit his sturdy shape. "It's Anna, my love. Can you hear me?"

The reply came, softly, from Sister Clotilde who had followed me into the room. "He hasn't regained consciousness yet."

"Where is Dr. Pagello?"

"He's gone, my child. It's late."

"What did he say? When will he be back?"

She was compassionately precise. "Tomorrow morning at eight-thirty. He's left an order for further X-rays, and these we'll do as soon as Sister Martha, our radiologist, comes on duty at six-thirty."

"Thank you, Sister." I dared not ask more questions lest there be answers for those, too.

"You must try not to worry," she said. "We're doing everything that we can."

I made no reply, despising the rude construction of bottles and tubes that entrapped Simon as much as the accident responsible for it. Were my thoughts so audible? Apparently they were to Sister Clotilde who attempted to lead them elsewhere.

"This door belongs to the closet, quite small. Over there is the bathroom, larger, of course. It surprises us how many patients would wish these dimensions reversed."

She paused, glancing at the window with an expectant smile, and I heard then the ringing of a carillon.

"The ten o'clock bells. Our convent is just this side of the hospital. But you'll see for yourself when you come back tomorrow."

"I wasn't planning to leave."

"Wouldn't it be better for you to go home and rest?"

"I'd rather stay, at least until Mr. West has come round."

Sister Clotilde's look was as warm and direct as her voice. "We have no way of telling when he might regain consciousness, my child. Dr. Pagello is an excellent neurologist; that we know. For the rest we must have patience and faith."

I turned abruptly from the direction of the conversation and went to hang the muskrat cape in the closet, thinking how strange it was to be called my child by this nun who could be no more than thirty, my own age, if that.

"However, it is as you wish. I'll be glad to ring the sixth floor for you. We have a few rooms there which we try to keep free for family."

But that wasn't quite my wish, and anticipating a bureaucratic skirmish, perhaps with an entire religious community, I took up a staunch position on the far side of Simon's bed.

"I'll stay here with Mr. West, thanks," I said, and suddenly recollected a childhood self standing just as fierce and frightened by my younger brother's bed in a small hotel in North Africa, waiting for the manager to complain about the noise. We were wandering somewhere along the Sahara at that time, and our mother had gone out to hire camels for the next morning's expedition. "Look at them, children, look," Lisi had cried, wild-eyed with pleasure at the sight of those gangling creatures swaying across the pink horizon; far more excited than her children who, had the shameful truth been known, still yearned for a wooden horse whose trail was the lavender-scented back hall of a Central Park West apartment in New York City.

"I will see if it can be arranged," Sister Clotilde was saying. "But now, do you mind going to Sister Bernadette's office on the main floor? There are still the admitting papers to sign. It won't take long," she added in reply to my thoughts, "and I myself will be with Mr. West."

Arms folded across her habit, hands hidden from sight, she escorted me down the hall. "Is there anything you'd like first? A cup of camomile or some hot milk? No? You're quite sure? Well, perhaps later, then." And this tall, slender white nun, with the gentle nod of a spring lily, left me at the elevator.

Sister Clotilde's pale beauty, a pink candy box at the nurses' station, the gold fixtures on a marble water fountain—was there anything my attention did not fasten itself to that night? I looked hard at each detail, seeking reality everywhere but in the bandage wrapped around Simon's head, in his tranquil face.

I could trace even now the fluid limbs of the bronze crucifix hanging above his bed. I recall the undulating grain of the desk in the admitting office, and I still see Sister Bernadette in her dark blue habit, raising benevolent plump palms to reverse the tidal flow of my information.

"I'm Mr. West's closest kin, yes, certainly. In a manner of speaking," I told her. "No, I'm not Mrs. West. There is no Mrs. West. Well, there is Mrs. West, his mother, but she lives in England with Mr. West. The other Mr. West, his father.

My name is Anna Stewart, and officially the address is mine. That is, it's my apartment, although it's his address as well. I mean to say, Sister, that we live there together. We have been for nearly two years. Mr. West is a British citizen, of course, and as a concert pianist he does a certain amount of traveling, but for the most part, he's been living in Italy with me, at this address, composing—"

Sister Bernadette, a hooded owl with a ruffled forehead and beaky nose, blinked at the flapping of my tongue. "If you'll just put your signature on these, Miss Stewart," she murmured, sliding more triplicate forms across the desk to me.

"So many, Sister?" I felt I'd already been sitting hours on the edge of that austere chair.

"Italian officials have a curious fondness for stamping documents," she said, the smile of a religious quivering with the impatience of a weary administrator. "Now, here is another for the *polizia* and one more for the *questura*, and this pink one which is for our own files, and so it is done."

We bid each other good night then, Sister Bernadette's inflection no less relieved than mine, and I hurried down the hall to the elevator, rushing as though to catch its last flight, so intent that I didn't see Alex waiting for me.

"Anna." He came forward with his arms outstretched, and I was just surprised enough to fall gratefully into them, to rest my head against that well-tailored shoulder and breathe in the oddly androgynous smell of bitter cigars and a too-fragrant cologne. It was blessedly familiar, and for a moment I allowed myself to be comforted by this tall man whose thin aristocratic face was pulled long with concern, this silver-haired friend whom I had long ago secretly adopted as my father.

"Dearest girl. How is he? Lord, what a terrible thing."

Caught off-guard, held in silence, I could accept his comfort, but the moment Alex spoke I released myself from his embrace. "It could have been worse," I said. "He could have hurt his hands. How did you find out? Gina?"

"Yes, of course, Gina." There was a faint rebuke in his voice.

"Well, I hope she hasn't called my mother."

"Not tell Lisi? But she's very fond of the boy." Another puzzled rebuke.

"Simon's going to be all right. There's no need to alarm everybody. I suppose Sofia knows, too?"

"Yes, and she says you shouldn't be alone tonight. I quite agree, so I've come to fetch you. I'll just look in on Simon for a moment."

"Oh, not now," I said quickly. "They'll never let you. It's too late."

To prove my point Sister Bernadette came out of her office, locked the door, and turned around to stare at my visitor. I hung back from her obvious dismay, but Alex, with his youthful, long-legged stride reached her side before she had finished that owlish blinking of hers.

"Good evening, Sister. I must apologize for loitering in your halls at this hour. The fact is, you have in your care a dear friend of mine. Indeed, you have two," he said with a fond nod at me. "Cherished colleagues, both of them. But again I beg your pardon. I'm Alexander Sareuth." This explanation was followed by a courtly bow and a compliment to Normandy's Sisters of the Divine Grace delivered in their own colloquial French; a perfect example of the urbane simplicity with which Alex soothed his actors and beguiled investors. Nor was the nun any less immune than they to his silvery charm.

"There, you see, it's quite all right," Alex said when she left. "The good sister has given me permission to go upstairs." How well I knew his slightly flushed expression, that complex look of triumph, coquettish vanity, and a thoroughly disarming self-mockery. "Come along, then."

But my consent was harder to get than Sister Bernadette's. "No." I snatched my hand away from his. "You can't see him, not tonight." It was an involuntary cry that startled us both.

"Poor Anna," he said. "It's been a dreadful shock. Such a

bizarre accident, so inexplicable. Come, let's sit down for a moment."

I resented the pity in his voice; resented having to sit down again, but I followed him, obedient and conciliatory, to the couch at the end of the hall. "Perhaps you and Sofia will come tomorrow when Simon's more himself."

He searched my face, much as I had done in the Patients' Baths mirror. "What exactly did the doctor say?"

"Nobody could believe the condition of Simon's hands in the emergency room. They're perfect, not even a scratch. I think he must have flung his arms up to protect them. Perhaps that's why he fell so hard." But this was hardly an answer, and to the wrong question, at that.

"I meant Dr. Pagello. What did he say about the head injuries?"

So Alex had called in the specialist. I should have recognized that well-organized solicitude. "Thanks, darling. It was good of you to arrange things so fast. Simon's nurse says he's an excellent man."

"I hear he's even better than his reputation," Alex said, smiling. It was his only concession to age, those folds of sun-wrinkled skin around his green eyes and the two deep creases that came with his smile. "Well? What does he think?"

"I don't know what Dr. Pagello thinks yet."

I got up from the couch, barely able to restrain myself from running, from flying back to Simon. Aware of this, and a good deal more, Alex, too, got quickly to his feet. Nor did he invoke Sofia's certain protestation on hearing that I was staying at the hospital, but with a kiss on my cheek he bid me a silent good night.

Dear Alex. I let him go away with his brow still creased in baffled lines over Simon's accident. And yet there was no mystery. I could have told him, had he asked, how sorrowfully simple the explanation was. Simon had followed the pipers; he had listened to the music of those woolly, leather-clad shepherds, to the strange tunes of their wooden flutes and sheepskin bagpipes, and followed them right into a herd of Fiats.

It was nearly Christmastime, yet December was as mellow and sweet as any other Roman month. Or, so it seemed, for the reds and oranges of the old palaces contrived to give the city a glow in the winter rain, a look of veiled sunshine. There was a smell of the countryside in our ancient neighborhood, of roasting chestnuts and spicy young firs. Hay filled the nativity corner of the Spanish Steps, and Piazza Navona was enclosed in the warm gaudy scent of fresh candy canes and *torrone*.

But what really heralded the holiday season were the shepherds who, following a tradition centuries old, climbed down from the Abruzzi mountains to serenade the Madonna of roadside shrines. In pairs they wandered through Rome, the *zampognaro* with his bagpipe on one side of the street, the *pifferaro* playing a flute on the other, their plaintive notes joining in the air high above the crowds.

How Simon loved these primitive musicians. He took pleasure in every provincial detail—the thick slabs of leather they wore as sandals, the thongs that trussed their heavy woollen stockings to the knee, the rough sheepskin vests and hats. But most of all he was enthralled by the music of their crude instruments.

"Will you look at that bagpipe, Anna," he'd say, stopping abruptly on the sidewalk. "Why, it's nothing more than a bloody tire. Damn, he's turning the corner. Well, let's go along for a bit, shall we? Really it's quite remarkable, that marvelous tune being squeezed out of a bulbous old inner tube." Or "Come listen to the pipers, Anna," he'd cry, flinging open the shutters and hanging out the window to throw coins down into the street. "Hardly matters whether they're playing a lovely pastoral piece or some banal Christmas carol, it's all got the sound of Mesopotamia to it."

Only a few hours before the accident I'd been sitting at my

desk, enjoying a perverse security in its disorder, in the scattered papers and cheap lined notebooks with which I hoped to construct a new novel.

But the security I enjoyed was, of course, based on more than disorder. As I worked I could hear Simon at the piano, not through the *palazzo*'s thick walls but out of his window and into mine. Carried on the sharp updraft of espresso, along with the street noises came fragments of his concerto, outbursts of an almost savage buoyancy followed by passages as exotic and melancholy as love.

At about five o'clock Simon himself came into my room. His eyes were a dreamy blue, and there was a tender expression on his face, which love, in fact, never inspired, only work.

"Hullo," he said with a vague smile, as though he could no longer recall what had brought him there.

I got up from the desk and went to him, with open arms, anxious to remind him, but at that moment the sound of bagpipe and flute rose from the alleyway below my studio.

"Listen, the shepherds," Simon said. "Do you know, I think I could use some fresh air. Perhaps I'll take a walk, a preprandial stroll, as my old man says."

He returned my embrace like a hasty, well-mannered child. "I won't be long," he said, and off he went to find the pipers, trailing after them to Piazza del Popolo. His head turned absently in the direction of their mournful pagan notes, he started across the square and, startled, bewildered by the sudden cacophony of horns and shouts, fell beneath the wheels of the evening traffic.

"What an extraordinary thing to do," my mother said. "Yet it's so like Simon, isn't it? Poetic . . . untamed. Oh, I can understand it perfectly."

There was a telephone booth in the lobby of the hospital, and after Alex left I had rushed to call my mother in Switzerland. But I was too late. Her cousin Sofia, as I feared, had already got through, and Lisi was in a state of valiant alarm. She had packed her bag, she told me, and reserved a seat on the morning plane to Rome.

"Honestly, there's no reason for you to come. Simon's going to be all right. It's nothing, really. He was knocked down, an unfortunate accident, but he'll be fine." Speaking fast and recklessly, I went on until I had persuaded Lisi to cancel her trip.

"If it's what you want, dear. But are you quite sure? Sofia told me—"

I interrupted that report with another quick "Everything's going to be just fine."

"I'm sure of it," my mother replied stoutly, her confusion as audible as the humming on the line that connected us. "But, Annie dearest, Sofia said he was hit by *several* cars."

"Only Fiats. You know how small they are."

The sharp intake of her breath sounded clearly in my ear. "On second thought, I will catch that plane. Try to stay calm, darling. I'll be there very soon."

So I had to start my reassurances all over again. I was nothing if not calm, I said. "And Alex has already taken charge. He arranged for a neurologist to come in and see Simon, a Dr. Pagello."

"Dr. Pagello?" Lisi said. "That was the name of George Sand's lover. You remember, the doctor who took care of poor Musset when they were living together in Venice. I told you children the story years ago, once when we were in Piazza San Marco because that's where George Sand and Dr. Pagello used to meet."

I didn't remember, but I had no doubt she'd told us. There was precious little nineteenth-century gossip my brothers and I hadn't been privy to under her zestful tutelage. "Well, don't worry. I'm sure it's not the same man."

Lisi gave a startled giggle at this. Such a youthful sound in contrast to my lugubrious humor. But I had tricked her into it, and in the next solemn breath she asked for the neurologist's report.

"We haven't actually spoken yet," I admitted, "but I know he's going to say it's nothing serious. He'll probably recommend bed rest, that's all."

I then reminded Lisi that Villa Monte Sacre was one of the best hospitals in Rome and, before ringing off, cited Sister Clotilde as an example of its excellence. "She seems very knowledgeable, and so kind, too."

Well, that much was certainly true.

"The orderly has brought in another bed. As you see, only a small one would fit this space. I hope it will be comfortable enough," Sister Clotilde said when finally I got back to Simon's room.

"Dr. Alborghetti is the physician on duty tonight. He'll be looking in on Mr. West later. And I, also."

I thanked her for all she had done, but I was astonished to see Simon still so white, so immobile, and when she had gone I pushed my bed close to his, determined to rouse him myself.

"Darling," I called, "Sweetheart," and leaving my bed to get on his, I demanded that he listen, begged him to. "Simon," I hissed into his ear. I gave his lobe a vicious nip to restore its color, bit his neck, and when he failed to respond I threw my arms around him in a severe embrace. I was beginning to find this a profane and selfish sleep.

"It's time to change the dressings." Sister Clotilde and the beamish little nun with the medication cart surprised me during one of my loving attacks on Simon, and though they lowered their eyes and pretended not to have seen, I kept a warier vigil after that.

Back on my own bed, lying straight and stiff as Simon himself, I sorted out the events, the phrases with which I would regale him once the interminable night was over. What an extraordinary thing to do, Lisi had said, and I heard again the husky catch of comprehension in her voice when she added that she understood it perfectly.

And with good reason, for who knew more about following pipers than my mother? Had she lived in Victorian times she'd have marched in the idiosyncratic ranks of those ladies who tucked up their skirts to climb the Himalayas or collect native weapons in the Masai country, those romantic travelers who set off with equal aplomb for Zenobia's kingdom or a Turkish harem.

As it was, Lisi had to make do with leaving our father, perplexed but unprotesting, we were told, in New York and taking her three small children to Kiev, the city from which our grandmother had once similarly removed her. But that was only the first brief stop, the beginning of our nomadic life. Lisi's curiosity took us far beyond her Russian birthplace.

"Poor Matthew," she said of our father. "He just didn't have the makings of a vagabond." Matthew had, in fact, proven himself to be as immovable as the mountains with which she tried to tempt him. I recall my mother, more evangelist than temptress, sitting on the window seat in the huge apartment that overlooked Central Park, everything about her—tawny mane of hair, wide hazel eyes—reflecting the Sunday afternoon sunlight.

"Come sit beside me, children," she said to my brother Augustus and me while David, then a baby, slept in the nursery. "The book I'm going to read to you was written by a woman named Mary Kingsley, who wanted more than anything else to go to West Africa and 'lark about'. Are you ready?" This question, as indeed the whole performance, was addressed not to us but to our father who sat deep in his leather chair in a cloud of cigarette smoke that never seemed to lift. "Now listen. 'It was no desire to get killed and eaten that made me go and associate with the tribes with the worst reputation for cannibalism and human sacrifice, but just because such tribes were the best for me to study from what they meant by doing such things.'

"Did you hear that, Matthew?"

And my father, glancing up from his Sunday New York Times, nodded. "Interesting syntax."

Matthew was the managing editor of his father's publishing company, a ruminant man who took his work seriously and tended to keep pieces of it with him at all times, on the breakfast table, by the bed, stuffed in the pockets of his jacket. So Lisi would describe him to us, never failing to add that he was attractive, kind, and generous. As near as we could make out, the only vice our father had was a singular propensity for sitting. But even this Lisi did not blame on him so much as his profound attachment to the apartment he was born in, and which his parents gave him as a wedding gift.

After eight years of marriage spent on Central Park West, Lisi began to fear that Matthew's morbid disinclination to travel might stifle our intellectual growth, was certain it would her own, and so she went to work as an interpreter at the United Nations and began to save for our trip. I've no doubt Matthew would have sponsored her initial desire to return to Kiev; there was, after all, considerable wealth in the Stewart family. But, as Lisi said, there was independence in hers, and she could allow our father no more than his equal share of their children's expenses.

It was, ultimately, the death of our great-aunt Luisa, for whom Lisi was named, and a modest inheritance that made our exodus possible. I had just turned six, Augustus was four, and David barely two when Lisi, smiling all the day long, set about packing us up. It was a cheerful departure altogether. Matthew made vague allusions to joining us, and Lisi said we'd be back soon, though they both must have known the folly of their exchange.

After a month in Russia we went to Afghanistan, following the same route Lisi had taken with her mother. Somewhere along the way we picked up an old green Volkswagen, a car small enough, Lisi said, to fit on any train or ferry. By these means, visiting places out of season, staying in the cheapest pensions, we began to roam in earnest, our mother absorbing whole countries with a generous excitement.

"Look, children, the Golden Horn!" And "Go on, I bet you'll love it," she'd say, pointing to the pungent meats and glutinous sweets displayed beneath the flies of a street stall. "It doesn't necessarily taste the way it looks, you know."

They were inexhaustible and indiscriminate, Lisi's pleasures, and so, at her insistence, were ours. "Lean back and listen," a happy whisper exhorted us in the velvet and crystal splendor of La Scala. Or, in Algiers, when I or one of my brothers had to relieve himself: "Put your feet where those footprints are and crouch down," she'd say, no less enthusiastic over a series of primitive cement holes.

With what zeal did she take us to Vatican City and Jerusalem's Wailing Wall; to tiled mosques and Buddha on his lotus throne. "Beautiful expressions of a spiritual need, all of them, but we must ask ourselves, children, why so many?"

And when we paused in our travels, our little *randonnées*, as she called them, say for lunch in the deserted garden of an ancient pink palace in Constantinople, our instruction continued. Lisi would unpack a book, and as we children lay around her in a sunny tangled patch of wild flowers, she'd read to us from *Childe Harold's Pilgrimage* or Cato or Mrs. Gaskell. We never knew what incomprehensible lesson waited for us in that straw basket along with the bread and oranges and cheese.

"But, dearest Lisi," Sofia used to say, "one day the children will grow up. What's going to happen to them in the real world?"

And our surprised, affronted mother would reply: "But the real world is exactly what I'm showing them."

Sofia. This cousin of ours, whom we first met in Paris, was not the least of the remarkable landscapes Lisi introduced us to. A stupendous beauty, she was nearly six feet tall, much of that distance covered by exquisite legs. Though by then nearing forty, she was very much in her prime, with full round breasts, a slyly happy Rubens face, and reddish-gold hair that fell to her waist and was as genuine, she told us, as everything else.

There was little that Sofia did not tell us. By the time she was fifteen, "already big and ripe," she had been ogled and patted by half the gentlemen in Paris and a disconcerting number of women. At seventeen she married an older man, a wealthy count who owned an entire village in the south of France. But none of that mattered, she said, when at the age of thirty she fell in love with Alex, a talented Hungarian director several years her junior. In a matter of days, without a backward glance, she left her husband for him.

I understood it well, even then. Though I was far too shy to let him know, I felt a strong affinity with the keen-eyed, soft-spoken man who would collect me and my brothers at school in his low red sports car and take us to Rumpelmayer's for a special treat. Lean and debonair, he seemed far more our noble relation than the dyspeptic old count who long after he'd forgotten Sofia's name went on refusing to give her a divorce.

Paris became our home for a time. Careful though Lisi was, the travel funds had begun to run out, and she decided to settle down for a while. It was a pleasant novelty at first. We took roost in a crooked Left Bank street that never lost its smell of fresh hot bread, in an apartment that befitted our vagrant flock, an immense studio with a row of beds along a high balcony. Our mother went to work for the United Nations again, and Augustus, David, and I were put in a proper school. This sojourn lasted an unprecedented two years; a period of normal life, as Sofia called it, that left us children as anxious to get back on the road as Lisi.

When I first showed Simon a family photograph, one taken the summer after we left Paris, he held it under the bedside lamp for a long time, studying it with an undisguised glee. "What a motley bunch," he said. "You look like a circus troupe."

Motley, there was no doubt. Leaning against Simon's bare

shoulder, against the warm freckled skin that gave off my own scent, I gazed at the chubby David in lederhosen, solemn Augustus wearing the striped jersey of a Breton fisherman, a ten-year-old Anna suddenly gone too tall and thin, sticking up like a broom handle from the folds of a Roumanian skirt, and our mother in some long white airy thing she'd picked up in a souk. Lisi, with her energetic bush of hair and that casual sunlit beauty, looking as though she'd blown in from the Near East. How closely and with what proud smiles did we gather around the young woman people mistook for our older sister.

Yet I've not forgotten those moments on a train or in a hotel restaurant when a typical family might capture our attention. There'd be a child or two in ordinary clothes and a plain mother who had sitting across from her a solid, a manifest father. Ah, it made us fairly itch with discomfort.

"Tell us about Matthew," one of us was sure to demand.

"Yes, what's he really like?"

And Lisi would, once again, distribute among us her small stock of replies.

"We've heard that a thousand times," I'd say irritably.

"Yes. Try to remember something else." That would be Augustus, while David frowned and said, "I'm the only one who doesn't know my father at all."

"But you shall. One day soon you'll see him again," Lisi promised. "Meanwhile, my dears, what about me? What do I know about my father? Except, of course, that he was a bear."

This ploy never ceased to work. "Tell us about Grandfather Bear," the cry now went, and with obvious relief Lisi would launch into an animated description of our grandmother's wedding night, spent in the company of a husband arranged for her, a large burly widower she hardly knew, named Ryzanova.

"Go on, Lisi," Augustus urged, while David obligingly stuffed his mouth with a dirty kerchief so that we'd be able to hear above his expectant giggles.

"Well, then, after the ceremony they went to a country inn for their honeymoon. And that night, after dinner, Mr. Ryzanova went into the bathroom to get ready for bed—"

"While Grandmother waited nervously—" Augustus prompted.

"Yes, she sat huddled beneath the big eiderdown with her eyes riveted to the bathroom door. Finally, it opened, and her bridegroom appeared. He was dressed only in his pajama bottoms, and his chest and arms were covered with the thickest, blackest hair my young mother had ever seen."

" 'Why, Mr. Ryzanova, you are a bear!' she cried, and ran from the room as fast as she could."

"And did he catch her?" David asked.

"*Imbécile,*" said Augustus, with a precocious leer. "How else do you think he got to be our grandfather?"

The boys never tired of this story, but after a time it caused me a vague apprehension and, as I grew older, began to cast a curiously hirsute shadow over my girlhood dreams.

"I've brought a cup of camomile to help you sleep," Sister Clotilde said. Putting her tray down on the table, she went to Simon's bed and straightened with a quick, light touch the sheet that had been disarranged by my hand, not his. Despite my promptings, he was no less pale, no less still, had not so much as moved an eyelash.

"It's only a few hours now until morning. Then we shall be able to do more," she said, as though I'd spoken aloud. "It would be a good thing if you rest until then."

"I don't seem to be tired."

"As we need strength God sends it to us, that's true." Her smile was no less serene for the late hour, her head still high on that long, firm neck.

"And you, Sister? You don't get tired, working all night?"

Her smile broadened, amused as a young girl's. "Yes, certainly I do. But when one is doing His work, it doesn't seem so tiring." She paused at the door. "I'm going off duty now, but I'll see you tomorrow. Sister Cecile is at the desk if you need anything."

"Thank you, Sister Clotilde," I said, pronouncing her name for the first time. "Good night."

She nodded, started to leave, and paused again. Was it only a religious afterthought that made her glance back? Perhaps, and yet it seemed to me there was something shy flickering in her brown eyes, something impulsive in her low voice as she turned around to say, "I will pray for Mr. West, for you both."

"I want my slippers back," Gina telephoned me to say. "The floors look terrible. They haven't been polished in over a week. What do you want me to do, signora, buff the tiles with my behind? You bring the slippers home today, or I'm coming to the hospital to get them."

"Maybe tomorrow," I countered. "We'll talk then. I have to go now." But she kept right on, yapping away with the ferocious demands of a loving terrier. "Gina, calm down," I said, while the nun behind the desk turned away to busy herself at a file.

"Calm? *Ma che cosa dici?* You haven't been home for a week, you won't let me come there, I don't know how the signore is, and you say be calm. What are you wearing? What do the sisters think when they see you in my dusting slippers and no nightgown?"

"Gina, I really can't discuss that now. You shouldn't have called me at the nurses' station. It's a bother for the sisters."

"You shouldn't have disconnected the telephone in your room, *signora mia.* The sisters will understand if I want a clean floor. So will God. I'll be at the hospital at two o'clock." She hung up abruptly, cutting herself off to assure the last word, determined to invade our secluded hill, no matter how transparent, indeed, simple-minded the ruse.

That afternoon I left Simon's room a few minutes before two and got to the main entrance just in time to see her short, round figure barreling up the hospital drive. Punctual, breathless, her color high, Gina came bursting through the door in her good brown leather coat, a bunch of bananas in one hand and a suitcase in the other.

"I had to take three buses to get here. You might as well be in Naples," she said. "The bananas are for the signore, for later when he feels better." She placed them in my arm, a plump yellow bouquet. "And I packed you a suitcase."

"So I see."

"Don't the sisters feed you? You're so thin. And how pale you look. You're like a white stick."

"Thank you."

Gina's gaze reached my feet, and her cloth slippers. "Come over to the corner, quick." Blushing for me, she hurried across the lobby to a couch behind a statue of the Holy Virgin and took my new black suede pumps out of the suitcase.

"Hurry, Annabella, put them on before anybody else sees. O Santa Maria, look how nervy she is. Why don't you come home for a few days, you stubborn little she-goat?" Dropping the "signora" she had assumed with such punctilio the day Simon moved into the apartment, Gina let loose a torrent of childhood names over me. "You need a good beefsteak, my beanpole—I can see that—and a glass of red wine twice a day."

"The sisters serve plenty of both. You should see the amount of wine that gets guzzled up here." A right enough reply but delivered absently. Conversations with Gina took more heart than I had at the moment. Already I could feel the virulent unease that attacked whenever I left Simon. "I'm going back now, Gina, and so must you. I'll order a taxi to take you home."

"I just got here. Are you crazy?"

"Perhaps"—how else to explain my inability to stay away from the third floor, the fact that I was far more jealous of Simon asleep than ever I'd been in his waking days—"but I don't like to leave him alone."

"So? What are you waiting for? Let's go upstairs."

"I've told you a hundred times he can't have visitors."

"Who said I was going to visit?" Gina grabbed my suitcase. "I'm helping you up with your things, that's all."

"*Va bene.*" With the ungracious shrug she expected, I led her to the elevators.

"How quiet it is," she said, watching the visitors and patients who passed by as discreetly, as nearly invisible, as the nuns.

"Is the hospital always so still?" she asked when we got to the third floor.

I gazed with a queer pride at the hushed rooms and the sunny corridors with their green plants. "Always," I assured her.

"*O Dio,* how depressing." Gina's round, obstinate face suddenly gave way. "I've never seen such a gloomy place."

"You think it's gloomy?"

She returned my incredulous stare. "You don't? In our hospitals the beds are all together. You can laugh and cry and play cards with your neighbors." My head was pulled down to her level. "*Poverina.*" She planted firm, sad kisses on my cheeks and left, while I, with an inmate's relief, rushed back to Room 305.

I had, it seemed, grown accustomed to Villa Monte Sacre. The sound of the nuns' long skirts drifting through the hall lulled me like the tide of a gentle sea, and I heard in the convent bells the silvery promise of a distant buoy.

"It's Christ's voice, calling us to our duties and prayers," Sister Clotilde said.

Though I wondered at the order of her fervor, it didn't surprise me. She was a more passionate nurse than her sisters, than perhaps quite fit the mold. No matter where she might be on the floor or how busy, somehow she always knew what was happening in each room, would run with veil and skirts flying to answer an emergency. This nun had piqued my curiosity, no doubt about it. I puzzled over her ability to sum up a situation and make a decision within a moment's gracious nod; puzzled no less over the way her young girl's mouth would curve into the mysterious smile of a holy woman.

But then, I found the Sisters of the Divine Grace altogether mystifying, right down to their arcane language. It astounded me to see how much little Sister Marie and old Sister Berthe told each other in a glance. As for Sister Clotilde, she could divine my thoughts, too, with an alarming ease. And if she happened to be in attendance during one of Dr. Pagello's politely ominous visits, she radiated messages of good will at me straight across the room.

Simon would have delighted in her silent talk, in those shining semaphoric brown eyes. "Do you really think everything needs saying?" he used to ask, bewildered by my attempts to define some small stray emotion that had appeared to tighten, or loosen, our bond. "A pity people don't speak music to each other. No, I mean it, one knows where one is with a scale and notes, after all. But words. They never signify the same thing two days in a row. I swear they don't." His smile, corresponding to his half-serious jest, was irresistibly crooked. "When I speak, it seems I don't always mean what I say. When others speak, they hardly ever say what they mean. That's words for you, my darling. There's no trusting the little buggers."

Merciless, I now bombarded Simon with words, blathered away at him with furious endearments, adoring threats, slavish promises; in short, whatever I could get my tongue around, anything to make him turn from that sleep, to stir and wake, if only to plead for a moratorium on words, and shut my mouth with his.

"Miss Stewart?"

It was not the first time I looked up to find Sister Clotilde standing in the doorway.

"I thought I heard you calling," she said. "Did you need something? No?" She glanced at the large, bold-faced watch that nearly covered her wrist. "The dining room will be closing soon. Don't you want to go down? Sister Marie tells me you haven't had any dinner."

"Then Sister Marie is mistaken. I expect she was too busy to notice me leave."

"I see. Yes, it's quite possible she was," Sister Clotilde said, giving my lie the grace it lacked. "Well, we always keep something on hand in the third-floor pantry should you ever get hungry in the night. Fruit and cookies, that sort of thing, though tonight I noticed there were puddings, too." She smiled at me, and I suddenly minded that the glow she cast was as impersonal as the sunshine it reflected.

"How long have you been here at the Villa, Sister?"

"How long? It's been six years now since I left Normandy."

She was gazing down at her chapped hands, perhaps at her narrow wedding band; taken aback not so much, I think, by the personal question as by the way I had flung it at her.

"The mother house sent me to Rome to study and prepare myself for our mission in West Africa. That was always my hope, to work in one of the bush clinics. Instead, there turned out to be a need for me here." She spoke with a sweet simplicity, an expression of unquestioning acceptance. "And so, as you see, here I still am."

"What a shame." It burst from me, much as my question had.

"Oh, no," Sister Clotilde said softly. "It's God's will that I have remained here. He allows to happen what must happen for our own good."

She then recommended the pantry again and after another glance at her watch left me.

They were avid clock watchers, these nuns. For all that they might come to a friendly standstill, arms folded and hands put to rest, they went right on listening to some interior clockwork. Occasionally, I'd overhear a reprimand to the cleaning women whose green uniforms, passed from the old help to the new, were always too tight. "We have no time to daydream," Sister Cecile, a sallow, sharp nun, would say to a pair who stood gossiping over mop and bucket. "Time is precious." It was just the sort of conundrum Simon would have enjoyed; for the Villa with its distilled nunnery air was quite outside the time around which it so devoutly revolved.

And yet it wasn't timeless enough for me. Though I kept my gaze averted from the decorations in the hall, I was aware that Christmas had come and gone. I knew another day was being launched when the first medication cart rolled by. Midmorning I recognized in the wide complacent hips of the nurse's aides who came to turn the mattresses, throwing mine to air over the window sill with so cavalier a hand I'd think never to see it again. Petty, forgivable intrusions in themselves, they nevertheless conspired to bring the time closer to Dr. Pagello's visits.

These meetings, awaited with dread hope, never varied. First there was our customary exchange of greetings, the doctor's apprehensive, mine ingratiating. Then, rocking back and forth from heel to toe, one uneasy eye wandering toward Simon, Dr. Pagello would speak. "I've been, hmm, looking over the sisters' notes for yesterday, tch." Or "It occurs to me that we should ask Professore Giovannini to come down from Bologna for a consultation. An excellent neurologist and, by the way, a lover of music who, ah, much admires Mr. West." At length, between despondent hems and haws, he'd inform me that Simon showed no signs of coming out of his coma.

"We must have patience. He's going to be all right, Doctor, he really is," and with a firm, reassuring hand on his elbow I'd guide him to the door.

Dr. Pagello was not the only one to feel my steely optimism. When I spoke on the telephone to Lisi or to Simon's elderly parents, too fragile and bitter to undertake the trip to Rome, my voice rang with the same bravado. As for the friends who came to the hospital, with them I avoided the subject of illness altogether. Confronted by these uninvited guests in the third-floor lounge, I steered the conversation through shallow talk until it foundered.

"Is it warm enough to be staying out in the country?" I said to my poet friend Eleonora Romagnani, who sat entwined with her husband, an American artist named Richard Duncan. They rarely separated, this loving pair whose willowy bodies were always bending toward each other, touching lightly, as though blown together by the breeze at their hillside home. "Did you notice many tourists in town?" I asked Richard.

"Warm enough?" echoed Eleonora, who affected the elegant sensibilities of her poetry. "Tourists?" she repeated, startled out of her dark-eyed sympathy.

Sofia, who as a rule emerged only at night with some glittering tent pitched over her vast curves, came to see me alone one afternoon bound up in street clothes.

"What a pretty dress, Sofia. It's delicious, that color, like myrtle-berry ice cream. Where'd you buy it?" I asked.

"How long, dear heart, do you plan to go on like this?" was her reply, straight out as usual. "Nobody can get through to you anymore. Alex says you don't talk even to him."

"He means listen." An unfair retort, but with enough truth to bring out that indulgent smile Sofia always had for him.

When Margot came to visit, there was happily no time for talk. She had begun work on a new film, and her appearances at the hospital, either far too early in the morning or impossibly late at night, were confined to charming the nuns. Educated in a convent school in her native Burgundy, she was used to these performances and, I suspect, enjoyed them as much as the sisters.

"I am Margot Valadier." With dazzling humility she'd announce herself at the nurses' station.

"But what are you doing at the hospital at this hour?" asked the astonished sisters, sitting over their coffee and spiritual books. "Who let you in?"

Margot, dark curly head bent in contrition, slowly lifted her face to the nuns: large violet eyes set far apart, a nose that contains itself until the end when it gives a sudden little leap, a too-wide humorous mouth. In other words, an impudent face, outrageous in its beauty.

"The night guard," she confessed with a look of the purest repentance, and was not only forgiven but granted a brief visit, just time enough for me to applaud her scene, to whisper brava to this beguiling Magdalen, and assure her that everything was going well with Simon.

Company gone, I would rush back to my comatose lover. There were few tricks I didn't try in order to give him a jolt. When neither my touch nor my voice stirred him, I turned to Mozart for help, playing tapes night and day of the concertos Simon most loved.

As I sat next to his bed, listening with him, I'd admire his beautiful hands, study the outline of his broad thighs beneath the sheet, and stare hopefully at his feet, waiting for a toe to twitch. My cowardly gaze fluttered over him, resting everywhere but on his peaceful face, on the still, deserted planes that went from an arrogant jaw to a gently sloping brow; on those pale orbs that belonged to a cold monument.

Simon's eyes—they were like him, mercurial, a blue that changed from sky to sea. With his head cocked to catch an elusive melody playing through his thoughts, his eyes were a cloudy blue; an attack of childish glee or anger turned them green. And when he was sated with love, they would grow soft and dark.

"You do look to the very bottom of a fellow, don't you," he murmured, yielding his eyes to mine, keeping them open to my gaze. We had spent the afternoon in each other's arms and at six o'clock we were still in bed, our bodies subdued but still clinging together, unwilling or unable to break apart.

"No, don't move your head," I begged. "I won't be able to see your eyes."

"Heavens, woman, I begin to wonder what you expect to find in them."

"You," I told him, knowing all too well it was my own lost, submerged self I sought. With an adoring finger I traced the faint shadow beneath his eyes.

"Such a serious expression," he said. "What are you thinking?"

"That we ought to get up. I'm famished, aren't you?" This, too, was a lie. I'd suddenly thought of Lisi's story about Lady Bessborough and her legendary infatuation, how, betrayed by her young lover, she wrote across his portrait, "Eyes where I have looked my life away."

One day during our third week in the hospital, I glanced up from just such a reverie to find that Sister Clotilde had come into the room with that quick soft step of hers.

"Why, Sister, hello."

"Everybody looks so startled to see me in the daylight," she said, with her young girl's smile.

"Are you on day duty now?" I asked, watching as she took Simon's pulse, grateful for the tender way she had of holding his hand.

"No. I came early today to do some housecleaning in the pharmacy with Sister Marie." She checked Simon's intravenous entrapments, gave me a nod, and left the room, only to reappear the next moment.

"It occurred to me, Miss Stewart, that you haven't seen the patients' chapel yet. I'm still free for a while if you would like to visit it. It's on the seventh floor, so I'll be able to show you the main terrace, too. You can see St. Peter's from there." She already had my muskrat cape out of the closet. "And what a good thing if you got some fresh air on such a nice afternoon."

I didn't mind this nursing maneuver, curiously enough, but went with her to the elevator like an obedient charge.

"The hospital chapel is small but very special. I often go there when I've an extra moment in the night," Sister Clotilde said, and I wondered if she were recommending the seventh-floor chapel to me as she had the third-floor pantry.

"I'm an unbeliever, you know, Sister." I felt I'd better set things straight between us at once. "A confirmed atheist."

"Oh, yes?" she said politely, her expression unchanged except for a glimmer of amusement in her eyes at so earnest an avowal of faithlessness.

The seventh floor had not only the patients' chapel and terrace but also the maternity ward.

"This way," murmured Sister Clotilde, and I felt an unexpected pang as we passed doors decorated with wreaths of rosebuds and pink or blue ribbons.

"Our nursery," she said, smiling through the glass at a young nun with a bundled infant in her arms. "And there, at the end of the hall, is the chapel."

"I do see what you mean. It is special." I had intended to say this to please her, but in fact it was the truth. A few rows of wooden pews, an old altar steeped in candlelight and myrrh, a roughly carved Virgin Mary with evergreens at her feet, it was a pleasantly rustic corner to come across in the Villa.

"We didn't plan it that way, yet it could so easily be a country chapel," Sister Clotilde said. "For a moment I always think I'm back in Normandy."

I saw in a sidelong glance her swift genuflection, the long curve of her neck as she knelt, graceful, swanlike, in the folds of her white habit.

"Now we shall take some fresh air," she said, but her brisk professional manner as she led me out on the hospital roof didn't quite dispel the image I'd glimpsed of a swan maiden.

Silently we stood by the terrace wall, and I was, as she had kindly foreseen, soothed by the sight of the sunny terra-cotta city below us, by the convent's garden next door, where daffodils were blooming with an utter disregard for the season. And by that profound serenity of hers.

"We are, all of us, His children," she murmured. "He knows the great loss you already suffer, but He never gives a cross, my dear, without the strength to bear it."

"It must be reassuring to have that belief," I said, surprised at the wistfulness of my infidel's reply.

"I couldn't imagine being without it. I was very young, only a child, when I learned to love Him." As she looked down at the convent garden, the narrow band of dark hair outside her veil caught the sunlight, showed the reddish gleam of a chestnut hidden by an early snow.

"And you, Miss Stewart," she asked, turning her gaze back on me, "you had no belief even in childhood?"

I shook my head, smiling, as I thought of Lisi, so pious a heretic. How else to describe those zealous bedtime readings from the great literary sinners, the nights little David, curled up warm and pink beside me, fell asleep on the words of Voltaire or Marlowe. "We were brought up, my brothers and I, in a strictly heathen household. Fairies, pixies, sylphs—that's what we put our faith in," I said lightly. "My mother was all for good magic and gentle spirits."

"But you didn't think God might also be that?" Sister Clotilde asked after a moment's hesitation.

Now I hesitated; though I had no use for her god, I was loath to offend her. "There was too much even then that didn't make sense to me. Condemning a skeptic no matter how virtuous, yet saving the wicked sinner. No, he never struck me as merciful, let alone rational." It was a mild sounding nihilism, all the more so for my having unconsciously adopted her soft religious tone.

"It's not always easy to understand the way He moves. The will of God is a magnificent mystery."

"But it would have to be a cruel god indeed who allows his people such suffering. Haven't you, as a nurse, Sister, sometimes wondered?"

"Yes, of course, I've wondered," she said, "but not doubted. I've had doubts of myself, perhaps, my worthiness of His love, but never of Him. This life is nothing, but its reward, to be happy with Him for eternity, that's what makes our earthly sorrows possible to bear."

Her face took on a radiance as she spoke, and feeling a queer regret for the great, the antipodean distance between us, I brought the conversation back to childhood beliefs. As we took a turn around the terrace I described the leprechaun Augustus claimed he saw when we were in Killarney and the ricotta tree Gina swore grew in her mother's yard.

"Gina has never stopped insisting on that tree. She still talks about those fresh white blooms of ricotta, even today."

"A ricotta tree." Sister Clotilde gave a delighted laugh. "When I was a girl in Normandy, I lived for a time on a dairy farm, and I can assure her that Camembert, at least, doesn't grow on trees."

A light-hearted remark, yet didn't I perceive a shadow behind her smile? So intent was I on my scrutiny that I failed to notice Sister Cecile approaching us until Sister Clotilde, sensing the silent footsteps, turned around.

"Sister Marie doesn't know whether to begin the work in the pharmacy without you." Sister Cecile squinted, using the sun's mild glare as an excuse to frown, for she regarded my presence in the hospital with something less than tolerance. "What shall I tell her? Will you be much longer?"

"We're coming now. I didn't realize the time. Thank you for reminding me." Sister Clotilde accepted graciously the criticism implicit in the other nun's manner, but her cheeks bore a faint red mark, as though slapped, and she kept Sister Cecile's stern silence all the way back to the third floor.

Later that night, as I sat in the dimly lit room thinking about the afternoon, reconstructing the terrace scene, I felt my own flush of guilt. Not because in seeking to comfort me Sister Clotilde had lost track of the time, but for the pleasure this knowledge gave me. Or had my pleasure come more simply, more honestly from, say her warm perceptive gaze or that sudden irrepressible laugh?

Such was the direction of my drowsy thoughts, and I let them go. I always felt easier after midnight, when the lights were low and the objects that surrounded me took on a hazy, benign familiarity. This was my hour of truce with the hospital room. No; it was more than a truce. There was something reassuring in the silhouette of the upholstered chair with its rounded open arms. I knew if I turned my head toward the lamp I'd see in its glow only the picture of a young golden-haired saint with a sweetly demented expression.

And Simon—at this time of night, the opening and closing of the door, the coif of a passing nun, lent a false mobility to his face. Deluded by this, by a virile shadow that I remembered from another wall, I rested, followed my somnambulant thoughts back to the terrace and the ricotta tree that was such a puzzlement to my brothers and me. Did Gina really believe in this botanical fairy tale herself, or was she simply too obstinate ever to admit to teasing?

When she first came to work for our family, we children, following a delicate aroma, a light but well-defined trail of spicy chocolate, to the kitchen, would find her beating crème de cacao into a bowl of ricotta. Black hair pulled back in a tight bun, cheeks a deep pink, she'd bustle away at the long marble table, ignoring us. Then, after a moment, with an ill-concealed smile, "Who told you I was in here?" she'd say, mixing lavish, heady amounts of cinnamon and nutmeg with the cheese. "I'm busy. Whatever you want has to wait."

"But it's only that we want." David would point at the bowl with a chubby hand.

"Just a spoonful, please? We're starving, and it smells like heaven." Augustus tried out some Italian theatricality, while I, suspecting I had got too old to beg with charm, confined myself to a lofty, "So we're having the chocolate ricotta pie for dinner, I see."

"Is that what you see, my Annabella?" Gina, proud and mysterious about her work, would throw me a glance of scornful merriment. "That's what you think I'm baking?"

In the end we were always treated to a generous taste of the pie filling, and the ricotta tree. Though even David considered himself beyond the age of this simple fable, we would perch ourselves around the kitchen to listen rigidly wide-eyed.

"You don't believe me? All right, but you're making a big mistake," Gina would exclaim if so much as a glance of skepticism escaped us. "You think I don't have enough work to do here without inventing stories to tell you? Who'd know better than me if what I tell you is true or not? Wasn't I the one who saw her mother go out to that tree every morning and bring back a bucket of cheese? Such fresh, moist buds of ricotta like you've never seen."

"Oh, come on, Gina," Augustus or I was bound to burst out at this point. "We're not stupid *turisti*, you know. Ricotta, once and for all, doesn't grow on trees. It's made from ewe's milk."

"Naturally. Did I ever say it wasn't? All I said was that when I was a little girl in Sicily we had, in our backyard, a ricotta tree."

I speak of Gina's coming to work for us, but it would be more accurate to say that we were the ones who came to her. She was the housekeeper of the apartment we rented and was as fixed there as the colossal mural cemented to the dining-room wall, a portrait of gigantic flamingos constructed from a million bits of coral by the owner's dowager mother. The owner himself was leaving for Brazil, and in a grand gesture, the desire to present a *bella figura* overriding not just greed but good sense, rented his immense apartment to Lisi for next to nothing. Though the velvet furnishings had obviously seen his patrician family through several generations, we children thought this threadbare opulence, balding and shiny even in the vague light of the Venetian gondola lanterns, the height of luxury.

Sofia, who had recently moved to Rome with Alex when he began producing his own films, confirmed our opinion.

"Much better than the usual gypsy camp," she said. "A *palazzo* near the Spanish Steps, two drawing rooms and enough bedrooms for a bordello. Really, I couldn't have done better myself," she complimented Lisi. "Think of it. We'll be neighborhood cousins now." She took Augustus and David and me, one by one, and pressed us to her magnificent bosom, inhaling deeply, as though gathering a bunch of wild flowers. "It's time they had a chance to live in the real world, *enfin*."

Lisi meant for us to stay in Rome only long enough to make the extra money for an expedition to India, but this siren city lulled her restless spirit as it had done with so many travelers before her. Consoled by the words of other enchanted wanderers, the joyous laments of Goethe and Stendhal, she walked around Rome for the next few years with the low, soft cries of an insatiate dove. "Look, oh, look," as she pulled us into a courtyard for a glimpse of a fountain and yellow roses on an old palace wall. "Ah, smell that sauce," she'd say, stopping in a small terra-cotta alleyway to sniff under an open window. "Ssh, listen," as an aria or lyrical argument came drifting down to us.

Not even the Eternal City, however, could completely satisfy Lisi's wanderlust. We did eventually make our journey to India, and from time to time roamed in other directions. The difference was that we now had a gypsy camp in Rome.

It was during this period, shortly after we moved into the apartment, that our father telephoned one Sunday afternoon to announce his arrival in Rome. The boys and I, too inured to sharing a hotel room to enjoy privacy, were sprawled around my large back bedroom reading when we heard the incredible news.

"Your father's here," Lisi called, running down the long hall to us in a Japanese kimono and a cloud of beige hair. "He's just flown in from New York." Amazement, triumph, perplexity lit her face in turn. "Now do you believe me?" she said with a broad uncertain smile.

It was more than six years since we had left New York, and though Lisi had continued to assure us that Matthew would come to Europe for a visit, we'd given up believing in it ages ago. Nor did we any longer expect her to take us back to New York, as our father occasionally suggested. She had, I know, been tempted by the idea more than once, but always, at the last moment, she backed away from it like a half-wild creature not daring to risk captivity again.

As for my brothers and me, this absent parent of ours, this unknown father had become too vague a memory to be more than a theoretical deprivation. Lisi's promise of a reunion with him was the golden beam cast by a nursery lamp, a childhood balm whose healing measures lay mainly in the ritual of reassurance.

Hurt and upset about something entirely different, I would direct sullen complaints to my mother. "Matthew's never going to come to see us, is he? Doesn't he care at all? Isn't he even curious about his own children?"

And Lisi, recognizing the symptoms of an unrelated injury, would stop whatever she was doing and take me on her lap long after I had, despairingly, renounced it.

"Of course he does," she'd say. "Matthew cares very much about you, about all of you." A fairly dubious statement, which she'd quickly substantiate with a catalogue of good deeds: the enthusiastic notes he always sent in reply to news and photographs of us; his half of our financing, which never faltered; the generous birthday checks that found their way to us in the most remote countries; the trips he'd have taken to see us had not business always interfered.

"Matthew in Rome. Can you imagine. I'm every bit as surprised as you are, if you want to know," Lisi said to us that Sunday. "But we mustn't stand here gawking at one another, my loves. We've got to get ready. Your father wants us to have dinner with him at the Grand Hotel."

"The Grand, of all places," Augustus said. "Why's he staying there?"

"Why can't he stay with us?" David demanded.

I kept silent, ashamed of my one thought, a fledgling of a thought that, nevertheless, had flown swiftly to the closet. What could I possibly wear? Did I own anything ordinary enough, ravishing enough to meet my father?

Halfway through my twelfth year, precariously balanced on the taut nerve that stretched between my child and woman selves, I was dumb with apprehension that evening. And, oh, so critical of our group as we stood waiting for Matthew in the *fin-de-siècle* formality of the Grand's lobby. Would he think any less of his fatherhood than he already did when he found us clustered around the marble pillar like tumbleweeds? Even I, who most resembled him, had Lisi's sun-bleached careless look cast over me like some kind of nomadic caul, was unmistakably one of her windblown tribe.

"There's Matthew." Lisi said. "Look, David, that's your father coming down the stairs."

Tall, with the slight patient stoop to his shoulders that I dimly recalled, Matthew not only hurried toward us but recognized and claimed my brothers and me with an eager embrace. His arms linked with Lisi's and mine, he then led us into the royal pink dining room like any paterfamilias out for a Sunday dinner.

"Now, then, children," he said when a corps of waiters had done with our ceremonious seating. "What would you like to order for this special occasion? Anna? Augustus? David? What's your favorite dinner?"

How pleasantly this mild-mannered stranger gazed at us through his tortoise-shell glasses, how kindly he offered us our choice of food while I sat eying him with such filial hunger. For his sake I pretended to study the menu, but over the top of it I stared, voraciously, at him, at our straight black hair, our sober gray eyes and wide cheekbones. Special occasion, could he really have said that? I looked to Augustus for confirmation of our father's genius for understatement, but he was either reading the menu or had taken refuge behind its tall pages. Lisi? She was asking her estranged husband about his flight from New York. But I wasn't fooled by her enraptured gaze. It was the expression she always wore when encountering an unexpected place or situation.

Only David seemed to be perfectly at ease. "Do you know, I learned to ride a camel when we were in Algeria," he said to

Matthew. "We stayed right near the desert, and Lisi and Annie were the only females in the whole village. *Au moins*, they were the only ones you could see. Oh, except for the Frenchwoman who owned the hotel. She kept monkeys. In fact, there were more monkeys than guests."

Overjoyed to be looking upon this chimerical father, David chattered away at him, seeking to bridge their separation with his entire stock of memorabilia. "Do you like venison and whipped cream? I don't mean together, *natürlich*. When we were in Yugoslavia we used to have whipped cream for breakfast and venison for dinner, every day."

Not even the flamboyant parade of waiters arriving with our appetizers distracted my little brother. Gazing steadily up at Matthew, he rambled on with the broad interests, the savoir-faire of a well-traveled midget. "Is that so? You don't say," commented our father, looking as though he didn't know whether to take David on his lap or give him a cigar.

Augustus, meanwhile, ate his prawn cocktail and mine with a certain cynical gusto. As for me, I had no appetite. Sucking on a rough sesame breadstick, I examined Matthew's gray suit and pin-striped shirt, proud and suspicious of the way he blended into the crowd of diplomats and international financiers who were our fellow diners.

"And then there was an extraordinary Asiatic bird," David said. "They call it a tailorbird because of the way it sews leaves together to make a nest."

"*Bugiardo!*" Augustus finally exploded into speech. "*Stupido.* You've never seen a tailorbird in your bloody little life."

"I didn't say I saw it." David's plump face was red and crest-fallen. "I was just telling him about the tailorbird. I thought he'd like to hear about it."

"Oh, but I did, son," Matthew assured him. "And I think you know an amazing lot for somebody your age."

Beaming with pleasure at his father's praise, David gave a shrug. "*Ich weiss nicht all,*" he quoted, "*doch viel ist mir bekannt.*"

"I don't understand everything"—Augustus turned to Matthew with a rapid, almost simultaneous translation—"nevertheless I know a lot."

"Faust," I rapped out just as quickly, having no wish to be excluded from this shining, shameful performance.

"Oh, children," Lisi murmured, breathing out a rare dismay. But Matthew only laughed. "You've done quite a job with them," he told her, and though my heart trembled at this ambiguous remark, he continued smiling upon us that evening in such a way that I began to wonder and hope. A tiny quivering expectation that did not survive the next day.

They had lunch together alone then, Lisi and Matthew, and I learned subsequently just how little we had to do with that smile. As involuntary as a babe's his smiling was, the bemused unfocused smile of a man in love. It was no desire for a rapprochement that had brought our father to Europe. He had come to ask Lisi to make their separation final, to divorce him, because there was a lady in New York he wished to marry.

"A what?" I was aghast, frightened to look at my mother lest I see those clear topaz eyes flawed by pain.

"Well, that's what Matthew called her. She's a novelist. One he publishes, it seems."

"A lady novelist, fancy that," I said, my mouth turned down with the bitter amusement I thought Lisi was hiding. But did I really think that, or was I simply hoping for a reflection of my own jealousy? It was Lisi, after all, who had bolted from the Central Park West apartment.

"So you see, one way or another," she said, deriving a healthy pleasure from the irony, "I did succeed in getting him out of his chair and across the ocean."

Matthew took leave of us the next day with those same eager embraces. "I really hope, Anna, that you and your brothers will come to New York and stay with me, anytime you like," he said, but we never saw him again. He married his lady novelist that following spring and, since he still maintained the same friendly distance with Lisi, we heard over the next five years each time she presented him with a child or book. There was talk of my visiting with him and his new family when I returned to the United States to enter college, but by then it was too late. Matthew's heart, without giving any warning, came to a rude, abrupt stop as he sat reading a manuscript in his old leather chair.

"Ah, no," said Lisi with sad wonder, and supplied the final twist of irony to their story by using his legacy to buy a home in a little village tucked between two Swiss alps.

"Really, I don't believe it. Settling down with the children, now?" Sofia said. "I think, my dearest Lisi, you've closed the barn door after the horses."

Dear Sofia, she might have put it more politely, perhaps, but certainly no better. In David there were already glimpses of the bold adventurer who would publish the first volume of his literary travels before he was twenty-one. Augustus, clinging to the habit of flight yet seeking stability, had begun the scientific studies that would lead him to a distinguished academic career in cosmology. And I, accustomed to trailing in the wake of Lisi's vigorous peregrinations, I became an uneasy wanderer on my own, drawn always in the direction of those stronger than myself.

When Matthew left us in Rome after that visit and the small, selfish hope of a reconciliation between my parents was finally extinguished, I told myself it scarcely mattered. We had got along very well without him all this time. A father was a luxury at this point, not a necessity, I told myself, and at the same time turned to Alex to fill the role. Or, to be more exact, I now began to realize that our charming, indulgent cousin had been playing the part for some time. Dressed in three-piece Valentino suits, high-collared shirts, and precisely knotted Pucci ties, he looked the perfect surrogate father. Even his prematurely silver hair, such a vivid contrast to that youthful, tanned face, seemed an extravagant gesture of Old World propriety.

On the occasional Sunday, we'd all stroll up to Villa Borghese together, like the other Roman families, Gina used to say, sending us off with her stern smile of approval. Having made by now my tentative, somewhat reluctant choice of sides, I'd sit between Lisi and Sofia at a garden café while our men played soccer, noting with pride that not even then did the irreproachable Alex loosen his tie or remove his jacket.

When Lisi went back to work and put us into school again, my brothers and I often played hooky and took refuge in the apartment he shared with Sofia. And the rest of the world, as we once heard her shout above the noise of their many guests. It wasn't jealousy that inspired her complaint but, as she told Lisi, a simple desire for peace. Actors, writers, production assistants were always hanging about the apartment. The telephone and the doorbell never ceased ringing, and there was a waiter from a nearby café who, like some film extra, kept wandering in with a tray of sliding cups and saucers. Nevertheless, in the midst of this commotion, Alex would find the time and the space, on a couch heaped with books and scripts, to sit down with me.

"So, now we can talk." His tone was as solicitous as it had just been for his leading lady. "How's the world treating you, Anna?"

"Oh, the world, it's no problem. But having to go to school again is a dreadful bore." And concealing, under the cover of scholastic ennui, the heart of my distress—a fellow student loved or a teacher despised—I'd allow him to ferret it out, to give me advice as wily and oblique as my confidence.

But it was not only my troubles we celebrated. Once when I had won an essay contest, Alex took me to the Caffè Greco, a long, dim, antique omnibus of a café, unchanged since it was filled with the literary smoke of its nineteenth-century patrons.

"A paradiso for the young lady," he told the waiter in the black frock coat, and as we sat in our corner of maroon velvet and clouded mirrors he raised his glass to me.

"Your career, my dear," he said, his long face creased in a smile that knew so well how to flatter even as it teased.

"Let's have another champagne, shall we, Alex?"

"Certainly not." His shaggy black eyebrows, at such odds with that refined silver hair, were lowered in censure that wasn't altogether mock. "You're not so grown up as all that."

I was already more than a little intoxicated anyway, not from that innocent champagne punch but because Alex had bought me my first drink, and because the waiter had taken him for my father.

And yet it's not completely true, not quite accurate to describe his manner with me as fatherly. I was not unaware that in his teasing compliments and lingering smile there was that faint sexual accent more commonly referred to as avuncular.

"My dear child, if your legs get any longer I won't be able to keep up with you"; and "What am I doing? Why, just sitting here waiting for my favorite girl to grow up"; and "What a scruffy outfit. Don't you think those old jeans are just a bit too tight?"

"I believe that daughter of yours has blossomed, Lisi."

"Why, yes, she has, hasn't she," my mother said with a startled look. Nothing astounded her more than these rare confrontations with time—suddenly to notice that David was almost as tall as Augustus; that a white hair was growing wild in her thick golden mane.

When the time came for me to return to the United States for my first year of college, it was Alex who helped with the practical matters and showed a concern over details that gave me a prudish shock.

"Come along, Anna. I'm going to take you to the chocolate shop for a last childhood treat," he said one day when he and Sofia were visiting us in Rosten, for by this time we were living in our Swiss village. "You shall stuff yourself with sweets to your heart's content."

Clearly he had more than my greediness on his mind, but he kept whatever it was to himself until we were sitting over our cakes and tea at the confectionery shop.

"It's going to be very different, you know, being away on your own."

"Yes, I expect so." Embarrassed by that hollow-sounding nonchalance, I took another small chocolate cake, breathing in its dark, sweet perfume.

"University life, especially in these liberal days, well, it's not quite what you're used to, is it?"

"Agreed."

"I hope you don't imagine that you're going to stay squirreled away with your books."

What was on his mind, this dear old friend who sat across from me without a smile in his green eyes, who kept stroking his chin as though he'd only just discovered it.

"You're going to be among people your own age now. Young men."

Ecco. He spat it out at last. I should have guessed that's what it was all about.

"But then," Alex said, lowering his voice, "I trust Lisi wouldn't send you off without making sure you were . . . well prepared."

This was no vote of confidence for my mother but a bald question, and the answer was that I had been surprised, even slightly shocked by her offer to take me to a gynecologist in Zurich. I had no intention, however, of admitting this to Alex. My fatherly confidant had gone too far. I was more than offended, I was scandalized. It was too much, this widespread family anxiety to make my fall from virtue as comfortable and safe as possible.

"Prepared?" I said with a dubious air. "Well, yes, Lisi did give me a few helpful hints. She told me that the women Casanova made love to always, ah, inserted half a lemon for protection. And crocodile dung and honey were considered very effective contraceptives in Cleopatra's time, she said."

It was a good enough parody of my mother to make Alex blanch. "Oh, Lord," he groaned, and I had the rare pleasure of seeing his total loss of countenance before, unable to contain myself, I burst into laughter.

"Why, you devil. You wicked brat. You deserve to be spanked for that," he said, reaching out to grab me by the wrist.

"Just you try it," I replied with a silly smirk, never more childish than now, on the brink of womanhood.

But how different that year in the United States was from anything we had imagined. My university, with too much sensitivity, thought to make its students from abroad feel at home by billeting them together in an international house. More a shy alien in my native land than anywhere else, I did, after all, spend much of the time squirreled away with my books. A consolation I enjoyed and yet so readily gave up for a new one when, in the second term, I met a law student, a tall, angular South American with an aquiline nose, a pensive manner, and black eyes that in a single piercing glance located my half-hidden, tremulous libido.

He was a moody young man whose muted conversation never developed beyond the basic need for an hour spent in my bed. But what else was there to discuss? My lover and I neither had common interests nor invented them. We never went out, not even to parties or dances on the campus. From the beginning our time together was confined to the darker pleasures of bed. At first I put these brief single-minded interludes down to the fact that he was a dedicated scholar. Those sullen looks of his I attributed to shyness, and his brooding silence I considered an aristocratic reticence. By the time I realized my lover suffered from that deep melancholy the medieval physiologists called the black choler, it was too late. I was anxiously, shamelessly addicted to his long, lean body, his musky scent, and his silent passion.

As for my protection, this intimate stranger practiced a method no less primitive than our affair, trusted in nothing but his own exquisite timing and the towel that waited on a chair to receive him. An expert, courteous lover, he would take me to my pleasure and then, when my arms wanted most to hold him, he would wrench away to plunge himself, with the thin, unnatural smile of a dark angel, into the nubby depths of that pink Turkish bath towel.

Our encounters followed the same brief pattern. He came to my room, greeted me in a low, grave voice, and, unbuttoning his shirt, looked at the chair to make sure the towel was in place. The day that pink towel received not only his seed but his first glance, I knew the time had come, if not already passed, to end our mésalliance. But how? My treacherous body could not be trusted to leave him; he would have to leave me. It was, in the end, his very black choler, his humorless spirit that saved me, inspired me to arrange four pink face cloths next to the Turkish towel, a pair on either side.

That evening when he walked into my room and glanced at the chair, he stopped short at the sight of my family group.

"Four little ones," I said in reply to his puzzled scowl. "You're to be congratulated."

He gave a baleful look at the litter of face cloths and another at me while I, beginning to feel giddy under that black glare, rattled on: "There's no safe cycle on the washing machine, you see. It was bound to happen sooner or later."

He buttoned his shirt, directed at me a final glower, and walked out of my life only a trifle more brooding and silent than he had entered it.

"Miss Stewart? Wouldn't you be more comfortable lying down?"

I was roused from my libertine sleep by Sister Clotilde and a chorus of virginal voices coming from the convent. Leaning over Simon's bed I had dozed off, my head, with its unfaithful memories, resting against his hand.

"It's dawn," Sister Clotilde murmured.

"Yes, I hear," I said, listening to the day break like crystal in the high, piercingly sweet voices of the nuns.

3

"If you have a moment, signora," Dr. Pagello said on the morning that began Simon's fifth week at Villa Monte Sacre. "I'd like to suggest— The fact is, Dr. Giovannini and I think it might be wise, helpful to you, a good idea, *insomma*, if the three of us could sit down together and discuss the, ah, present situation."

"Actually, I'm rather busy right now," I replied. "Tomorrow would be more convenient." I'd have gone to any lengths, indeed already had done so, to avoid a discussion.

"But the professor goes back to Bologna today."

"Unhappily, this is true. Though I assure you, dearest lady, I've no wish to."

That crooning came from Dr. Giovannini himself, a slender, stylish man who suffered from dark good looks and a small, compulsive gallantry.

"Not to worry," he added. "There's still time to talk. I suggest we find some place more comfortable for Miss Stewart, a setting more worthy of our *bella signora*."

"*Pardon.*" Sister Marie was rolling her cart into Simon's room.

"And I'm sure the good sister will be relieved to have us out from under her capable feet. Isn't that right, *Suora?*" Dr. Giovannini said with a smile that turned her round cheeks a ripe color.

"Hmmm . . . yes. Let's see . . . well, there's the visitors' lounge." Dr. Pagello's dithering was, for once, false.

"*Benissimo! Perfetto!*" Just as spurious was this feverish endorsement from Dr. Giovannini who, taking advantage of his own excitement, put an arm through mine and swept me down the hall.

Round velvet sofa pillows left lying flat on their backs, Our Lady of Lourdes smelling faintly of last night's cigar smoke, the ruffled bottom of a chair cover hiked up to reveal an elegantly turned, vain little claw—we had surprised the fashionable lounge in its morning deshabille. Yet despite the early hour we were not alone. In a corner of the room three Arab women filled, indeed were overflowing, a sofa upholstered in a rose pattern. Silent, harmonious, they sat side by side, perfectly still in a sea of white filmy stuff that streamed and swirled and flowed around them.

"Oh, yes, now this is better," Dr. Giovannini said, "really much better."

Were they expecting word from their stricken spouse, that trio of veiled wives in mournful white, those sisterly odalisques waiting impassive and obedient among the damask roses?

"What about here? This looks comfortable," Dr. Pagello was saying. "A nice, quiet spot, eh?"

The youngest of the three, sitting in the middle, returned my glance, gazing over her yashmak with the dark, curving, seductive eyes of a houri.

"Miss Stewart, my goodness. We're waiting for you, please." Dr. Pagello had erupted into English, but his hands, ignoring that fine Oxford accent, were clasping each other in fervid Italianate prayer, were moving rapidly the short distance between supplication and fury. "Do sit down, I beg of you."

"What we thought, you see," Dr. Giovannini said, sinking down into the couch beside me, his head of black marcelled waves close to mine, "was that we should all relax and in a friendly way review the facts of the case."

"For three weeks, even more," Dr. Pagello broke in, "Mr. West showed no signs of improvement. However, despite our being unable to give any, ah, favorable prognosis, his condition was at that point, let's say, negatively stable. But, *signora mia*, in the last fortnight this is no longer true! And now, as we've discussed once or twice already—eh?—we must accept the unhappy facts of a quickly deteriorating situation. It is . . . I am so very sorry . . . quite altogether irreversible. *Capisce?*" he asked, pressing a handkerchief to his moist brow.

"*Cara signora*," the other crooned, "we're just a trifle concerned, Dr. Pagello and I, that perhaps you haven't fully grasped the gravity of this situation."

"It's not so uncommon, the desire to resist such knowledge."

"On the other hand, an intelligent, attractive young woman like yourself, a writer, naturally has the capacity and the wish, I'm sure, to fully appreciate what is happening."

"*Capisce?*" This sad, anxious little cry of Dr. Pagello's could no longer be denied.

"Yes, of course, I understand. I do quite see what you're getting at. Naturally, I'm aware of Mr. West's condition. But all the same I'm still . . . hopeful."

I felt a moment's guilt for the despairing look that passed between those well-meaning, kindhearted physicians, but I had broken it to them as gently as I could. Hopeful was far too mild a word to describe my crazed belief, my hectic conviction that Fortune would save us in her next capricious fling. Why not, after all? Like a gambler whose steady daily losses have taught him nothing but obsession, I stood alert, expectant, rooted in green baize.

"Could you tell me what the actual odds are, Dr. Pagello?"

"The odds, Miss Stewart?"

"Why, yes, the odds of his surviving."

Dr. Pagello took off his glasses and turned to his colleague with the vulnerable, trusting gaze of the myopic. "How would you answer that, Fabrizio?"

The other shrugged, was silent for a moment, and then gave me his resilient smile. "But you know, dear lady, that's not what we can consider a realistic question. You're asking for a miracle and, alas," he said with modest rue, "we are not the ones to grant it. The chances of Mr. West's recovery might be maybe one in eighty or ninety thousand."

I fell eagerly, gratefully upon this grudging and improbable calculation.

"The point is there's a chance," I told my mother when she called from Rosten. "We can't discount anything as unpredictable as luck. After all, it's not as though the doctors said the odds were one in a million. Oh, I'm not completely crazy. I know it's going to take incredibly good luck, but then, how can the probability of Simon's recovery be any less than his accident? And if one really begins to think about it, why, just imagine the staggering odds there were against Simon and me ever meeting each other."

Lisi, who no longer tried to question or reason, who listened in a faithful, distressed silence, murmured: "Well, it's not exactly illogical, what you're saying."

"Why don't we leave it that I'll call you," I told her, "as soon as there's some good news."

"What's that? Hello?" In a moment of craven love, Lisi ducked behind a cloud, took refuge in the faint, faulty long-distance connection. "Anna? I can barely hear you, dearest," and her voice drifted off in alpine atmosphere, leaving our respective telephone operators to finish the conversation.

"*Pronto!*" a deep masculine demand. "*C'è nessuno?*"

"*C'est Geneve, signor,*" a young, throaty reply. "*Je mon partie perds.*"

"*Che voce, mademoiselle. Come bella, come romantica!*"

When the sensitive, languid Eleonara, coming to the hospital one afternoon without her faithful Richard, got caught in the path of my soaring spirits, she simply drooped that pretty head of hers and wilted. But Margot was another story.

"Anna, *chère amie,* I'm going to come right out with it," she warned, stopping to visit me one night on her way home from the studio, "I'm going to speak my mind like a flatfooted country girl."

"Good," I replied; for it was the offstage, unglamorous, tough Margot I liked best. The Margot who thrust her broad shoulders forward when she was touched or concerned, lifted her short square chin, and said belligerently: "We're good friends, after all, so why shouldn't I say exactly what I'm thinking. Right?"

"Oh, absolutely. So?"

"Have you been drinking opium?"

"Have I *what?*"

"Yes, you heard me. Opium, liquid opium. You don't have to pretend with me. Once, when I was on tour, I ended up in a convent hospital near Palermo. Never mind what for, and I happen to know that when a patient's in a bad way—no, don't interrupt, if you're not a patient, then you're the next best thing—some dear, soft-hearted sister of mercy will creep in with a shot glass of opium and a nice hot cup of camomile to wash it down."

"Not really." I gave an astonished laugh. This was one of Margot's better flatfooted performances.

"Oh, Anna, it isn't funny at all," she protested. "You see, I've good reason to be suspicious."

Toward the end of the week, Alex and Sofia came to Villa Monte Sacre for dinner, and we sat together over a plain but nonetheless interminable meal. Unlike the lounges, the dining room was neither handsome nor comfortable, but, reflecting the order's sterner view of the basic necessities of life, had been painted a pale, vague green and left at the bottom of the villa.

"I was just having a long talk with Dr. Pagello," Alex had said when he telephoned me that morning.

"I don't think there is any other kind. And?"

I sensed rather than heard his sigh. "And nothing. Nothing you don't already know, darling. Except that Sofia and I are hoping the Sisters of the Divine Grace will give us our dinner tonight."

I didn't bother to protest. I knew that mild tone from childhood. It was the disguise of an iron will, and to reinforce it he was bringing Sofia.

By seven that evening, I had lined my eyes with kohl, brushed rouge high on my cheeks, and was waiting in the hall.

"Dear heart." Sofia caught me at once in an affectionate tangle of her glittering fishnet shawl, but Alex stood quietly by.

"Anna," he said finally. It was almost a question, pronounced like that. He stared at my face, searching so hard for a trace of his Anna that he looked strangely lost, and for a moment I longed to throw my arms around him and burrow into that smooth suede shoulder.

"My God, darling, why do you stand there grinning like a monkey?" This frankly dismayed question came, of course, from Sofia.

"Was I?" and still with a grin, I suppose, for it was none of my doing, that rictus, I led them down the hall.

"Good evening." Sister Cecile nodded coolly as she came along with a small white-haired woman in a wheelchair.

"That's the Contessa Dolcetti," I whispered as they went by, Sister Cecile pushing rather too fast that tiny elderly child whose haughty beakish nose and bright black eyes peered up from a nest of peach-colored silk, whose little blue satin ballerina slippers pointed down, feeling delicately for the bottom of the chair.

"The *contessina* has a heart problem," I said, wondering why Sister Cecile and her new patient should appear more clearly defined, more real than my cousins, whom I felt I had conjured up from memory. Though I walked between them, my eyes traveling politely from one to the other, I was far more aware of old Sister Berthe stepping out of the elevator and standing in the hall with the lowered gaze, the remote expression of one still in transit. And the way Sister Clotilde glanced up from the desk at the nurses' station to give my visitors a quick look of recognition, and me a pleased smile, which clearly said: "Yes, I heard. Your friends are having dinner with you. I'm glad. Take your time, my dear. I'm here now to watch over him."

Linking my arms with theirs, I guided Alex and Sofia through the villa with a cheerful hospitality I never felt for guests in my own home. Did they want to see the charming country chapel upstairs or the view of St. Peter's from the big terrace? Should we take the elevator or walk down the four flights to the dining room?

"Guess who was admitted yesterday," I said. "The American ambassador. He's got influenza. Very mild, noncontagious, and, according to Sister Marie, nothing to write home about. And down this hall in the room at the end, there's a boy named Luca who's got the face of a faun. He's only ten years old but already a talented artist, Sister Clotilde says. She's quite mad about him. He's been crippled all his life, poor child, never able to walk. He comes from a town near Naples, and all the villagers chipped in to send him and his grandmother to Rome to see if there's any sort of orthopedic surgery that will help.

"Oh, look, Alex, quick. See that girl in the frothy negligee, that blonde wisp who looks like she's drowning in whipped cream? Well, she's the daughter of a famous German industrialist, I've forgotten who, and she's come here to have her nose reset. That's exactly how she put it. But, wait, that's not all. She has a burning desire to be an actress, you see, only she says they won't take her seriously in Berlin because she's too short, and so she's planning to get herself stretched."

"Do you know," Alex said with a grave smile, "I don't think I've ever heard you with so much to say."

"Or so little," sighed Sofia.

It was no love of gossip, however, that kept my tongue wagging, but a vain wish to change their dolorous faces, a primeval suspicion that those woeful expressions might influence Fate. Downstairs in the small restaurant, which smelled of ripe apples and cheap white wine, where guests spoke in hushed voices and traded curious glances, I went on with my foolish chattering. I picked at my food, squawked when I knocked over my wineglass; in short, gave a good enough imitation of a drunken magpie to confuse myself as well as Alex and Sofia.

And yet later, as I sat beside Simon in the Villa's dusky midnight, that high, wild confidence of mine suddenly gave way and fell to my feet with the sickening thud of a wounded bird.

"Sister Clotilde!" My involuntary cry, as surprising as my sudden fear, attracted the wrong nun. The coiffed shadow I glimpsed in the hall belonged to weary Sister Bernadette in her blue habit.

"What is it, my child?" she whispered, blinking into the dim room.

"I'm sorry. I thought you were . . . I thought I saw Sister Clotilde. I . . . forgot to tell her something."

"She's in with the little boy, I think. Sister Berthe seems to have had trouble getting him to sleep."

I murmured something unintelligible even to myself and rushed past Sister Bernadette, aware of those round eyes following me down the hall and yet unable to slow my step until I came to Luca's door.

"So now, *mon petit*, you've got a glass of water and apricot juice and your crayons."

Standing in the shadow of the half-opened door I listened to Sister Clotilde with her young patient, my heart already eased by a balm not intended for it.

"Come, Luca, put your head down on the pillow." I could see her as she leaned over the boy, her smiling face the younger and more innocent of the two. "I shall fix your blanket just so, like this, and when you're asleep your guardian angel will come and sit right there to protect you."

"It's not always my guardian angel who sits there, Sister." The bedlamp caught out the yellow gleam in Luca's eyes. Large hazel eyes, unusually clear and bright, they lit up a narrow face and showed the precocious cynicism that hid in the corners of a sensitive mouth.

"Oh? Who sits there, then?"

"The little monk, Sister."

"A little monk? No, I don't think so. Lie still, my child, and let me finish tucking you in."

"Well, he's not really a little monk. They only call him that because he's small and fat and wears a big hat. As soon as you fall asleep, Sister, this *monaciello* comes and jumps right up on top of you. Usually he just sits there, but sometimes he pulls your covers off and leads you to buried treasure."

"What a story." Sister Clotilde gave that startled laugh of hers, and then with a sweet sobriety: "It could be the devil himself who sits there tempting you, my child. You must turn your back on him and look only to your guardian angel. Now, tell me good night." With this soft, maternal command she kissed him and turned out the light.

"Why, Miss Stewart," she said, coming out of the room, one auburn brow arched with concern to find me waiting in the hall.

"I was taking a little walk."

"Good. It helps to exercise when you can." But she had perceived my despair as clearly as if it had color and form. "What is it, my child? Is there anything I can do for you?"

"Oh, no. I just happened to see Luca's light as I was passing by."

"It's hard for him to rest when he's always in bed. And then often in the night . . ." She paused. "Well, the night can seem threatening at times."

"I suppose so." Surprising vagueness from one who only moments ago had come running, terrified, to hide her face in these serene skirts. "He's lucky to have you here. You're very good with him."

Sister Clotilde, coloring, raised a hand to ward off my compliment. "Luca's an exceptional patient. He suffers heroically. When he asks for crayons and paper, that's when I understand he's in pain. Or when he teases."

Arms patiently folded, she stood with her straight back to the wall, her eyes steady on mine, a warm friendly gaze that invited me to say what was on my mind or simply listen.

"Luca can be quite a mischief-maker, but we shall miss him when he leaves. No, no indeed, he's not being sent away without hope," she said in reply to my look. "On the contrary. He's to have surgery that will, *Deo volente*, enable him to walk. But it's a complex procedure, done only one stage at a time, so his grandmama will take him home to build him up first."

"That's good news." Only the most perfunctory remark, it seemed, could pass the fright still lodged in my throat.

"Yes, we're very pleased. They've been doing this particular operation for some time now in an orthopedic clinic in Sweden with excellent results, and Dr. Ibernesi expects the same for Luca. We shall all be praying for it."

An impulsive hand left its refuge and reached out to mine. "You know, my dear, Mr. West is also in our prayers every day. Tonight Luca, too, was praying for him. The prayers of the young have great power with our merciful Lord."

"The Lord who lets that little boy suffer?"

Her smile, like her reply, was charitable to us both. "There are times when God gives those He loves best a special trial."

I shook my head in sad protest. "I don't suppose I shall ever be able to understand your God."

"My God?" she said softly. "Yes, it's true I belong to Him, but He belongs to us all. His ways are inscrutable to me, too, at times, but I know there's no hazard in His plan."

Oh, how I longed to penetrate the mystery, the invulnerable secret behind her smile.

"Why Simon, Sister? Why him?" My dread spoke up at last, and in that hushed white corridor I whispered to her the catechism of an atheistic child. "Why did it have to happen to Simon? If his accident wasn't hazard, Sister, then isn't it all the more terrible?"

"We cannot always expect to understand what He chooses for us."

"But why would He choose this for Simon, a young man, a good man, who's made the world more beautiful with his music?"

"Oh, my dear," she said, her brown eyes shining into mine. "I've seen the deep love you have for Mr. West, and I can imagine your agony. If only you could find comfort in the thought that it's because the Almighty loves you so much that He singles you out for such a trial."

And I, with a quiet rational hysteria, persisted, determined to comprehend the mind of a deity whose existence I denied. "But, Sister, why would a merciful God want anyone to suffer? There's no logic—"

"Ah, logic, no," Sister Clotilde agreed, smiling.

I smiled, too, soothed for the moment, not by her sweetly uttered paradoxes but by that quick, generous smile; the way she plunged her hands deep into the pockets of her habit, moving down the hall with the swift silent stride of a country girl unhampered by long skirts.

As for me, I went back to Simon's bed and let loose the shameless fingers that still tried to insinuate themselves between his. My cheek, stubborn as my hand, found a familiar resting place on a chest whose chaste white cover and vague breathing it hardly knew.

Our luck can still turn, I assured myself as I had done Lisi, and once again took up my string of suppositions; recalled such fortuitous happenings as made Dr. Giovannini's odds seem reasonable; counted the foolish impulses, the chance acquaintances, the random paths; the vagaries of Fortune, in other words, which had led me to Simon.

If Lisi and her mother before her had not been bolters, if I hadn't received from my kinswomen the uncertain desires of a vagabond, would I have left that pleasant green campus in Massachusetts to wander from one European university to another?

And suppose a certain French poet, a professor at the Sorbonne, had not come to lecture at the University of Barcelona when I was studying there? This man, for whom I conceived an uneasy passion, was excessively hairy. His full, vigorous beard was merely the polite form, the outward sign of a wild, rambling black growth that covered his chest and limbs, clung to the small of his back, flourished in his ears and escaped in tendrils from his nostrils. O Grandfather Bear, were you the cause of my strange malady which, though brief, resulted in a move to the Sorbonne?

In Paris, nothing more than wind and rain were responsible for my turning a corner to dash into a small English bookstore, a very personal sort of room with floral drapes and rare volumes that smelled of Gauloises and rose water. It clearly wasn't meant for anybody else, that tiny shop, but its owner and her stout gray cat. In an attempt to avoid tripping over the latter I fell against the only other customer, a thin narrow-chested young man who gave a little shriek.

"Oh, it's okay, mam'zelle. I guess I'll live." His smile was as soft and slow as his words. "Though you just might have to carry me back home. Don't look like that, honey. I didn't mean Georgia, for goodness' sake."

Such was my introduction to Henry Lee Merchant, a gifted painter who never stayed sober long enough to finish a canvas; an imperious child who distrusted the women he understood too well. Yet we became good friends that year, Henry Lee and I, and it was because of him that I came to know Suzanne Valadon.

No, that's not entirely true. I already knew her, better than was necessary. This nineteenth-century painter was another of the independent, resolute women who visited our childhood like a company of staunch aunts, free spirits Lisi would summon up and proudly point to soaring above the conventions of their day.

During the period our family lived in Paris we spent most Saturday afternoons following Lisi as she blazed new trails for us through the museums of the city.

"Look, children, you can tell by the uncompromising lines that these are Valadon nudes," she said one day, gathering my brothers and me in front of harshly voluptuous figures, disenchanted women with sprawling, intemperate buttocks and small startled breasts.

"Oh, Suzanne Valadon may have been influenced somewhat by the Impressionists, but she was much too busy searching for her own truth to give *this* for schools and rules," our mother said with a smart snap of her fingers. " 'You must have the courage to look the model in the face if you want to reach the soul,' that was her creed. And it's no secret, children," Lisi said, drawing us closer to confide those turn-of-the-century tidbits of hers, "that she lived as daringly as she painted. She thought nothing of causing a scandal by sliding down the Moulin banister, and because it was her dream to be an acrobat, she joined a circus."

"What else did she do?" a rapt, hopeful Augustus asked whenever Lisi paused for breath.

"What else? Well, when she was a young girl she posed for all the famous painters of her time and more often than not fell in love with them. Oh, yes, she took her pleasures as casually as any man. And later on, when people would ask who had fathered her son, Utrillo, she'd say, 'It is too difficult for me to tell you, because I really haven't the slightest idea.' "

By now Lisi's teachings had attracted a crowd of attentive and amused men. With what relish did they listen to our young mother who, caught in a shaft of museum light, glowed like a divinely inspired gospeler, unaware of this audience until I gave her a prudish, mean poke.

"But we must ask ourselves why, children," she said then, raising her chin, though not her thoughtful voice, "why it is that a woman's independence seems to be a quality only other women admire."

Some fourteen years later, because my new Georgian friend idolized Utrillo and tried to imitate him, not, alas, as a painter but as an alcoholic, Suzanne Valadon came back into my life.

"Hey, Miss Anna, you in there?" The lonely Henry Lee, who usually stayed up all night, would bang on my door at seven in the morning. "You know how late it is, honey?" Swaying under an armload of groceries, he'd come into my room, filling it with the smell of hot baguettes and freshly ground coffee, but always for my breakfast alone. He never showed interest in any food but the elusive bits of fruit that happened to bob up in a glass of liquor.

"*Bonjour*, sugarfoot." The kiss he brushed on my cheek was already well flavored with sharp, licorice absinthe.

"I thought you were going to stay home and paint today."

"That's tomorrow you're talking about." His tone was defiant, but deep in his lovely, strange lavender eyes there was entreaty. "So are we going to hunt down those Utrillos or not?"

Thus would Henry Lee and I begin another round of the museums and, just as inevitably, the bistros.

"You ought to be locked up like your idol, with nothing in the room but paints," I'd venture every so often, worried by the pallid skin and the delicate tremors that rippled over this friend who seemed never to achieve the intoxication he thirsted for. "I wouldn't even leave you the turpentine."

"I bet you wouldn't." A sly look of affection filtered through his long blond eyelashes. "I don't believe I've ever known such as old stick-in-the-mud in my whole life. Why don't you just mind your own business, Miss Wet Blanket, and *ferme ta boîte* for a change, *d'accord?*"

But I never paid much attention to what Henry Lee said, certainly no more than he. I loved the sound of him, the way he sang his words with the deep, sweet rasp of a blues singer. "I mean you're turning into a real old *trouble-fête*, honey, you know that?" and raising a graceful, too-thin arm, Henry Lee would order another two drinks, for himself.

It was only natural that Utrillo's countless churches, his city streets without end, would bring Suzanne Valadon to my mind: the girl-mother who made such tender crayon sketches of "My Utrillo," who thought to cure her son by making a painter of him and succeeded only in teaching him another addiction.

"Come along with me, sister. Don't you know springtime was made just for sitting on the old Butte." Guile alone saved Henry

Lee's smile from being too pretty. "I know a café where you can sit forever, and when you look up at the trees you can see Sacré-Coeur shining through the leaves like another sun."

There was hardly a day that spring we didn't wander up to the Butte. Fragrant lilacs and artful roses turned those steep winding streets back to country lanes, and my thoughts went with them. Back to the young Valadon who called Montmartre her "beautiful village," to the little milliner's apprentice who made hats out of birds and feathers, and dreamed of flying through the air on a trapeze. How she intrigued me, this illegitimate daughter of a sewing maid who so blithely invented a different father for herself every day, claiming, as mood struck, to be the daughter of a wealthy old aristocrat or a young criminal.

Now it was I who dragged Henry Lee around, looking everywhere for the model who called herself Suzanne and spent her rest periods bent over a sketch pad. Is she Calliope or Clio, Thalia or Urania, or did Puvis de Chavannes envision her as all the Muses in the Sacred Grove? She was only seventeen when she became the mistress of the fifty-eight-year-old painter, a somewhat incestuous affair, surely? Nor was she much older when she posed for Renoir's nudes . . . Renoir, her senior by twenty-four years, was he another father?

And, yes, Lisi, we must ask ourselves, those of us who regret Matthew still, was it Valadon's search for a father that fascinated me the most, slowly fired me with the rather curious ambition of writing a novel based on her life?

That summer both Henry Lee and I finished our Paris studies, and one day in August, a hot, still, urban desert of an afternoon, I went to his studio to help him pack up for Georgia.

"Looky here, hon," he said, beckoning me to a corner furnished indiscriminately with canvases and bottles. "I don't believe you ever saw my study of 'Miss Anna.' You want to keep it for a souvenir?"

I still have that elegant charcoal drawing, but I cannot say even now whether Henry Lee's unconscious was responsible for it, or his cunning. I didn't dare ask. Nor can I truly say how much of myself I saw in that slender, boyish figure. Cheekbones heightened by the straight dark fall of hair, yes; the somewhat masculine severity of a direct gaze beneath thick, undeflected brows, perhaps; but that dimpled chin propped up by a languid hand and the bow-shaped mouth with its secretive smile, they belonged to Henry Lee.

At the end of August I received my degree in medieval history and went back to our Swiss village, where I bought a schoolgirl's batch of cheap lined notebooks and pens.

"Going to begin all over again?" Augustus teased.

"I'm writing a book, a sort of novel, about Suzanne Valadon."

"A book about Valadon?" A beatific smile rose over Lisi's face. "What a splendid idea." she said, and tiptoed off to Southeast Asia with my brothers so that I would have the necessary solitude for work.

All through the winter and well into the spring, I stayed at the top of the chalet in a long dormer room with wooden beams and a squat stone fireplace that comforted more than warmed. My desk faced a triangular window, the perfect frame for a remote mountain range, but I ignored the drama of stern white alps reaching for the tenderness of a blue sky.

Piling the desk high with my kindergarten supplies, I sat cross-legged on the bed and wrote with my back to the view, my eyes fixed on a nineteenth-century Montmartre, a hill village where sheep and cows grazed near windmills, and a little girl, climbing a crooked vine-covered street to her convent school, stopped to draw pictures on the pavement.

The Blue Room received a certain amount of calm praise upon its publication, but later, when it appeared transformed into a film produced and directed by Alexander Sareuth, starring Margot Valadier, with music by Simon West, it was what the press called "an overwhelming success."

Just as Alex had predicted.

"I like *The Blue Room*, Anna," he told me one winter weekend when he and Sofia were visiting Rosten. "I like it very much. You've got quite a film there."

"Oh, have I?" In three strides I had crossed the room to where he was toasting himself by the fire, his stiff-collared shirt and firmly knotted tie only partially concealed beneath a ski sweater. "A film you say?" This was hardly the commendation I'd hoped for, and I snatched the brand-new, sleek author's copy of *The Blue Room* away from him, my neophyte's pride wounded. "You're crazy."

"Like a fox," remarked Sofia, who was playing backgammon at the table with Lisi.

Had Alex heard neither of us? Unperturbed, he went on smiling into the fire, gazing at heaven only knew what pictures leaping in the flames. Rosten's bright cold sun had given a winter's burnish to that tanned youthful face of his, and now the firelight was casting it in bronze. "I think I'd like to direct this one myself," he murmured.

This one, indeed. I wanted to kick those long legs that were stretched out in such comfortable, impeccable confidence.

"Margot Valadier would be the perfect Valadon, of course."

"Margot Valadier?" I was horrified. "Why she's a . . . a pretty little actress!"

"But of course, dear girl." Alex turned his bronze and silver head around to give me a puzzled look. "Whatever's the matter with you tonight?"

"Nothing. Except I don't understand why you can't ever read a book without seeing an international Technicolor movie. Why isn't it enough for a book to be a book."

"Aha, inviolate, you mean," said my old friend with a kind, maddeningly understanding smile.

"No, I don't." But my quick hot protest told us both he was right.

"I feel just as you do, and if you permit me to buy the film rights, then you must promise to do the adaptation yourself."

"Me? Do you really imagine I'd be interested in making a feature presentation out of my book? No, thanks. Anyway, what do I know about writing a screenplay?"

"Forgive me, darling, but did you know so very much about writing a novel? One only learns in the doing, don't you agree? Now what's so funny about that?"

Not really funny, no. I'd been thinking how often in my jealous adolescence I had listened to him wrap that same silky voice around some petulant actress.

"I'll be there to help you with the screenplay if you need me, but I don't think you will. Anybody clever enough to have put such a marvelous book together—"

"Can take it apart." the irreverent Sofia broke in.

Alex laughed. "Don't listen to her," he said, unembarrassed.

It interested me that she was still the only one who could make him laugh. An amused smile or a quizzical one, a persuasive smile or one of pure affection—Alex had, at the ready, any number of charming smiles for others, but Sofia alone could arouse him to laughter, make him throw back his silvery head in a gratified outburst of that particular pleasure.

Had so very much, in fact, changed between them since Sofia's abdication several years earlier? This decision of hers to leave him had come as a surprise even to Alex, I suspect, although he kept his own counsel and would merely put on his Madonna face, as she described it, when anybody mentioned her move to the country.

"I'm going to retire," Sofia had confided to Lisi. In her late fifties, with a broader back, perhaps, a thickened waist, she was still an imposing beauty.

"Retire?" my baffled mother asked. "From what?"

"Not from what, from whom," Sofia replied. "I think it's time for me to leave my darling Alex. I want to sit in the country where there are no telephone calls, no doorbells ringing. And nobody sitting across the table with a sad expression when he sees me eating too much pasta. In other words, dear

Lisi, I want to be left in peace. I want to be as old and fat as I really am, almost."

And yet, though Alex's name began to appear with shocking regularity in the Italian scandal sheets, linked with this countess or that actress, it was still Sofia one saw at his side. Sofia, with a hearty, good-natured sigh, still turned up at her old post for Alex's parties, and not until the last guests had gone and the great *palazzo* door below slammed shut, did she kiss him good-bye.

"*Au revoir, mon amour,*" and gathering up her white Persian cat, Sofia would depart for her own home, for the country place which in the end turned out to be no farther away than the apartment directly above the one she had shared so many years with Alex. A duplex at the top of the old palace, it was surrounded by terraces; by a sunny quiet garden with grape arbors and yellow roses and a pink, frivolously wrought dining table.

"Are you paying any attention at all, Anna?" Alex said. "Because I can prove to you, in your own words, how right Margot Valadier is for the part. We couldn't do better if we had Suzanne Valadon herself."

Alex had retrieved my book from the table and was rapidly thumbing through its pages. "Here we are. Now listen to this description. 'One meter and fifty-four centimeters tall, blue eyes and a turned-up nose.' Wait, wait, there's more. Yes, here where Valadon's young husband speaks of her as 'having something of both an Amazon and a fairy.' So there you are." Alex shut the book triumphantly. "Doesn't that exactly describe Margot? Really the only question now is how soon you think you can come to Rome and get started on the screenplay. Well?"

And at my continued silence, my rigid uncertainty: "Come on, child, tell the truth. Doesn't the idea of making a film with your old cousin intrigue you just the least bit?"

"Not the least," I assured him.

.   .   .

"Oh, Miss Stewart, you're still awake? Didn't you sleep at all tonight?" Sister Clotilde gave me a look of genuine dismay. "It's not good to let yourself get exhausted."

I watched her bend over Simon, moving a gentle, persistent stethoscope across his chest, listening intently, pausing, and listening again. In another moment I knew she'd glance up at me with opaque eyes and one delicate line etched in a smooth brow.

"Try to get some rest now," she murmured. "I'll check back soon."

How many times during the night, and for how many nights, had this scene taken place between us? I was no longer sure; my memory had made good its escape.

Alex, with his deft, insistent hand, had arranged for everything, and within a few months of my loud protests I was back in Rome, installed in the old apartment.

"O Santa Maria, just look at her! Imagine it, my little Annabella, my pretty beanpole, writing a movie for the maestro," cried Gina. "But you better not think anything else has changed around here, young lady. It's Thursday, the gnocchi are in the oven, and mind you're home at one o'clock sharp for dinner."

Amazingly, I could see no changes. Gina's cheeks were still the smooth pink of the azaleas. It was a familiar bar boy at the corner café who gave my cappuccino a hefty dose of cinnamon, and the old *portiere* next door, sitting in the doorway of the *palazzo* he guarded so affably, looked up from his newspaper with the same toothless smile. No, I wasn't at all sorry to be back in this affectionate, effusive Rome, who paints herself in such earthy colors, whose corners of baroque splendor spring up in so impulsive, generous a manner.

Nor was I any the sorrier, it seemed, and this is the point, to be making a film of *The Blue Room*. For one thing, a fact that cannot be ignored, I was at last to earn my own keep, and quite a handsome one at that. I admit, also, to liking the challenge of preparing the book for action, in the tactful, nervous words of Ugo Rossetti, Alex's co-producer. What's more, it definitely gave me a thrill to see the set designs for the Mollier Circus and the first costume sketches for, yes, Margot Valadier.

And if I were to take this honesty a step further, wouldn't I confess to enjoying, most of all, the conferences with Alex; his paternal murmurs of praise over certain scenes and those furtive, sidelong glances of pride I knew I was meant to catch but which nevertheless succeeded in flattering me.

"About the music," he said one day when I had dropped in at the Bella Vista Productions offices. "What would you think of Simon West for the score?"

"Marvelous. Why not Saint-Saëns or Ravel while you're at it?"

"So you approve. Good."

"Approve? I love his music. He'd be perfect."

"But?" Alex supplied, his eyes reflecting amusement, and patience, as he waited for my doubt to raise its snobbish head.

"West doesn't do that sort of thing, does he? And he must be ancient by now. It's a lovely idea, but an artist like West would never want to compose for the sound track of a movie."

"The medium is not without its classics," Alex murmured, and I blushed at so undeservedly mild a reproach from one who had several such films to his credit. "In any case, we're very close to making a deal."

"A deal with West? You're not joking? You've already talked to him?"

"Of course we've talked, silly girl. He's in Rome. What a lucky coincidence, eh? Apparently somebody lent him a villa to work in for a while."

"But has he read *The Blue Room*? What did he say? Did he like it? Do you really think he'll do the music?"

"Oh, come, Anna. We're not asking him to compose the score for a spaghetti Western. This is going to be a very distinguished film. I might even lose money on it," Alex said with a teasing smile, and then added casually, too casually: "By the way, we're expecting you at a party Sunday. Don't look alarmed; it's nothing special. Just an ordinary Sunday fete. Margot's coming, and Eleonora and Richard will be there." Alex paused, glancing over the papers on his desk. "Ugo said he was bringing a new investor, some sheik, and his entourage, which means half of Saudi Arabia, no doubt. Oh, and Simon West is coming. I thought it would be a pleasant way for us all to meet."

If I hadn't known my old friend so well, I might really have believed that his concentration was more on those papers than on his guest list.

"And there'll be a few friends of Sofia's from the Bolshoi. They're in town, you know. Et cetera, et cetera, et cetera."

"Sunday, you said?" I had every intention of excusing myself by claiming another engagement, but I was betrayed by a dull, sluggish brain that blinked foolishly at my urgency and came up with nothing but a stammer of thanks.

I knew what those Sunday gatherings were like. All of Rome would be there and, by Alex's own admission, half of Saudi Arabia. But my reluctance went beyond a natural disinclination for those affairs. I was awed by the thought of meeting Simon West, particularly in such a mob. I'd have much preferred a business meeting at the studio, or even the chaotic production offices. Almost anywhere, in fact, but at one of these fetes in a crowd of Alex's et ceteras.

What a din greeted me that Sunday evening, a loud babble of French and Arabic and Serbo-Croation. Had Largo Argentina been the chief square of Babylon, and Alex's *palazzo* the wondrous tower, I doubt there would have been a greater confusion of languages and guests. Such, anyway, were my unsociable thoughts as I set myself adrift among the ultrachic women whose hair was in long, writhing tangles or cropped short and plastered back to reveal a startling masculine beauty; the American "cowboy" actors who were all wearing the same rugged, craggy features and a Western décolletage that exposed the smoothest of bronzed chests.

I was more or less headed in the direction of Alex's study, an old refuge, when I caught a glimpse of him standing near it, deep in conversation with a large, imposing gentleman who had the nose of a hawk and the fragmented white beard of a mountain goat. Simon West, I was sure of it, and with the perverse speed of those born shy I turned back into the crowd.

"*Carissima*, long time no see." I had thought it was Sofia's cat rubbing against my leg, but this purr belonged to a midget named Milo, an actor friend of Alex's. "My, how you've grown," he said, looking up at me with his soft, whiskery smile.

Sofia signaled to me then with a flaming chiffon scarf, and as I began to make my way to her side of the room, I passed a young man with an extraordinary pair of blue eyes, a vivid cornflower blue. My appraisal also took in a corduroy suit that didn't quite fit and whose tightness emphasized a broad chest and heavy thighs. It was the muscular bulge of his thighs and the way he stood with a certain solid grace, his canvas shoes pointing outward, that led me to think he was one of Sofia's friends from the Bolshoi Ballet. And, yes, I noticed, too, his flirtatious manner as he talked to a young actress in a red toga. As I walked by, he glanced up, and I was no less dazzled by that blue flash than was the girl.

"Anna, *come sta?*" said the dark, melancholy Eleonora. She was sitting on the lap of her husband, Richard, one arm draped around his neck. How lightly they wound themselves around each other, this amorous pair, like the tenderest of flora.

"Miss Stewart, wait up. Hold on a minute, will you?" That breathless Irish voice belonged to Margot Valadier's secretary, Cathleen, a devoted fan of eighteen who proudly called herself nursemaid.

"A bit mad tonight, isn't it? Margot's sent me to fetch you. Come on, we're over there on the other side. Lord, what a crush. 'Tis worse than feeding the pigs." Jostled from behind, Cathleen spilled the glass of red wine she was carrying, and "Oh, damnation!" said this beautiful gawky blond with a wild blush. "Oh, shite! Oh, fuchk!" she cried in a transport of Celtic embarrassment.

"Anna, over here." called Margot who was holding court around the piano.

Alex had been right, of course. The too-large, mannish khaki jumpsuit, those short dark curls caught back in a provocatively untidy knot, the wide gamine's smile that showed in a reckless flash her small white teeth could well have belonged to Suzanne Valadon herself.

"We must talk, *chérie.*" In all truth, I never imagined that we'd have anything to say to each other, Margot Valadier and I, but to my surprise we were already friends. She had a charming way of insisting on it.

"You've got to help me, Anna. You're the only one who understands," she said. "I want to do the aerial somersault myself. *Je dois le faire.* Believe me, I've done far riskier things in my life than fly on a trapeze. We must get Alex to agree. I simply won't have a stunt woman performing for me. Catch Valadon with a stand-in. *She'd* never have allowed it. *She* wouldn't let anybody stop her."

As Margot was speaking I noticed Alex taking Simon West into the dining room. His long tête-à-tête with the composer was giving me hope. A second glass of wine made the decision for me. I would go back across the mobbed room and join them. This resolution, however, did not keep me from taking the long peripheral route, or from a wistful recollection of the Sundays my brothers and I had watched the goings on from the safety of Alex's study, or, better yet, the alcove library, where we would find the odd glass of spumante abandoned, sweet and flat, on a bookshelf.

Once again I passed the dancer with the brilliant eyes. This time I wondered if they weren't too bright, too flashy, like the blue satin a pimp might choose to wear. Yes, they were almost a tawdry blue, those eyes, I decided, and responding to a light touch on my shoulder, turned around to stare directly into them.

"You look ready to bolt." That was the first thing he said to me. Then, "You're an American, aren't you?" He laughed at my confusion. It was the only unlovely thing about him, that crow of his.

"Now why do you suppose the English always expect to be recognized? They simply assume it, you know. I'm not sure they could do without it, whilst the Americans are always so surprised when they're identified, not to say a bit offended, some of them." The blue eyes, kinder than their master, told me: This is sheer gibberish. Pay no attention.

"So are you visiting or do you live here?" he asked. "Tourist, transient, expatriot, or what?"

I greeted this echo from my childhood with a rueful smile. How could he know his innocent question had followed Lisi's tribe halfway around the globe?

"I'm working here." He was hardly a member of the Bolshoi troupe, this outspoken Englishman who was encircling me with waves of such eccentric vitality.

"And you?" I asked, an offhand query that masked a real desire to know.

"I expect I'll be staying in Italy for a bit longer anyway." I had anticipated that noncommittal shrug. His stance, the soiled canvas shoes and rumpled corduroy, the pencil in his jacket pocket where a handkerchief might have been, it was more than a casual attitude, all that. It was a state of freedom.

"I don't know Rome that well, really," he said. "I've always had to pass through far too quickly. A one-night-stand sort of thing."

"It's a good time to get acquainted."

"Oh, yes, spring. I see what you mean."

Did he? I certainly wasn't paying any attention to what I said. Instead I was discovering that his eyes changed their shade of blue as swiftly as his mobile face its expression, that he was not as young as I had first supposed. Somewhere in the middle of his thirties, I reckoned by the narrow lines that had entrenched themselves on either side of his mouth and across a high sloping forehead. But it was his hands that fascinated me the most. They might have been borrowed for the evening, so elegantly, with such unexpected grace, did they emerge from his too-short jacket sleeves. Slender, long, aesthetic fingers— I glanced away, startled not by my urge to reach for them, but by the sudden warmth in my limbs that presaged their touch.

He, meanwhile, was surveying me with the frankly curious gaze of a savage, a scrutiny that made me think I'd have done better to wear a toga or crop all my hair.

"You won't take it for impertinence, will you, if I ask how you happen to be in this crowd?"

So he agreed. An angry, humiliated child's taunt leaped to my tongue: I was invited; weren't you? But what I said was: "I don't think I would have come if I hadn't been told that Simon West was going to be here."

"Then you're a fan of his," he cried, on that surprised, triumphant note with which one hails a fellow devotee of some obscure pleasure.

"You're as great a fan, obviously," said I, eager enough to knot the bond between us.

How can I describe the expressions that passed over his face— the complexity of embarrassment, pride, and coquetry, the smirking, sly tone of intimacy with which he confessed: "Afraid I know him too well for that."

I blushed, not for his indiscretion but my own. "I see." What else was there to say after so clear a declaration of his proclivities. "Well, it was nice talking to you."

"Oh, don't go. Wait a minute. I don't even know your name. Look, let's get out of here, shall we?" His eyes had turned a softer, darker blue. "I can tell you anything you want to know about West, more, very likely." One side of his mouth curved into a crooked, untrustworthy, irresistible appeal. "You see, the fact is I need rescuing. Somewhere in this crowd there lurks an old novelist, one of those formidable feminists, I'm sure, whose book I was supposed to have read."

And while I stared at him dumbly, overcome with anger, and relief, Alex suddenly materialized before us with a self-congratulatory look, a satisfied little smile that told me things had gone according to his script, his staging.

"So, Anna, Mr. West," he said, not bothering to hide from

me the pleasure he took in his machination, "it looks as though my two guests of honor have already met each other."

O dulcis Virgo Maria . . . It pierced through my reverie, that high, pure cry for mercy, and I went to the window and drew aside the curtains. The orange-colored convent, singled out by the evening sun, was itself a flaming sunset, and I stood, with folded arms, listening to the Sisters of the Divine Grace sing, warming myself in their vespertine glow.

"Excuse me, Miss Stewart. I was looking for Sister Clotilde." I jumped at Sister Cecile's voice. Why did her footsteps seem stealthy to me, the other nuns' merely soft? "I thought I saw her coming into your room."

"Yes, she was here, just for a minute." I had no idea what that contrite note was doing in my voice. Surely there was no need to apologize to this nun for the benevolence that was bringing her sister here with increasing frequency. "I think she may be down the hall. Sister Berthe said the *contessa* was threatening to have another coronary if she wasn't allowed to go home. She's an adorable old thing, isn't she, the way she goes whizzing down the hall in her wheelchair. Is it true she ran into the supper cart on purpose last night?"

Sister Cecile, ignoring my prattle, picked up Simon's hand, straining with a frown to catch his pulse.

"Sometimes I think the *contessina* creates a fuss just to get Sister Clotilde's attention, the way Luca did. Well, whatever the trouble was, I bet Sister has calmed her down by now. She's remarkably good with the patients, isn't she?"

"Yes, Miss Stewart, she is." Sister Cecile came to stand beside me at the window. "God has seen fit to give Sister Clotilde a special talent. She's an excellent nurse and an extremely industrious one. But, like the rest of us, she is only His instrument. There's only one true aim in the religious life, my dear, one desire alone, and that's to please our Lord. It is our single constant dedication," she said slowly, quietly. "Nothing else matters but serving Him, absolutely nothing."

I had no reply to this, nor did I know if one were expected. These sentiments were more or less familiar to me by now, but never had I heard them stated so deliberately, with so meaningful a smile. And what, after all, was that meaning to me?

"Dr. Pagello's already in the hospital," Sister Cecile said, straightening the curtains, "and I believe Dr. Giovannini is on his way." She moved the chair closer to the table, pushed my suitcase out of sight, and, with a pleasant nod, left the room.

"That's *my* suitcase." After seven months of living with Simon, after seven wanton, besotted months, I came home to find him in the bedroom packing his clothes. Astonished and frightened, I pointed an accusatory, ridiculous finger. "What are you doing with my suitcase?"

"Anna, hullo," he said, in that tone of faint surprise with which he often greeted me. "I'm borrowing it, darling. It's much bigger than mine, and nicer. You don't mind, do you?" One hand was absently dropping underwear into the suitcase while the other, precise and loving, smoothed sheets of music between layers of shirts. "Anyway, mine's got a sinister little tear right by the zip. Just the sort to suddenly give way and spill out its guts." And with a smile of sweet insouciance, he continued his preparations to abandon me.

True, we had never stopped to exchange vows; my careless lover had made no promises, but I thought, fervently hoped, it was because there was no need.

"I'll walk home with you, if you like," he had said the night of Alex's party. "We've a lot to discuss, haven't we? I'm very eager to read *The Blue Room*, you know. Fully intended to, even before I met you, of course. It's a rather intriguing notion, isn't it, setting a novel to music."

That walk lasted nearly a week. I agreed—oh, how willingly—to show him my town, a Rome I'd never seen sprawled out in quite so sensual and languorous a mood. Alarmed by the feverish weakness I felt for this stranger, I led him through a maze of terra-cotta alleys and moonlit ruins, not knowing whether I meant to escape or ensnare. And all the while shocked at the devious ways I found to give myself to him, a bittersweet *tartufo* embedded in whipped cream, a glimpse through a *palazzo* window of cherubim embracing on a Renaissance ceiling, the twilight music of a campanile that tilted in the dusky blue sky as though harkening to its own bells.

At the end of the week, we drove out to the country to Simon's borrowed villa and collected his suitcase, a handsome tweed overcoat he never wore, and an old recorder in a shabby leather case, the "baroque plaything" he never traveled without.

"Mr. West is going to be staying with us," I told Gina when we got back to the apartment.

"*Si, signora,*" she said, tightening her lips over this first *signora* not in protest but to suppress a smile, to hide the approval that brought a dark red flush of excitement to her cheeks.

"Why so quiet?" Simon asked, glancing up from his packing. "Dear me, you are looking rather peaked; d'you know that? I suppose we ought to be sensible and make an early night of it. Especially since I have to leave at the crack of dawn."

I sat down on the bed slowly, in the groping, apprehensive way of the infirm and the heartbroken.

"Heavens, woman, aren't you speaking to me anymore?"

"You're really going to leave, Simon?" I said, raising my eyes to meet his at last. "Tomorrow?"

"Yes, of course. Why so surprised? I told you ages ago."

"You told me?"

"Forgot all about it, hey? This is the week of the Symphony Hall business. . . . Oh, Lord." Simon gave me a stricken look, letting his shoes fall into the suitcase. "But I was certain I told you the day Nicholas rang up. I know I meant to."

He came to put a conciliatory arm around me, a touch my shoulder welcomed slavishly and which I pushed off with a violent gesture.

"You're quite right to beat me up. I'm a forgetful brute, an absent-minded lout. All the same, you will forgive me, darling, won't you? You must; I don't have time to kill myself before I leave. Is that another snarl, or, dare I hope, a smile? Ah, good. Well, the news, if such it can still be called, is that Nicholas is organizing a London engagement for me, and I promised to fly over and discuss things. There's talk of my playing either a Schumann or Brahms program for four evenings. That's what we have to decide. But definitely I shall be conducting West's Piano Concerto in D Minor for the other two."

"Oh, Simon, that's marvelous." I threw my arms around him in a vigorous embrace, joyful for him, yes, but more so for me.

"So you see there's good reason for my plea of insanity, ain't there? And now if you can only tell me where my suede jacket is, all will be right with our world."

"Why do you want that old rag? Better ask Gina. She's probably polishing the silver with it. You're certainly taking a lot with you for just a week."

"Not really. I'm leaving my recorder. And do, please, for heaven's sake, keep Gina away from it, will you? That precious thing's far too sensitive to be fooled around with. One shake of a feather duster and it'll have a nervous collapse. I've left it on the closet shelf. Out of her reach, I hope."

I went to the dressing table and began to brush my hair, hiding the memory his words had evoked behind a curtain of thick black hair—foolish, persistent thoughts of Josef and his sewing machine.

When Lisi bought the chalet in Rosten, it was Josef who came in reply to her advertisement for a housekeeper. A pale blond boy in a blue serge suit, he appeared at the door with a trunk at his side and an old portable Singer sewing machine under his arm. His treasure, he called it, his *Schatz*. Only twenty-four years old, he already had a parcel of references to prove that he excelled in tailoring, cooking, gardening, and drifting. Though now, he assured Lisi, he was more than ready to settle down, to turn the chalet into a "proper home for the madame's children." But it was really madame he adopted, this maternal young man who rolled out great lengths of strudel dough on the kitchen table at one moment and a bolt of wool jersey the next.

"Dear madame," Josef would say, gazing at our mother with an adoring, critical eye, "why don't I make you something new to wear into Zurich tomorrow? Something a bit more stylish." Rushing to the linen closet, he'd take his sewing machine down from the shelf, and by the next morning Lisi would have a new dress and Josef a matching narrow-waisted shirt with flowing sleeves.

"What are you doing?" Simon asked. "I thought I was forgiven. You're not sitting there sulking, are you?"

"Of course not. Why would I be?" I replied, thinking of the day Josef packed up his trunk. *"Ach, Gott. Ich muss jetzt gehn,"* he sighed. Yet he steadfastly refused to say good-bye, because he was returning "so soon, almost at once." He was only taking the shortest holiday, he insisted, and then only because of his sick grandmother.

"But Josef, you've packed all your things," Lisi said gently. She understood very well that the time had come for this drifter to leave and guessed that he could bring himself neither to confess it nor to say a final farewell to the family he had mothered for more than a year.

"No, dear madame, not all my things. I'm not taking my treasure on so short a trip," Josef said, opening the linen closet, where, to our surprise, the old Singer sewing machine still sat on the top shelf. Confident now of his return, we casually waved him off, only to discover when he didn't come back that he had packed the sewing machine and left behind the case—a loving coward's decoy.

"While I'm in England," Simon was saying, "I might pop down to Dorset and spend the weekend with my parents."

He so rarely spoke of his family, seemed so totally unattached, that I'd never given his parents much thought. Yet now, shamelessly, resolutely, I said: "I'd love to go along with you to meet them."

He was buckling my suitcase shut and looked up in amazement. "Meet them? Why on earth for?"

I wanted to plunge deep into those sea-blue eyes and tell him the truth: Because I'm afraid to let you leave me, afraid of going to the closet and finding an empty recorder case on the shelf.

"Why?" I said. "Why, because they're your parents. What better reason?"

"Well, yes, I suppose so" was the vague reply. "It's a rather good idea, actually. I wonder I didn't think of it. Only, you'll have to find another suitcase for yourself."

"I'm here," Sister Clotilde murmured. "Sister Berthe tells me there's been no change in Mr. West."

"I don't think so, no. You're on duty early, Sister."

"Late," she corrected with a kind smile for my confusion. "Reverend Mother has given me permission to stay on in case you need me."

Thank you. Oh, I do really thank you. I may no longer recognize late from early, but the relief I feel when you're with me is unmistakable.

"Sister Clotilde?" A nurse's aide, standing at the door, interrupted my silent communication.

"Please ring if you need anything, Miss Stewart," Sister Clotilde said. "I'll look in again as soon as I can."

Simon and I didn't stay the weekend in Dorset with his family after all. Instead, we decided to drive on to Cornwall, if I can call that bedroom farce, that disorderly midnight flight from the West home a decision.

We ought to have given his parents more notice of our visit. Simon meant to, assumed he had, and in the end rang up at the last moment, just as we were leaving London. It was really better this way, he told me. Otherwise they'd have had all that time to fuss and fret. Much better to surprise them.

"Well, this is certainly a surprise." The Wests greeted us, oh, so stiffly. "Quite a surprise indeed."

For my part, I was no less surprised. It was hard to believe that these two dry sticks had sparked such a flame as Simon; that this formal Georgian house, which despite its highly polished surfaces had an atmosphere of such dusty silence, was his habitat. Only the piano in the drawing room had, with its expansive gleam of white ivory, a welcoming, happy look. And, in fact, it was this handsome baby grand Simon rushed to sit beside and caress.

"Your friend speaks English extremely well for an Italian, dear." Mrs. West pointed at me with her long, curving beak, a fitting handle for a face with delft blue eyes and fair, deeply lined skin that had the gloss of mended porcelain.

"Anna's an American, Mother. Didn't I mention that?"

"Is she really? An American? I'm not sure I'd have guessed. Where in America does she come from? Boston?"

Mrs. West followed this question with a leisurely selection of others to do with my family and schooling. More unnerving yet, they were all directed at Simon, who turned to me so often for the answers that I might have been, indeed began to feel like, someone he'd just picked up on the road to Dorset.

Tall, wooden Mr. West meanwhile sat folded up in his chair, his gold-rimmed glasses focused on his wife. "Are you cold? D'you want your shawl? Or are you too warm?" he kept asking with an irritable affection. But for this and an occasional nervous, bored bark, he was a very quiet man.

Tired from the long drive, discomposed by Mrs. West's relentless curiosity on the one hand and her husband's total indifference on the other, I longed for escape. Surely any moment now my hostess would take me upstairs to whatever refuge was to be mine for the weekend? But no. I was shown around the gardens, discreetly directed to the downstairs powder room, and given tea. Only another stroll, this time to the riverbank, separated tea from dinner, and that solemn meal, with its pale grudging wine, was in turn followed by a family concert.

Simon, dreamy and masterful at his boyhood piano, playing a Chopin waltz, mazurkas, an ardent, almost martial polonaise. I watched his straight, disciplined back and that unruly head of sandy hair with as maternal and fatuous an eye as Mrs. West.

"Oh, my pet, how well I remember when you first learned those pieces," she said. "Do play on. I'm sure your friend is as eager as we are to hear more. There can't be many such fireside recitals on the Continent."

Simon, with an absent, lazy smile and swift conjurer's hands flying over the keyboard . . . now Beethoven's cuckoo, now the nightingale. I was charmed by this glimpse of a Dorset youth, a shadowy golden boy, charmed and vaguely jealous, and finally too weary to feel anything but the desire to be alone. How much longer would my lips put up with this heavy smile? What a luxury solitude was, after all. I yearned to be quiet, motionless except to turn the pages of a book.

"Well done, my boy. I should say that deserved some more cognac," Mr. West declared.

"Do you really think we need it, dear? The fire's warmed everything up so nicely."

Nonetheless, Mrs. West allowed her glass to be refilled, accepted at last the offer of a shawl, and eventually requested a pillow for her head. Mr. West, as the night wore on, barked more frequently and every now and then, with the quick, precarious gait of a circus dog, tottered from the room, quite possibly to go out and relieve himself at a favorite tree. But neither one of this amazing pair seemed to have any need for sleep.

"It's getting late, Mother. I imagine Anna's as ready for bed as I am. What with the drive down and all, we've had rather a long day of it."

"I know you have, poor dears," Mrs. West sympathized, but whenever I made a move to get up from the sofa, she restrained me with a quick hand and a firm "Oh, surely not yet. Such a quiet creature she is, Simon. But still waters—"

And so another hour passed. "What about you, Father? Aren't you ready to call it a night?"

"Why, it's not even half past twelve." Mr. West's reply sounded curiously like a rebuke.

Did this rigid, custodial couple intend to stay up all night rather than risk letting Simon and his "friend" go to bed? I'd long since realized there was no chance of our sleeping in the same room; now I began to wonder if under the same roof.

"Well, you two night owls have my permission to carry on for as long as you like," Simon said, "but if Anna and I don't go upstairs soon, we're likely to drop right here on your Persian rug, and very comfortable it looks, doesn't it, Anna?"

"Heavens, everybody, do you see what time it is," his mother cried in capitulation.

I was given a bedroom next door to the Wests and, predictably, at the opposite end of the hall from Simon. A virtuous pink-and-white room whose walls were covered with prudent rosebuds. Exhausted, I fell upon the bed, telling myself I would stretch out for just a moment, and then unpack, and then undress, and then wash.

The creaking of the hall floorboards woke me first; next came the plaintive cry of my door, opened too slowly, followed by a loud "Who's there?" from Mr. West in the next room.

"Sssh," said Simon, "it's me." Simon, who, if he dressed for bed at all—"Surely one of the oddest pretensions of civilized man?"—wore a pair of old flannel pajama bottoms, was now standing by my bed shimmering in peacock blue silk pajamas, a matching robe, and a paisley ascot.

"It's you, is it? Are you sure?"

"Very funny. She likes keeping a few things here for me."

"Son?" This apprehensive call from Mrs. West proved too much for my badly frayed nerves, and they gave way, releasing a torrent of giggles.

"Shut up," Simon whispered. "Have you gone crazy?"

Alas, I had, but the knowledge was only fuel to my childish mirth, as indeed everything seemed to be; the loud rasping of the bedsprings when Simon sat down, his own unwilling cackles, the censorious slam of a parental door. Drunkenly, there's no other word for it, I rolled into his arms, and our mouths met in mid-laughter, a light kiss that took itself too seriously, deepened into an earnest quest that brought me to my feet, sober and reeling.

"Anna." But I backed away from the wistful mouth that uttered so lordly a command, turned from the blue eyes threatening to descend over me again like a turbulent sky.

"Not here . . . I couldn't."

"Let's go then. Come on, get your suitcase."

"Go?" Astounded, I watched him creep to the window. "Go where?"

"Why, wherever you like, my darling. Cornwall would be nice, I think."

"Simon, you fool, wait. We can't just sneak out the window in the middle of the night."

"Of course we can. The roof's quite flat at this side," he said, easing up the window sash. "You can imagine the row if we tried leaving by the front door. Sssh, for God's sake, don't have another giggle fit now."

"But look at you. You can't go anywhere like that."

"Why not?" he said, tucking the ascot into his robe. "It's a very respectable sort of outfit."

One tempestuous scene followed another on that drive to Cornwall. A haunted, melodramatic peninsula it was, with its bleak moorlands and misty cliffside castles. Habit kept my face turned to the car window and the addictive pleasure of a new vista, but my thoughts were back in that virginal bedroom where I had been so stirred by Simon's kiss, by the silky touch of those absurd, iridescent pajamas.

"Simon, be careful. You're driving awfully fast, aren't you?"

His answer was to press his foot down on the gas pedal. "Not nearly fast enough for two waifs without shelter. A pair of run-aways who have to find a hotel with floorboards that don't creak and a bed—"

I put my hand over his mouth to protect myself from words that I knew could leave me as weak with desire as his touch, but he kissed my hand. "Don't," I murmured against the soft pressure of his lips in my palm. "Oh, Simon." Scandalized by my incontinence, I pulled my hand away and put it to rest lightly on our combined thighs, thinking this a refuge. But there was no longer a neutral place for us to meet.

"Soon," he promised. "We'll be there soon," and taking his hand from the wheel he embraced mine. For an embrace is what it was. Our hands, united in longing, molded themselves to each other, fingers interlocked with the passionate strength of limbs, mounts touching, palm pressed into palm.

"Ah, do you feel that?" In his moan I heard my own awe and desire. "Our hands are coupling."

Coupling. A curious word for Simon to choose, and so exact. How I loved him for that genteel accuracy and how I wanted him, this primitive in his paisley ascot. My palm, submissive, straining, pressed itself into his.

"Yes, they're coupling," I echoed, exulting in the word, as I did in the sound of tearing brakes when Simon pulled off the road, as I exulted in the rough damp heather we fell upon.

"I'm surprised, Sister," Dr. Pagello said. "I thought it would be yesterday, certainly last night."

"His heart is still strong," Sister Clotilde murmured.

"The heart," said the young resident doctor, "is full of surprises. How many times has it made a liar out of you, Professore?"

"It can fool us, but not for very long. Too bad, eh? In this case, another few hours, perhaps, another day at the most."

Standing at the window, gazing out at the gray wet morning, I heard clearly this sotto voce conversation, but I didn't turn around until Sister Clotilde gave a discreet pluck at my sleeve. Then, in the silent way of her sisters, I followed her from the room.

"I thought while the doctors are here you might want to go downstairs for breakfast," she said, and, at my look of surprise, "It's important that you keep up your strength." A pause, and then: "You must be prepared now, my child. The doctor says—"

I don't know what appeal Sister Clotilde read in the harsh gesture I used to cut her off, but her response was quick and, in its way, as helpless.

"Oh, my dear. I have prayed to God to show me the way to ease your pain. I wish so much that you could know Mr. West isn't really leaving you. Our earthly life is not the end. The good Lord is waiting even now to receive this soul who is so precious to Him."

Warmed by Sister Clotilde's fervor, the generous way she offered me her simple beliefs, I gave her a grateful, unconvinced nod and started back into the room.

"Wait, Miss Stewart. About breakfast," she said. "If you're not going down to the dining room, I shall ask for a tray to be sent up. Will you take cereal or eggs?"

"What about the broiled mackerel in oats?" Simon asked, our first morning in Cornwall. "Although I must say grilled bacon and tomatoes sound rather tasty, don't they?" He turned the page of the handwritten menu with such amorous haste it might have been a billet-doux the innkeeper's daughter had slipped under our door. "And so does fresh trout steamed with butter and oregano. Oh, but wait, there's walnut flapjacks," he looked at me with an innocent, helpless greed, "and gooseberries with clotted cream."

"Why don't we order the lot?" I, too, was gluttonous that weekend, insatiable, and yet so simply satisfied.

Cornwall's literary landscape did not altogether escape my notice. I recognized that strange flat Dozmary pool into which Bedivere flung Arthur's sword, and though I knew Lisi had a vagabond's scorn for picture postcards, how could I resist sending her Virginia Woolf's "distant, austere" lighthouse? But as clear as the Godrevy Lighthouse, as distinct as Swinburne's "wind-hollowed heights and gusty bays," is the memory of a picnic: the fresh-crabmeat-and-cucumber salad, thick brown bread, and an elixirish blackberry wine that we took to a cliff covered with bluebells and yellow daisies, high above the sea.

"Look, we have a friend," said Simon, when the sea gull who came to snatch at our sandwiches stayed on, hovering with a fierce docility between sea and sky.

O Cornwall, with your sweet sunny coves that know so much more than they admit, your green guileless meadows that lead to such sudden jagged cliffs, did I fall in love with you because you had the same compelling appeal, the same mixture of savagery and gentleness as Simon?

I knew, without lifting my head from Simon's bed, that Sister Clotilde had gone to stand by the window. She was there in the room with me nearly all the time now. Sister Marie and Sister Berthe came to the door for whispered consultations and sometimes Sister Cecile called her away, but when next I looked around she would be back, reading the prayer book she took from her pocket or simply standing still with folded arms, watching over us. Whereas the other Sisters of the Divine Grace came into the room with calm looks of compassion, Sister Clotilde's face was white and strained, and it seemed to me that she bowed her head as much in pain as in meditation.

"It's raining again." I glanced around as Sister Clotilde shut the window. It was not much after four o'clock but the sky was already black, and she drew the curtains, shutting away the sad dark rain.

"Are you all right?" she whispered.

I nodded and turned back to the bed without speaking, startled and ashamed of the imagination that so clearly heard the rain mixed with the pounding of a wild sea.

There was a rainstorm the night before we were to leave Cornwall, and when we woke in the morning it was raining still. I expected Simon to be restless and anxious to leave the too-authentic old fishermen's inn, our small dormer room, so crowded, with only a lumpy bed, a chipped water basin, and the damp, misty memories of another century.

And I? I desired nothing more than to stay fitted into the warm curve of his back, my mouth so close to his sunburned skin that I breathed in its saltiness. Too content, too selfish to part with this moment, I listened to the rain and crashing waves without stirring, kept my eyes shut, and my breaths deep and evenly spaced.

"I know you're awake," Simon said. "You're really such a rotten liar, Anna, you can't fake sleep. Listen to that howling wind. Still, it's not without a kind of charm, all that poignant ferocity, don't you think, like a siren's requiem?"

He turned over and pulled my head down to rest on his chest. "Do you hear the waves?" he said. "What a mad thrashing about. Pure bravado, if you ask me. All the same, I'm glad we're not at sea. In fact, I wish we could go on staying here in this squashed little room of ours."

He gazed at me with such a trusting, tame look in his blue eyes that I felt a sudden guilt, a moment's fright for him.

"Just listen to that gale. Queer prehistoric sounds, aren't they? Come closer. We're much better off hidden away here. We'll stay like stowaways and let this old raft of a bed go rocking and tossing through the storm."

The storm that would rock our bed, the tempest he promised me was our own, and I threw myself on top of him, covering my friend's body with mine. Yes, we had become friends in Cornwall, my lover and I, and lest he see how protective and vulnerable this discovery made me, I buried my face against his shoulder, stayed there with my lips pressed on the small pulse that throbbed in the hollow of his neck.

Simon's chest heaved beneath me with a single, forceful thump that made my head fly up.

"His soul will soon be at peace," murmured Sister Clotilde with a gleam of tears in her eyes, not for him, I knew, but for me.

Utterly still for a moment, his heart gave another great thump, and thumped again, and with these few loud wild beats drummed itself out.

5

"Do you think a terrible tragedy comes on its own, without direction or help? You imagine that it just decides to happen all by itself? Well, excuse me, but there's a lot you don't know yet, *maestra mia.*"

"I know a crazy woman when I see one."

"And I don't?" Gina's rejoinder was quick, sharp, and pained. "A terrace with a rosebush and two pepper plants isn't a farm. What's wrong with your black silk dress? Tell me. Didn't I have it cleaned and pressed, all ready when you came home from the hospital? But no, you have to climb into the same trousers every day, the same big ugly sweater like a roughneck *contadino*. Do you think the neighbors haven't noticed? Do you imagine the whole *palazzo* is blind? Do you know what you look like? A goatherd."

"And you act like a witch. Since when have you taken up sorcery, that's what I want to know."

"Hold your tongue, you wicked thing. *Cattiva!*"

"*Strega!*"

Such was the abuse Gina and I were hurling at each other across the kitchen—the easy contempt of two old cronies surprised into rage, robust insults accentuated by the banging of pot lids and the smell of garlic frying in olive oil.

What had led me to storm Gina's citadel, to fly in the face of that savory armament? It began when I discovered that a notebook of mine was missing. This notebook, the smallest of a half-dozen that held the random notes for my novel, contained nothing important, nor had I any special fondness for it. On the contrary, it was a cheap *quadretto* with a glaring yellow cover and, worse, pages that were not lined but sported a pattern of blue checks. Its only virtue was its size. It was small enough to tuck into a pocket, and I used to do just that, taking it along with me in case I should get caught in a mild shower of thought while on a stroll in the Borghese Gardens.

But I was neither strolling in the park nor writing these days, and the search for that notebook was purely automatic, the work of a mere but well-trained reflex. Most of what I did was, for I had returned to my apartment with the uncertain step of a lost traveler, relieved and grateful when habit showed up to guide me.

Each morning at nine o'clock, my hands warming themselves around a second bowl of hot milk flavored with leftover espresso, I went to the desk in my studio and—and nothing. I simply sat there, a visitor who gave a respectful glance of recognition to the stout Italian dictionary and its even heavier companion, Roget's International Thesaurus, and admired the arrangement of lilac and blue pens in a crystal vase. After a while, one finger might venture forth to trace, seriously, precisely, the carved rose that, like a fancy garter, decorated the thick legs of my Bavarian desk. Just as studious was the attention to the alignment of stacked notebooks, and that was as far as habit, grown weak and addled, would take me.

No, that's not altogether true. An eager candor tempts me into the realm of lies. I did, naturally, read over the notes for my novel, and the pieces of description, the bits of dialogue, the rash plans and promises, left me not only unmoved but mystified. Urgent and cryptic, those breathless scrawls seemed to be addressed to somebody else in a private language of love.

Nevertheless, I continued to follow my old routine and, as I sat at the desk on this particular morning, it finally occurred to me that I was staring at an incomplete set of notebooks. Absent was the *quadretto*, and thinking I must have left it in some jacket, I went to my bedroom closet, looked into the pocket of a favorite blazer and saw an improbable heap of sugar. A glance into the left-hand pocket revealed the gleam of another deposit, the breast pocket a third. With the awful foreknowledge, the divine certainty usually reserved for bizarre dreams, I went from dress to skirt to trousers, and, as I expected, found a similar leaving in every pocket.

Furious, baffled and disgusted, I flew to the kitchen, my peculiarly defiled clothes in my arms.

"What the devil's been going on in my closet?"

Gina lowered the flame beneath a steaming pot, adjusted the lid on another, and without turning around from the stove said: "I don't know what you're talking about."

"Oh, no? It's very clear what I'm talking about. I'm talking about my clothes."

"Your clothes?" She stirred the sauce in the iron skillet slowly and calmly, but her militant shoulders, the sudden rigidity of her plump buttocks under that tight housedress told me she was ready for battle. "You want to discuss clothes? Then I'll tell you something, *tesora mia*. The poorest widow in Messina wouldn't wear such an ugly black sweater."

"I'm not wearing it because it's black." That swift vicious bark of mine startled us both. "I'm wearing it because I'm cold. And if you're so anxious to tell me something," I said, throwing my things down on the table, "tell me why everything I own is full of sugar."

Gina raised the flame under a saucepan of simmering tomatoes, and all I had by way of response was that soft, insolent sputter.

"Oh, what an obstinate beast you are. Will you turn around. Look at this. Sugar in every single pocket."

"You're wrong," she said with a brief glance over her shoulder. "It's salt. Foolish girl. Why would anybody put sugar in your pockets?"

"I'm warning you, Gina, I don't have time for this craziness. Do you hear me? *Mulo!* You'd better start talking. I'm in a hurry. I can't stand around here waiting any longer."

"You're in a hurry?" Still facing the stove, she reached up and jabbed a hairpin deeper into her tight black bun, a warrior's thrust. "Hurry for what, my Annabella? To go sit on the terrace by yourself, mourning like a tomboy in the top of a tree?"

"It's none of your business where I sit. Busybody!" In my fury I kicked the table, gratified when the butter dish crashed to the floor.

"*Madonna.*" Gina's back winced at the mess. "Why are you carrying on so much? What do you want me to do, let the sauce burn? It's not like you to be so angry."

"It's not like you to salt my clothes."

She turned to me then with a hot, sad, defiant face. "All right. I did it. I did it to ward off the evil eye. I did it so whoever put a curse on you can't cause you any more harm."

"Oh, Gina." Was I going to throttle or hug her? "Nobody's put a curse on me. That's rubbish, it's nonsense."

"Nonsense is it? Tell me more, madame." She yanked open the oven, prodded a chicken that sat roasting under a thatch of sage leaves and sprigs of rosemary, and just as quickly slammed the door shut against that warm aromatic gust of the country-side. "You think a great misfortune comes without an invitation? Is that what you think?"

"I think you're a lunatic. Why would anyone put the evil eye on me? Who do I know who'd want to do a thing like that? Who do I know, for that matter, who could?"

"If you had been born in my village," replied the disdainful Gina, "you wouldn't have to ask such questions."

Oh, the range and affection of that scorn; the arrogant, worried sniff at yesterday's cream, the loving hand that whipped a bowl of egg whites until they rose in their own graceful, fragile defense.

"So sometimes you don't know who has the *malocchio*, sometimes a curse falls on your head by accident. When you were children, didn't I always warn you to be careful where you walk, to go to the other side of the street if you saw somebody coming toward you with crossed eyes."

"Yes. And didn't David break his ankle running away from some innocent cross-eyed girl on Via del Corso?"

"A disaster is never innocent. If David hadn't run away, he'd have broken something worse."

Wild rebukes, sensational cries—our scene continued for some moments more, rivaling, and I've no doubt surpassing, the dramatic outbursts heard on occasion from the other apartments in the old palace, those truly passionate scenes that issue not from the bedroom but the kitchen.

In the end it was no return of sense or sensibility, but a raw, painful throat that served to remind me that I was, after all, the mistress here, was I not? Conclusively, I pronounced Gina a loud-mouth and a witch, took up my clothes, and, with a grand display of nonchalance, left the room, emptying pockets of salt along the way.

But she had the last word. "Hoyden! Thank God the sisters at Monte Sacre can't see my fine lady now. You in your goat-herd's outfit. Tell me, *maschiotta*, when you unzip those pants can you piss farther than any other woman?"

Her bellicose cry followed me out of the kitchen and down the long foyer, a shadowy path with forest-green draperies and burnt-umber portraits, followed me, I confess, straight to a gilded looking-glass. An ancient oval whose gold leaves were beginning to wither and fall, this *settecento* piece had, like the foyer itself, a somewhat dim, remote character.

But the mist crystallized within the glass, those antique clouds, did not obscure a pair of blue jeans that emphasized long, straight legs; nor the bulky cardigan that hinted, perversely, at a slender waist and small breasts. A winter sun had roughly colored high cheeks that were now in command of a face grown thinner; and unshed tears had turned the eyes a deeper gray, given them the hard luster of certain agates one sees in a shallow stream. The mouth . . . the mouth put an end to this scrutiny with a derisive, unbecoming smile at the goatherd.

The relief Gina expressed on behalf of the Sisters of the Divine Grace, so fortunately spared my fall from fashion, could not have been better delivered from the stage of the Teatro

93

dell'Opera. How rapturously she thanked God for the blessing, and what an odd pang I felt. Did my fierce glower succeed in concealing that sudden—was it possible—nostalgia for the hospital? Her words had brought on a positive flurry of white veils, and for an instant I could hear the soothing murmur of long skirts rushing down a corridor, feel the warmth of Sister Clotilde's quick, bright smile.

The building's internal telephone rang in the kitchen, and Gina's welcoming shouts to the grocery boy reminded me that it was getting close to midday. The sun would have turned the corner of the *palazzo* by now, well on its way to the small terrace above my bedroom, and I hurried there to meet it.

A tomboy in a treetop? If that's what pleased Gina's bucolic imagination, let her think it. But she was wrong, quite wrong, to suppose I sat up there mourning Simon. Not at all. While my anxious Fury, my loving Hecate poured her grief into saucepans, into the unceasing preparations of lavish feasts for one, I slumbered on the warm red tiles like a Roman cat.

There was a logical enough reason. I was suffering from a chill that would not leave me. I was cold to the bones, and I hoped to ease this unusual condition in the sunshine. The truth of the matter is, I had once again been betrayed by my body, for though I had no intention of sorrowing after Simon, it never let up a shivery lament. And if on occasion I was moved to hug my midriff and rock that lorn ache, it was only the helpless, self-conscious care one gives to another's anguish, to a foundling affliction. No, I never believed that wretched, ignominious bundle of misery belonged to Simon and me.

Allegro con brio, those were the last words he wrote, a light penciled phrase dashed off above a few bars of music. I found it on a crumpled bit of paper under the piano. As though I needed a clue to tell me how mourning would have bored him, how offended he'd be by sorrow. Oh, Simon, you were fleeter, briefer, more transitory than ever I suspected but would I grieve a shooting star, could I bury a fallen comet?

So did I deceive myself with the pretty fancies, the lyrical sophistry of a coward. It was nothing more or less than fear that kept me from mourning Simon. I was, quite simply, terrified to confront so overwhelming, so breath-taking an absence. I dared not look behind me lest I catch sight of a phantom lover, nor did I pick up a ringing telephone without a macabre hesitation. And when my guard was down and he came barging into my head, I listened to him with a cowering heart that could scarcely contain itself waiting for the *mise en scène* to lift, for him to go and leave an empty mind behind.

Leave it free, rather, for white windmills turning in an Aegean breeze, or a pink stork balanced on a minaret, or remote hills holding aloft a secret lake that blooms with yellow iris. It was not to lull myself that I recalled such vistas, but to tempt and stir. Surely the time had come to leave Rome, to move on, and yet a queer sort of lethargy kept me from making even a brief trip to Rosten.

"What do you think about my flying home next weekend?" I had been saying to Lisi for nearly a month now. "I'm really longing for a visit." This was true, though it seemed to matter little to my sloth. "I should be able to get everything organized by Thursday or Friday."

"That would be lovely, darling. Thursdays are better for travel, of course." My patient, gallant mother copied perfectly a tone as vague as it was positive. "There's less of a crowd—"

Her words faded from the line and were replaced by a thundering "The Assyrian came down like the wolf on the fold / And his cohorts were gleaming in purple and gold." This snatch of Sennacherib was the chant, the tribal code with which we children, mocking and thrilled, had followed our foot-loose mother from one continent of cheap pensions to another, and the sonorous voice now on the telephone belonged to my brother David.

"Well? What about it? Are you sure you don't want to come

with me?" He had recently signed a contract for a new travel book and was about to set off on a year's exploration of river life on the Indian subcontinent.

"The Punjab! Think of it, Annie. Bengal, Tibet!" he exclaimed, offering lavishly the only consolation he knew. "The itinerary's changed a bit. I'm starting off now with a houseboat on the Tsangpo. How'd you like that?"

"Oh, David, I'd love it. Who wouldn't?"

"Then come along. It will be like old times. Augustus says definitely he'll be out after the spring term. The silly ass. Do you know he lost his head and invited Sarah-the-don along? Good Lord, it's not exactly an afternoon's punting at Oxford. Oh, well, *qu'il fasse comme il lui plaît*. Perhaps we can all meet in Calcutta when Lisi comes out. That would be fun, wouldn't it?"

"Great fun."

"Well, what are you waiting for? Pack up. *Fai presto, cara.*"

What was I waiting for? I had no idea. Nothing. And yet, despite the tender tug of our nomadic bond, I lingered on the terrace, continued to sit, irresolute, in a landscape of sloping red-tiled roofs and orange domes.

This high, quiet spot was particularly attractive to me in the middle of the day. Not just for the sunshine but because from noon until one o'clock, the hour that signals the siesta, my ancient neighborhood was a chaotic place. Last-minute shoppers flocked into the streets while the merchants, impatient to get home, reached up precipitate hands for the iron grilles that locked away their shops with an irrefutable clang. It was once my favorite time of day, that zestful hour, but now I found the noise and exuberance uncomfortable. I knew too well the siesta where that wave of activity subsides, recalled more clearly than I wished a false twilight created by empty streets and closed shutters.

"They're jolly clever, aren't they?" Simon had murmured in my arms.

"Who?" I asked, holding him tight against me, not letting his head turn from its resting place on my breast. "Who are?"

"Why, the Italians." His lips moved slowly, deliberately, against my skin. "Oh, so clever, to have invented a day with two nights."

A piece of tile fell to the terrace, scattering my thoughts. It was the fault of a roving cat, a big sleek animal the same russet color as the roof. He leaped to the cupola of the church next door, turned to me with a challenging stare, and when I did not move, continued on his way, stalking across the top of Rome.

The terrace was not my only refuge. In the late afternoon, an unaccountable need for a similar retreat took me to my bedroom, where the walls were a rich, confident blue and the immense bed, with its golden grogram cover, had the peaceful, inviting look of a field of shorn wheat.

Above a pretty white escritoire, too pretty to write upon, hung the portrait of the mother duchess who once ruled this vast apartment. Her beauty and hauteur were summed up by Boldini in a swift commanding black line that swept from her chignon to the hem of a swirling skirt. With an imperious chin she pointed across the room to a wall that, like the one in the dining room, was covered by an awesome bequest. This tapestry depicted the underworld of the Lorelei, a colossal floating mélange of fish and sea anemones constructed from a million minute coral and amber beads. My attention often drifted to it when I was reading, and I would put down my book to wonder whether suffering a grand passion, or the lack of it, had inspired the duchessa to such heroic patience.

"Dear heart, why are you staring at that hideous thing? May I come in? You didn't hear me? Are those dreadful beads so fascinating?" My cousin Sofia, rigged out in a great white cape, sailed unannounced into the bedroom in a stream of distressed greetings. "This is exactly what Alex worries about."

"Oh, is it?" Indignantly, I stood up. "I thought he'd have more interesting things to worry about," I said, giving her an embrace warmer than my words. "And what brings you down from your ivy tower, my darling Sofia?"

"Shopping. I was just around the corner and I thought I'd stop by for a minute."

"Shopping in the rush hour?" That wasn't like my cousin. "Whatever for?"

"New sandals. I've given up on shoes. Once I began gardening in earnest, I thought why shouldn't the feet have their freedom and fresh air, too." She pulled up her flowing white trouser leg and pointed a sandaled foot at me. "You see?"

It was, as one would expect from Sofia, a big, bold, handsome foot, a robust bunch of toes with rosy pink nails. But had they been attached to a less stylish figure, wouldn't they seem a shade too robust, a trifle overblown?

"So, Anna?" The toes in question began to wriggle under my pensive eye. "What do you think? Why don't you come along with me and get a pair? You're quite sure not? Well, dearest, I'll be off then."

No sooner had I seen Sofia out the door than the turtledoves, as she called Eleonora and Richard, arrived. They, too, it seemed, were shopping around and so decided to drop in. Actually, they were hoping to find that antique shop with the picture frames I once mentioned; did I happen to remember? Stay for tea? *Grazie mille*, tea's the very thing she was longing for, Eleonora assured me with her tristful smile.

Such was the simple pretext a central apartment offered friends who were more disturbed by my solitude than I.

"It's so pleasant in here," Eleonora said, as I led them to the sitting room, which, furnished in a single shade of aged, undiluted burgundy, already had a mellow evening glow.

Too kind, too solicitous, they lingered over tea and, like their hostess, discreetly refrained from commenting on the host's absence.

"So what's it been like in your hills?" I asked.

"Quiet, very quiet," replied Richard, whose blond good looks were a perfect contrast to the dark Eleonora. "In other words, ideal for my work."

"And yours?" I asked the poet.

"Oh, mine. I sit under the wisteria with a handful of sweet new grapes and I listen to the river, and that seems like poetry enough" was the pretty reply. "I hate to leave our hideaway even for a day. Richard's lucky, a painter needs only solitude. I had to come into Rome twice last week to work with my translator. It's really so tiresome having to dress and go to a city. It's a bore, and an interruption, *non è vero?*"

These caressing words were directed at her husband, whose reply was an intimate smile, an eloquent look that said entirely too much about the pleasures this couple found in their secluded country life.

"I know you weren't the most sociable person even when . . . even when you were sociable," Eleonora told me, "but now the weather's getting warm, perhaps you'll drive out to see us soon."

"That would be nice."

They then asked for directions to the antique shop and, the way made clear, left arm in arm, companionable lovers, and my shameful pang of envy followed them.

Later on, or the next day, Gina, who complained about the parade in our hall with a pleased grimace, opened the door to Margot.

"No, I don't believe it," the latter said breathlessly, her arms full of packages, her face pink and astonished as she glanced at the hall clock. "It can't possibly be six-thirty. I have an appointment for seven. I'm sure that's wrong. The kitchen clock isn't the same as this, is it?"

"Heavens, what a shopping spree you've been on. Yes, of course, the kitchen clock's the same."

"Why 'of course'?" Out went the short, square chin, up flew the dark eyebrows, and I was treated to the street-urchin charm that Margot's fans thrive on. "In my town, the main square has a clock outside the old inn, one on the yellow schoolhouse, another at the Hôtel de Ville, a pretty little clock tower makes four, and when I was a girl none of them ever agreed. If anybody pointed this out to the mayor—he owned the pharmacy in the square—he'd be sure to reply, 'Upon my word'—yes, that's how he talked, like an old English squire—'Upon my word, what's the point in having four clocks if they all say the same thing.' "

Margot kissed me hello then, a brief pause before going straight into the next routine. "Your friend has behaved very foolishly today. She bought everything in sight, threw her money around the shops like an idiot. Would you believe such extravagance, darling? I didn't even leave myself the cab fare home. Lucky you live in the neighborhood, eh?" She delivered these lines perfectly, with just a hint of prevarication, an accomplished actress giving the self-conscious performance of a novice liar.

When Margot went to Paris to do a television play, it was her devoted secretary, Cathleen, who came to visit. "Margot said to tell you she's never in her life seen a worse script than what they gave her." Or "She said I should come over and get Gina's recipe for her cheese pie." But I was touched by this awkward young dissembler. I enjoyed her shy silence and, even more, her rapid, blushing outbursts.

"Oh, 'tis a terrible hot day." With a fetching gaucherie, Cathleen lifted her long hair above a high collar, letting two handfuls of fine yellow silk slip carelessly through her fingers. "It being still winter, I mean."

"Why don't you take off your wrap?" The dark shawl flung over a long brown dress was not an unusual costume for her. She made a point of covering as much of herself as she could with floor-length dresses, heavy square-toed boots, and garden hats, trying to hide, along with her beauty, such wild, uncertain emotions.

"I hope Margot's getting enough rest in old Paris. She forgets 'tis work she's doing until she drops from it. Mario thinks I carry on like a demented mother hen, but you know what our Margot's like. She can't look after herself at all properly."

"She'll be fine. It's only for a few more days. You haven't said much about Mario lately. How is he?"

"Oh, him. He's right enough." An indifferent reply, for Cathleen was cavalier about her man. "He came round to help me plant some rosebushes to surprise Margot. He's a dab hand with the flowers, I'll say that for him, though nowhere near as good as my dad. 'Tis a true work of art, our garden at home. Everybody says so. But whatever my dad touches turns into a masterpiece; he can't help it, poor old bugger."

"I remember seeing such beautiful gardens when we were in Ireland. Perhaps one of them was yours."

"If Margot could hear us carrying on about Irish gardens. She'd think I was homesick or something. Go take yourself off on a holiday, she'd tell me. A holiday. 'Tis the last thing I need. And who'd take care of her? Anyway, I don't want to go home," she announced, her round face flaming.

"Oh, Cathleen—" The sympathetic murmur that escaped me caused that fierce red to spread to the very rim of her big candid blue eyes.

"Well, 'tis different since the old boy's taken up with Kat. Not that I give a fhuck what they do. Oh, I'm not saying I don't miss him. Her, too, for that matter. We grew up together, didn't we? I just don't feel like hanging around with them, that's all."

"Of course you don't."

"Sometimes I dream I'm back, though. Like the other night, I had a real corker. There I was in Killarney, tearing down the road in a big old school bus. 'Twas a bit mad, see, because the driver was my dad and the bus was full of girls with long blond hair. I couldn't see any of their faces, but I knew they were all me."

Thus, compulsively, did Cathleen sum up her profound attachments; the one to her glamorous employer, the other to an artist father who in his vigorous mid-life became the lover of her best friend.

During this period I had another regular visitor, and if I've waited until now to speak of Alex and the calls he paid, stopping in each evening on his way home, if I've saved them until last—ah, well, I suppose that childish instinct tells how I felt about those brief visits.

"Oh, maestro, it's you." Gina, rushing to answer his peremptory ring, contrived in that simple greeting to convey expectation, surprise, and her boundless admiration.

"*Buona sera*, ladies. No, thanks, I'll keep my coat. I've only come by to say hello." Busy with the production plans for his new film, Alex rarely stayed longer than it took to exchange a conspiratorial glance with Gina, and hold out a pair of paternal arms to me.

"How did it go today?" By staying still in his embrace, by breathing in the scent of a harsh tobacco sweetened by cologne and exhaling in a long sigh, by my tremulous silence, I answered him.

"Yes, I know. Poor darling, I understand. I miss Simon, too. We all do, those of us who were fortunate enough to know him and those who knew only his music. But even to know the music is to love the man, and at least that remains to us." The deep murmur continued, as reassuring and comfortable as the shoulder where my head burrowed, seeking a childhood refuge. "It's very sad, but you're still so young, and time has its own way of dealing with tragedy. You'll see, dearest girl, I promise you. One day this will seem no more than a bad dream, *un mauvais quart d'heure*, as they say."

"Oh, that's what they say, is it?" My old friend had murmured a little too much, and, shocked and wounded by his crowning reassurance, I gave him a rough push away. "Pah! What do you do, bathe in that filthy jasmine stuff? Sofia's right, you smell like a real cocotte."

One afternoon Alex came by earlier than usual and found me at my desk in the studio.

"You're working on your book again," he declared. It was his peculiar civility to launch personal questions in the guise of statements and wait, a patient half-smile his mark of interrogation.

"Wrong. I'm trying to decide whether or not to do the household accounts. What's your moral inclination, to pay bills today or tomorrow?"

Alex's smile remained patient, and though I was tempted to outwait him, in the end I gave him his answer. "If you must know, I still haven't put so much as two words down on paper."

"But writing a book," said the gregarious film maker, "is a lonely thing to do at the best of times, or so I would imagine."

"Still, it might be easier if I were some place else, away from . . . from everything that happened. I've been thinking about Greece."

"Why, you little ingrate. You'd leave Rome, would you?" he asked, giving a wry twist to his smile. "Leave your old cousin with his pockets full of chocolate, would you?"

It's true. Alex consoled me, as he had done through the ills and woes of my girlhood, by bringing a daily supply of sweets, which I snatched at with a disgraceful, perplexing greed. Thin, elegant, gold-wrapped bars of chocolate appeared next to the cigars in his jacket, while the outer compartment of his briefcase bulged with caramels and heavy chunks of a dark country chocolate filled with raisins and hazelnuts. There was even a revolting pastoral set of pink marzipan pigs and red truffles; marzipan which I detest and yet seized upon no less gluttonously.

"I wish you'd stop treating me like a spoiled brat," I complained. "But since you've gone to the trouble, at least sit down and have a drink while I devour these loathsome things."

"I really shouldn't. Ugo's waiting at the apartment to discuss the budget. Well, maybe I'll have one glass of wine with you first. You're a much prettier sight than he is." Alex unbuttoned his suede coat, but kept it on as he sat down on the small sofa opposite my desk. "It won't surprise you to hear that my partner is already threatening suicide. And murder, naturally. I don't know how he thinks a film like *The Revolutionary Princess* can be made without costing money. Of course, it's going to be an expensive project, but, frankly, I haven't been so excited about a film or a woman since *The Blue Room*. Anna, did you hear me?"

"Yes, yes." I replied in the hearty tone that underlines inattention. "This is your princess, right?"

"My princess." He gave a low, offended cry. "Why, she's Italy's Jeanne d'Arc. She was like a tigress trying to free her country from the Austrians, a beautiful, courageous revolutionary who raised her own regiment of volunteers and fought beside them in the fields of Piedmont. Oh, she was fantastic."

It wasn't Alex's style, this sort of raving, and I felt a prick of jealousy at his excitement, at the light the princess had sparked in his green eyes. "Well, I'm sorry. I can't help it if I've never heard of her."

"That's what everyone says," he replied, strangely elated by his heroine's obscurity. "But they'll hear, they'll hear. It's going to give me the greatest pleasure to introduce this fascinating woman to history."

"Very obliging of you, and so modest, as usual."

"When the princess was an exile in France," he went right on, with his imperturbable smile, "she kept a brilliant salon. She was a very talented writer herself, by the way. All the Parisians were mad about her."

I wondered if I should get up and turn on the lamp. Dusk fell more quickly in my studio than in the other rooms, indeed, than in the streets outside. Like the foyer, the walls were hung with an antique dark-green velvet, and in the gloaming its worn patches had the pale golden gleam of forest moss.

"Anna, are you listening to me?"

"I don't have any choice, do I? You were saying that Princess What's-her-name—"

"Pay attention. I'm going to tell you her name. If I recall correctly, the unexpurgated version goes like this" He paused to take a deep, proud schoolboy's breath. "Princess Maria Cristina Beatrice Teresa Barbara Leopolda Clotilda Melchiora Giulia Margherita Laura Trivulzio-Belgiojoso."

I sat up with an interest that brought a pleased smile to his face. "Did you say Clotilda? Isn't that a coincidence."

"A coincidence," said the puzzled Alex. "What coincidence?"

"Why, the nun at the hospital. Don't you remember? She's called Sister Clotilde."

It did not take much to bring her to mind. I had only to glimpse a communion child in bridal dress on the steps of a church, or a pair of elderly nuns holding each other's hand as they ran across a traffic-filled piazza, to be reminded of that tender, vigilant nurse. But once faced with an image of her patient, my thoughts would take fright and run. Nor was there any telling where they might turn up to seek refuge next.

One day I stopped at the Piazza di Spagna to buy some flowers, and as I hesitated over a bunch of daisies that were all tarted up for city life, almost unrecognizable with their good-natured, simple heads dyed magenta and royal blue, I noticed a family act on the Spanish Steps.

A single glance at those young performers in their eclectic dress—one wore an embroidered Greek vest, another a Colombian shawl—gave back a reflection of my entire childhood. A brother and three sisters, they all had straight, wheat-colored hair clipped by a determined, unprofessional hand, and beneath their uneven fringes that expression of innocence and worldliness peculiar to vagabond children. The boy, who was the eldest, played a violin, accompanied by one of the girls on a piccolo. Another child flung herself about in an abandoned jig which revealed a Slovenian-looking pair of long flannel drawers, while the youngest sat on the steps, a black-and-white pup clasped in her arms.

It was to pay for the inoculations of this newly acquired pet that they performed, the children explained, circulating among the audience with straw baskets at the end of a musical set. They addressed the crowd in Italian, but to one another spoke the curiously unaccented, amalgamated English of American wanderers, their sentences held together with bits of French and German. Loudly muttered invectives, for the most part, they were aimed at the less generous spectators.

Once, I'd have called it a lively, amusing scene, but now those youngsters, so reminiscent of Lisi's troupe, left me with vague, sad, unanswerable questions about them, about us.

What an oblique, hazy shaft of unease had filtered into the vivid tableaux of Rome. Sun-flaked baroque façades I found shabby and desolate; lovers sharing a public embrace—he astride a motor scooter, she standing on the sidewalk—were dismissed as contortionists. I knew perfectly well the old gypsy beggar woman who sat on the corner of my street was an accomplished and successful tragedienne, yet the sight of her moved me to an anxious pity.

The same was true of the prostitutes who waited on the roads leading to the country, and for them my compassion was sharpened by the memory of certain callow, gleeful speculations.

The school my brothers and I had attended during our first stay in Rome was at the city's outer limits, and every morning our bus passed a roadside clearing where a small pack of wild-maned creatures in brief skirts and white rabbit-fur jackets was gathered.

Augustus, not surprisingly, was the one who identified them as whores. I say not surprisingly because my younger brother was, as Lisi put it, extremely quick at picking things up. He had, in fact, an amazing scatalogical gift, an unerring instinct that enabled him to divine the nearest toilet in whatever strange, remote corner we happened to land, and to absorb, in a matter of hours, the most obscene words and gestures that particular foreign place had to offer.

"Yes, they're *puttane*, all right," Augustus said as we gazed through the school-bus window at the circle of robust women warming their huge pink thighs by a fire made from old boxes and rubbish.

"Really?" I asked. "Are you sure?"

"*Certissimo*," he replied with a lickerish little laugh. "What did you suppose they were doing out here?"

I blushed in shame and refused to tell him. At that time I was more or less planted in the formal gardens of the nineteenth-century English novel and had simply thought they were convivial rural folk waiting for a public conveyance. In a way, of course, I was right.

"Look! There're the *puttane*!" Augustus continued to cry as we drove past the campfire voluptuaries. "Did you see them, David?"

"Well, there's not that much to see, is there?" I said, vexed by this daily excitement. "If what you say is true, where are their customers? And anyway how can . . . where do they—" The lack of privacy puzzled me. Those Rabelaisian women were much too tall for the low scrubby bushes and too wide for the furled cypress.

"Silly fool," said Augustus. "They do it in the cars that pick them up."

"They do it in the trucks, *dummkopf*," echoed David.

Nor did the matter end there. Under my brother's expert guidance this topic of conversation lasted longer and had more variations than I, for one, would have dreamed possible.

"What shall we try for the pasta course?" Lisi asked, taking us out to sample one of the restaurants in our new neighborhood.

"I know what I want," said Augustus who had been studying the menu with a distinctly pleased air. "I'll have the *spaghetti con salsa puttanesca*," he told the waiter, and, lordly, beneficent, added, "My little brother will have the *salsa puttanesca,* too. Won't you, David?"

"*Je crois bien,*" replied the little brother.

"That sounds interesting," Lisi said, turning her wide smile on the waiter, already savoring the delights of the unknown. What kind of sauce is it?"

"Oh, it's just a simple country sauce signora," was the disconcerted reply.

"It's a sauce made from this, that, and the other," said a more brazen waiter, who, charmed by our mother's voracious curiosity, took over the explanation with a respectful leer. "Olives, peas, maybe anchovies, sometimes mushrooms. Whatever's on hand goes into the pot. That's why it's called *puttanesca.* How shall I say it, *signora?* Like certain women, everybody goes with it." And Augustus, proud leader of this gastronomical discovery, beamed around the table, radiating Lisi's own kind of tutorial joy.

So did my thoughts wander and circle, often going quite out of their way to avoid each other, and in this manner three, then four desultory weeks passed. Tomorrow you really have to make some definite plans, I told myself, but the next day found me wrapped in my huge black cardigan and back on the terrace, contemplating nothing more than a lofty terrain where red geraniums thrive and only swallows stir the air between dome and pinnacle.

"Signorina." Gina was calling to me from below. "Annabella. Are you up there? I'm back from the market."

"So I see."

"You wouldn't believe the artichokes they had this morning, prettier than the flowers, but so dear. I bought two big beauties, and it cost a fortune. But everything was expensive today, except the clams, and they were too cheap. Well, are you coming down or not?"

She had climbed halfway up the spiral stairway to the terrace, as high as she ever cared to go, and stood securely fitted in the curve of the balustrade, waving a handful of letters at me. "Here's the post," she said. "I put the carnations on your desk, and now I'm going to the kitchen where nobody can bother me anymore."

In that batch of mail was a square white envelope that bore the imprint of Villa Monte Sacre and came, I was surprised and pleased to see, from Sister Clotilde. A letter of condolence, it was composed in English with an occasional literal translation from the French to blame for an awkward phrase, a charming mistake that I could plainly hear.

"Once again I would like to express my great sympathy in your grief over the one you loved so much," Sister Clotilde began, and with the gentle ardor of a small flowery script went on to speak of man's sorrows and joys, the world's frailty and the good Lord's endurance. She assured me that "God's will is the Magnificent Mystery at the center of Christian life," asked Him to bless me, and then ended on a most unexpected and puzzling note. "Dear Miss Stewart, you have taught me a great deal. I will never forget you."

Pious and platitudinous, it was nevertheless a warm letter and a curious one. Though, come to that, no more curious than the way I rushed to telephone the hospital, or my disappointment when I was told that Sister Clotilde was at the convent and wouldn't be on duty until evening.

And just why was I calling? To tell the nun what? That I had received her letter? Was all this simply to say thanks for a message that came in large part from the god with whom I had no truck? These stricken little questions darted into my head at the last possible moment that night, when it was already too late, when I could hear the telephone ringing at the nurses' station on the third floor, and a cool voice, Sister Cecile's, perhaps, asked me please to wait a moment.

"Oh, Miss Stewart, hello," Sister Clotilde said, not in the least surprised to hear me. "How are you?"

"Just fine, thanks. Very fit, really." With this appalling heartiness there sprang up another vigorous lie. "I was awfully reluctant to disturb you at work."

"No, it's quite all right. We've had a quiet floor lately."

"Does that mean the *contessina* went home?"

"Oh, yes. She made a splendid recovery," the nun replied with a soft laugh. "And I'm glad, Miss Stewart, to hear such good tidings from you."

So familiar and comforting was Sister Clotilde's murmur in my ear that when I thanked her for the letter I found myself adding a hope that we might meet again someday. Her invitation to visit the convent one afternoon followed just as naturally, no less so our rather prompt agreement on Thursday of the coming week.

"*Come bella!*" a surprised Gina cried, catching sight of me as I left the apartment for the convent. "That's a very nice dress. Wait, let me have a look. You're wearing make-up, too. My lady is *molto* chic today. Where are you off to? Can't you wait one minute to answer? Good heavens, how impatient she is."

Such was my mute fluster. I couldn't have said why any more than I could have explained the care I had taken to look chic for a visit to a nun, or why I was so willing to return to the hill of my undoing.

Only a row of cypresses separated the convent of the Sisters of the Divine Grace from the hospital, and yet it sat at the top of a sloping drive with an air of utter isolation.

"Good afternoon, Miss Stewart." It was the beaming Sister Marie who answered the convent bell. "Please come in."

I murmured my thanks, staring at the vast, vaulted halls opening one unto another, struck by the peace and perfection of them.

"If you don't mind waiting in the reception room?" she said. "It's this way."

I might have wandered in from a blazing desert, so cool and soothing did the hallways seem, an oasis of white marble.

"Sister Clotilde will be with you shortly."

The reception room on the other hand, was small and narrow, furnished with tall, stiff chairs and a table covered with green serge—a room that clearly had no real interest in receiving. Much less in the pacing of an anxious guest who studied by turn a statue of the Sacred Heart, a photograph of His Holiness in Rouen, and a solitary window.

"Miss Stewart?"

I spun around from the window. "Oh, Sister, hello."

"I'm sorry to have kept you waiting."

"Please don't be. I was admiring the view." I spoke without thinking; for that window, as the nun's puzzled smile reminded me, looked onto nothing more inspirational than a circular drive. The truth is, I was startled by a slender, supple beauty my memory hadn't done justice to.

"Two of the nurse's aides didn't show up today, so we're busier than usual on the third floor."

"I've come at an inconvenient time then."

"No, it's fine. I have a free hour now. Do have a seat, won't you?"

We sat across the table from each other, and she gazed at me with dark eyes all the more lustrous for the white velvet they were displayed against. "I'm glad to find you looking so well, Miss Stewart."

"Thank you, Sister. And thanks for inviting me here. I've thought about all of you often. Did Sister Bernadette ever go for her holiday in Brussels?" I wanted nothing more than to sit quietly, with her kind of serenity, but my tongue had got loose and was rattling away. "Has Sister Agathe been transferred to the nursery? And how's Sister Marie getting on with her Italian lessons?" I was grabbing onto those nuns as though I were at a class reunion. "Is Sister Berthe still on the third floor with you?"

"She is indeed, the kind soul." Sister Clotilde put her chapped hands to rest beneath folded arms. "I hope you're comfortable enough in that chair. You're quite sure? Good. Tell me what news you have of your cousin, Miss Stewart. How has he been?"

"Who, Alex?" I don't know why this surprised me. I had inquired about her family, after all. "He's fine. In fact, he couldn't be better. He's producing a new film and thriving on the chaos."

"And you, my dear, are you writing something now? It was a book, I believe?"

"Was, yes. I haven't done any work lately. I'm afraid I've been extremely lazy."

"Lazy? Oh, no, I don't think so," she protested in quick charity. "The body must recuperate after a difficult time, just like the spirit, and I'm happy to see the good a rest has done you."

She was as tender a nurse in the reception room as on the ward, and if I had become aware again of an impersonal quality to her friendliness, a certain distance from which she shed her warmth—well, it didn't stop me from basking in it.

"And how is Luca?"

"We're expecting him back at the end of the month," she replied with a maternal glow I remembered well. "He's already gained three kilos. I think his *bonne-maman* has been stuffing him like a goose. Oh, yes, he's doing quite well, God bless him. We have such a lovely drawing he sent of the village market-place he sees from his window."

She interrupted herself, turning to the door in response to a knock so light and soft it might have been brushed on by an angel's wing.

"Thank you, Thérèse," Sister Clotilde said to the young novice who floated in with a tray of bottled juices. She was hardly more than a child, a thin, slight girl with an ecstatic smile.

"Sister," she murmured as she put down the tray and, still smiling, drifted right out again.

"Happy child."

"That happiness, it's the surest sign one has found one's true calling." A gentle reply to my tone of rude wonder. "There's a very special joy in being His bride," Sister Clotilde said, and dropped her gaze, leaving me to admire a pair of deep-set, full, smooth lids scarcely less beautiful than the eyes seeking a moment's seclusion beneath them.

Had she, too, been such a rapturous novice? Everything about her roused my curiosity; the way she sat in seeming comfort on a chair her back never touched, the narrow rim of dark hair that showed outside her veil. Was it or wasn't it auburn?

"Now what may I give you to drink, Miss Stewart? I asked for a variety, as you see, because I didn't remember what juice you like. Apricot, perhaps? The apple is also good, though nothing like the applejack we have in Normandy," she said with the sudden broad smile of a country girl.

"I don't think so, Sister. Thanks, anyway." I was the one who lowered her eyes now. Those stout pint bottles of thick syrupy juice seemed to contain the very essence of the hospital. In them I saw the pantry, with its left-over puddings and smell of ripe bananas, the long white corridor leading from it, and, at the end, Simon's room.

"I know how you grieve over Mr. West," Sister Clotilde said, "but, truly, you've not lost him. Your Simon is still close beside you, my child, loving you as he did."

Compassionate, bounteous, she heaped on me the very assurances from which I, so fainthearted, had fled. And yet I didn't mind the way she repeated his name. There wasn't a trace of the scandalized pity I heard in other voices. On the contrary, she rang it out like a joyous pronouncement.

"I wish you could find solace in this knowledge."

"I'm afraid it's quite beyond my grasp."

"Oh, but mine, too," she said, with no less serene a smile. "Who could possibly understand? There's no greater mystery than life and death. It's the incomprehensible which makes it so wonderful."

We had, once again, taken up our dialogue of the religious and the skeptic, and a peculiar one it was. I listened avidly, impressed not by the nun's innocent mysticism but the pure goodness with which she declared it, the sweet passion that brought color to her cheeks and turned her eyes nearly black. As for the heresy I uttered in return, it was mild, almost regretful. My argument was only with Sister Clotilde's tyrannical Bridegroom. I never doubted her.

"But reason rebels when there's no evidence of God's existence, no rational proof."

"Oh, proof," she said, a healthy Gallic shrug of a word. "When I was a young girl, I loved to feel the wind blowing in from the sea. I could follow its path and breathe its saltiness, but I never saw it."

And when, with sham diffidence, I murmured that the intellect could be a, well, a barrier to faith, and called upon Voltaire and Dostoevsky, those heretical giants of my childhood, to defend the point, Sister Clotilde's quick reply was Dante and Mauriac. "And, surely, you wouldn't accuse Lord Chesterton of lacking a wit?" she inquired with gentle amusement.

"You've read a great deal, Sister." This remark leaped out of my mouth like an eager question, and I regretted the swift, disturbed expression it caused.

"No, not really," she murmured. "Not so much as I would have liked. There wasn't always the opportunity. At least not until my fourteenth year, when I went to work as a maid in our mother house." A startling piece of information to me, all the more so for the cool detachment with which it was given. "Our convent was once a château belonging to the family of the Archbishop de Clemquelle and still had an excellent library, which the reverend mother permitted me to use."

Having done with this conscientious reply, Sister Clotilde gave a covert glance at her watch.

"It must be getting late," I said, rising from my chair. "I hope I haven't kept you too long."

"No, of course not," but she was on her feet, and the gracious smile that had greeted me was just as ready with its farewell.

"Well, good-bye then, Sister," I said, feeling a vague sadness, "and thank you."

"I'm sorry there wasn't more time, Miss Stewart. I wanted to show you our chapel and the garden. But perhaps you'll come again?"

"Yes, I'd like to, very much. I was hoping I could," and in that same confessional rush I dared ask one more question, the one that had been on my mind since I received her letter. "When I was in the hospital with Simon, my behavior was far from exemplary. It was dreadful. I carried on like a madwoman. So you can imagine, Sister, how puzzled I was by what you wrote in your letter. I mean, what could you have possibly learned from me?"

She gave me a little smile of surprise. "Why, love," she said.

Two weeks later I rang up the Villa again. This telephone conversation with Sister Clotilde was very much like the first, a brief pleasant chat that resulted, as I had hoped, in an invitation to return to the convent on the following Thursday.

"Bonjour, madame." An unfamiliar, stout sister opened the door to me with a shy smile of recognition. Was my visit anticipated by the entire religious community?

"Come in, please," she said. "Sister Clotilde will be down in a few moments."

She led the way to the reception room and then left to join two nuns who were passing through the hall in their nurse's capes.

"Good afternoon, Sisters," I said, and in their murmured reply, their benign nods, I detected the same curiosity. It was this quiver of interest, unconcealed by habits, that caused me to greet Sister Clotilde in so blunt a fashion.

"Well, I'm back again," I said as we sat down at the reception-room table, "but only to visit. That is, I hope you don't think I've come as a proselyte."

She laughed at my rude alarm. "No," she said softly. "I don't think that, no."

It wasn't concern over losing my impiety that prompted such a remark, of course, but the fear of a misunderstanding between us, and her kind gaze said she knew that, too. It told me, or so I imagined, that most assuredly she wished me the solace of faith, but just as I had come to feel oddly protective of her beliefs, so did she accept my skepticism.

In the next month I began to visit the convent regularly. Though I wondered at this unlikely impulse, I never hesitated in my flight to that white marble sanctuary and Sister Clotilde who seemed the very embodiment of its peace and purity. We met every Thursday afternoon at three, and while I waited from one week to the next for that tranquil hour, I flew in quite another direction.

Flight, flew—I've chosen those words with more care than exaggeration deserves. But how else can I describe the sudden, swift rising from my red-tiled aerie that was as compulsive as the torpor from which it emerged. What else to call the frenzied movement that landed me so abruptly in the home of the legendary Maria Antonelli.

"It's uncanny how much you resemble Princess Cristina," Alex was telling the actress. "You have just her sort of noble beauty."

"Really? Is that so?" Antonelli regarded him with amusement from her corner of the red velvet sofa. "How interesting," she said in that deep gravelly voice that comes up from God knows where, as the uneasy Ugo described it.

"Frankly, I'm going to be in trouble if I can't persuade you out of this retirement. There's simply no other actress who can play Italy's Joan of Arc."

"Those are kind words. Oh, yes, they are, they are. All the same, it's strange one hasn't heard more about such a marvelous princess."

"But she was very famous during the Risorgimento."

"The Risorgimento." Antonelli's beautiful, ravaged face was lit by a fierce smile. "I'm retired, yes, but that doesn't make me a contemporary of Garibaldi, my dear Signor Sareuth," she said, giving his unmelodic, un-Italianate name a charming lisp, far more of a lisp than it deserved.

There wasn't a sound of hers, not a gesture, that didn't have the style of a great and relentless performer. Her very features were a dramatic conflict; the thin, too-long nose that looked down on a short frivolous chin, a wide mouth that seemed to view its own generosity with a good-natured rue. Nothing so much as the eyes, however, those large black eyes, ineffably sad and gleaming with amusement, gave Antonelli her air of improvident, reckless sensuality.

She was, in other words, still a remarkable-looking woman. Yes, even though she had become heavier—a fact her black caftan did its best to hide—and, yes, despite the sallowness brought on by too much drinking. To tell the truth, I had been surprised when Alex first mentioned her for the part, wondering where in that magnificent intemperate prima donna he saw the slender, frail princess.

"Where?" he said. "Why, in her acting, dear girl. There isn't an actress half her age who's as exciting. Anyway, you forget the princess was almost forty when she went to battle."

"Yes, I know, but Margot—"

"Dear Margot is a delight. She's a gift to mankind. But she doesn't have the experience to handle a role like this. Besides, she's French."

"But, Alex, Antonelli has retired."

"We'll see" was his sanguine reply. "It's not the first time, you know. And when did she make the announcement? Right after her young lover ran off. Of course she's been too upset to work. Naturally she stays home and eats too much and drinks too much. What could be more normal? She'll be fine once she puts all that fury into acting. And what could be a better part for her to play right now than a woman who'd rather make war than love?"

Oh, that kind, manipulative hand. I'd recognize its touch anywhere.

"Miss Stewart, as you know, is working on the screenplay," he was now telling Antonelli. "Meanwhile, I'd like you to read the treatment. It's a bit sketchy, but it was done with skill as well as speed," he said, casting a smile at me. "At all events, you'll be able to see what a fascinating character the princess is."

"If you want to leave the treatment, I'll read it, but—"

"Men adored her, you know." Smoothly, suavely, he filled her every pause. "Heine, for instance, and Balzac and Liszt. But she couldn't have cared less about them or the prince she married. Her only desire was to liberate Italy."

"Well, and herself," said I, for like my kinswomen, she had been quick indeed to slip the marital knot.

"Oh, yes, to liberate herself, I feel sure of that!" cried Antonelli with a singular, hoarse passion.

"Who more able to understand her scorn of men," Alex murmured, "than one with the same beauty and strength?"

The director was giving quite a performance for the actress. I, too, was part of his show. "It might help if you come along, Anna. I happen to know how much she liked *The Blue Room*," he had said, and in a weak, vain moment I agreed.

"Spies and intrigue. My goodness, the *principessa* had an adventurous life. Think of her rowing up Lake Como at midnight to meet the conspirators. Imagine that gorgeous revolutionary leading her soldiers to war. Isn't this a role one could put one's whole heart and soul into?"

How urgently, amorously he hovered by the sofa, what an insistent cooing came from my old friend in his elegant dove-gray suit. I couldn't remember when I had seen him so handsome, so engaging, so meretricious, and I glanced away, out the French windows. In the Largo Argentina below, an old woman in an apron and sweater was hurrying to the ancient center with a newspaper-wrapped supper for the cats who lived there, black, gray, and tortoise vagrants who came out from the shadows to eat their pasta by the moonlit ruins.

"Oh, I'm sorry, Signor Sareuth," Antonelli was saying. "It's the telephone again." Did she jump up each time hoping to hear the boyish voice that had left her? "Please, have some more cake and wine. I'll be right back. Renato." She signaled to the butler, her hand flying into the air like a plump little bird. "Fill the signorina's glass."

But too much wine was the cause of my wandering attention, that and weariness. The one hour Alex had been granted to discuss his film had extended into five; into a dressmaker's fitting, an interview by an American journalist, a conversation with the cook as to whether the veal shank should be stewed or braised, and telephone calls by the dozen.

"Your wine, signorina." And into each of these intervals came the golden pourings of the young butler, himself as fair as a Veronese courtier.

Antonelli's renaissance apartment was in every way splendid and festive: rococo furniture with gilt flourishes, palms and laurels glittering on a shelf of cinematic trophies, a gallery of lovingly inscribed photographs from her leading men. Nor did the accolades end there. A peripheral but nonetheless tributary motif was carried out, I now observed, in the stucco garlands over the arched doorways and by a fresco of cherubs who held out offerings of fruit from the wall.

"You're very quiet over there, my girl," Alex said. "I hope our star isn't going to come back and find you asleep."

"Don't be silly." My head rested against the back of the chair only for a better view of the gilded heaven above me. The easier to see Apollo racing in his chariot toward the windows and the swarm of angels who spread their wings wide to shelter a goddess playing a lyre. Then again, perhaps it wasn't quite as celestial a ceiling as I had first thought, painted in those voluptuous blues and pagan reds. And wasn't she more nymph than angel, that provocative figure with a long neck curving so sensuously, abandoning itself to a cloud of dark hair?

"Dear me, such a funny look. What are you dreaming about?" Alex asked. "Or has the wine gone to my young cousin's head?"

"Yes." was my evasive reply. Why else would that heavenly and profane creature make me think of Sister Clotilde?

When I had gone to the convent last week, it was with the surprising news that I had begun work on the screenplay of *The Revolutionary Princess*. Surprising to me, that is. Sister Clotilde had merely given the small, secret smile of a holy woman.

"He sends us consolation when we least expect it," she said.

"Consolation?" I had taken the job as a means of escape, a promise of the strongest sort of opiate.

She looked at me across the narrow table, reading my unspoken thoughts with brown eyes that glowed in the shadow of their long dark lashes. "Perhaps you call it one thing and I another," she murmured. "Sometimes we have different words for the same thing, don't you think?"

"Yes, I suppose we do." In a curious way this was the most personal remark that had passed between us, and I smiled at her, more pleased than such a simple observation might warrant. "In any case, it was certainly unexpected."

Alex's suggestion that I write the screenplay had been so unexpected, in fact, that I had stared at him, not fully taking in his meaning. "Are you saying you don't have a scenario yet?"

"None whatsoever."

We were in my studio. I sat at the desk, where I had been writing letters, and Alex was installed on the small chintz sofa, which showed to definite advantage that youthful, casual lankiness of his.

"None whatsoever?"

"Not the briefest outline," he confessed, making no attempt to conceal the delight he took in my astonishment.

"I don't see anything so wonderful about that." It's true he was famous for his sang-froid in business matters, but to be this involved in a production and not know when and where the script was coming from, that was carrying things a bit far.

"But, of course, I knew. Hoped, I should say. The princess is your kind of woman, after all."

"My kind of woman, is she?"

"Naturally, I didn't want to push you into anything at a time like this. But if you had ever really listened, you might have realized I was trying to interest you in the project, however subtle my way."

I gave a startled laugh at my silver fox. If anything had kept me from such a realization, it was how unnaturally overt he'd been. I had not even recognized, for its unabashed flagrancy, the pretty trap he had set for me the evening before, when, like the neighborhood vigilante, he looked in, said hello, how is everything, and went on his way.

"Will the maestro be back later?" Gina asked, rushing into the living room a few minutes after he had gone.

"No. Why should he come back?"

"Poor man, he's been working too hard" was the answer. "He went away and left everything on the hall table. He forgot his briefcase, his umbrella, the newspapers."

And, as I soon discovered, squarely placed upon *Il Tempo*, a rare old book entitled *Oriental Harems and Scenery*, whose author was none other than Princess Cristina. So. In between revolutions, Alex's heroine had turned her formidable gaze upon the domestic habits of Asia Minor. "She studied the harem," according to the fine, sensational print of the foreword, "and tempted the women to precious disclosures concerning an unexplored world of passion and misfortune." Well, and well again.

"Should I take the maestro's things to his apartment?" Gina was untying her apron as she spoke.

"Don't bother. He'll send somebody over in the morning," I said, wondering where Alex had found this fragile volume, and an English translation at that. Published nearly a century and a half ago, it had a lively enough contents page: *Trouble with a Dragoman, Abnormal Practices, Women's Rights.*

"I've never seen him so forgetful," Gina fretted. "Suppose he doesn't remember where he left them?"

"No need to fuss. He's preoccupied with work, that's all," I murmured, my eye caught by a section called *Hasheesh Entertainment.* "I smoked hasheesh, I ate it, I drank it, but all in vain," wrote the earnest investigator.

"Where are you taking his book, *cara mia?*"

"To the sitting room," and, more easily addicted than the

author of these ingenuous revelations, I curled up on the old burgundy sofa and read late into the night.

It was Alex himself who came by the next morning to collect his things. "I see you've been reading the princess's book," he said, not at all surprised to find it on my studio desk. "Well, maybe now we can talk business."

"Business? What business?" I asked, but it was my look of slow comprehension he addressed.

"Yes, the screenplay. I'm going to come absolutely clean with you. The truth is, I left the book and everything else on purpose. A ploy, if you will. A deliberate, premeditated act of senility. There you have it." He could hardly have made a happier confession, or set greater store in the charm of his belated candor.

"Will you forgive your old cousin if he tells you he's guilty of going to the greatest lengths to find a first edition of *Oriental Harems*? Salt for the tail, as they say. Well? Come, Anna, you're not going to just sit there staring at me."

"I don't know what to say."

"You hesitate to involve yourself with such a low and cunning fellow, is that it?" He gave me the smile that concerned only his lower lip, a long, firmly rounded, clever lip that knew so well the art of tender, wistful teasing. "Well, our last collaboration didn't turn out too badly, did it? I suspect you'd find there are still rewards to working with me, if only monetary."

Darling, devious Alex. There was so little need to salt my tail and charm. I hesitated only in the doubt, and hope, that I would be as capable of writing *The Revolutionary Princess* as he assumed. And, between the two of us, wasn't I the more devious for remaining silent?

But that was the measure of my eagerness to have the job. Not for the monetary rewards, although I was reaching a low financial point and would soon enough need money, nor for the honest solace of hard work. I might have found that in my abandoned novel. No, it was to escape my ghostly lover, to flee an incoherent mourning, that I darted like a frantic wood creature toward the glaring light, into the noise and confusion of Bella Vista Productions.

"Well, Anna, what do you say? When can you start?"

"Right now, if you like."

During the next weeks I worked at a hectic pace, consuming the masses of research material piled on the desks and chairs in Alex's office and flying to Milan, then to Paris, and finally to London for more.

"The British Library? My dear Anna, you're writing for the cinema, not your doctorate."

"I thought you were one of the rare filmmakers who didn't insist on a distinction. That happens to be a quote, which you may or may not care to remember."

Alex's reply was a tolerant laugh, for himself as well as me. "I see that pretty mouth of yours is set. Do you know, you look abut twelve years old when you make that stubborn face. How well I remember. All right, if you've got it into your head that you need more research, then go. But hurry, child, hurry. I don't have to tell you how far behind schedule we are."

"I'll be as fast as I can."

Hidden in my exaggerated sigh of obedience was gratitude, not for his paternal indulgence but for the "Hurry"s, "Quickly"s, "We've got to have a treatment *subito*," ". . . a first draft *presto*," a this or that no later than the day after tomorrow. Soft-spoken alarms given with the most reasonable of smiles, they kept me toiling from dawn until midnight.

Except on Thursdays, when at two o'clock sharp I'd stop whatever I was doing. With a kind of religious punctilio I'd lay down a pen on an unfinished page or leave Alex's office in the middle of a conference.

"Hey, where are you going? We're not finished yet. Oh, yes. It's Thursday, isn't it?" he said with a quizzical look. "You're off to see the nun. And you can't wait a few minutes more?"

"Not if I want to get to the convent on time." It was a strange compulsion that insisted on this, since by now I knew perfectly well I'd arrive too early, and Sister Clotilde was almost certain to be late.

That day it was the bilious Sister Cecile who opened the convent door with a cool greeting and a thoughtful scrutiny that caused me to stammer.

"I seem to be a bit early."

"A bit," she agreed, and led me in silence through the great marble halls to the reception room. "If you don't mind waiting here."

"Not at all, Sister. Thank you."

I had, in fact, grown accustomed to that narrow, pious room and was quite content to sit there, anticipating Sister Clotilde's swift entrance, the swirl of white veil and skirts, her slightly breathless, "My dear Miss Stewart."

"Hello, Sister."

"I'm late," she said, taking a chair on the other side of the table, "as usual." Her smile was its own quick, bright self, but the mauve shadow under her eyes and the faint line that marred a perfect ivory brow suggested that she had been on duty for more than one shift.

"Is Luca all right?" The long-awaited operation had taken place several days before, and I hoped it was no complication of his that had kept her on the third floor all night.

"Oh, yes, he's coming along splendidly. *Dieu merci.* The first procedure, you know, it's the difficult, tricky one. There's an article about this same operation in a new medical journal from England." It was downright unholy, the excitement that flared in her eyes when she spoke of medicine. "I'll save it for you, if you'd like to read it."

"I would, thanks. And you'll tell me when Luca's allowed visitors?" I asked, with as much intention of pleasing her, I confess, as her young patient.

"Indeed I will. I know he'll want to thank you himself for the lovely flowers you sent. It was so thoughtful of you." She turned in her chair to face me more directly, a swerving movement that revealed a long, charming curve of white throat. "Sister Cecile said you got here rather early. I'm sorry you had such a wait. I was in the chapel."

"I'm the one who—" I put out a vaguely gesturing hand meant to stop her apology and offer mine, but that clumsy paw was just as inarticulate. How to explain the twinge of secular guilt I felt for taking what little spare time the nun had? "You'd tell me, Sister, if I were intruding?"

"Intruding? But of course you're not. I was expecting you today," and, in the professional manner with which she usually began our interviews: "Did you have a good week? You look fine, I'm pleased to say, as though you may have gained back a few pounds. You've been feeling quite well?"

"Very well, thanks. And you?" I dared reply for the first time, wondering how and when she had found any rest that day. Had she breakfasted in the afternoon light of an empty refectory; sat in the chapel, solitary and adoring, to fortify herself for yet another round of hospital duty? "You're not working too hard, Sister?"

"It's what I'm here for. And to do work in the service of Jesus isn't hard in the sense you mean." She folded her arms, and those strong shapely hands with their red, rough skin and short, blunt nails, so quick to seek their resting place, disappeared from sight. Was it only a disciplined repose they sought, or did a forbidden vanity tempt them to stay hidden beneath the wings of that white swan?

"I'm sure you're too busy with your writing nowadays to be out of doors much. It's such a nice afternoon, perhaps you'd like to sit in the garden?"

My temporal pang forgotten, I was already on my feet. "I'd love to."

Could any garden have better reflected the Sisters of the Divine Mercy: expansive lawns with uncompromising benches of granite, modest, glad-hearted red geranium borders, simple clusters of pure white gardenias. And the palm trees, one didn't catch them in any of their indolent attitudes here. Not for them the lounging about, the languid swaying of the tropical *flâneurs* at Piazza di Spagna. No, these palms held themselves perfectly erect, as upright and aloof as the nuns who walked beneath them with their prayer books and rosaries.

"It's so peaceful here, so pretty."

"Yes, we're very fortunate to have these pleasant grounds. And to have Guido taking care of them, God bless him. It's a wonder the way a man his age can keep up the whole place. But then, he doesn't waste his time bothering our novices the way the younger gardeners did."

It was the last note I expected her murmur to end on, and she smiled at my look of surprise, my naïveté.

"We're spiritual, my dear, not spirits. Naturally, we're aware of such human instincts. It would be impossible, I think, to run a hospital and not notice these feelings. It's one of the problems of working in the world, this peculiar attraction nuns have for men."

"Listen, you can hear the birds," I said, embarrassed for some reason by her down-to-earth talk.

"A sweet sound." She paused briefly by the cloister wall, an ancient barricade of rose-colored stones. "Sister Agathe says we have a new robin's nest with three eggs."

"They're lovely, aren't they? Simon used to think they were Easter eggs when he was a boy. Nor could I ever quite believe that exquisite color."

My musing earned me a shining glance. "That's where I see God's hand most clearly, in the special blue He's given to the robin's egg, or the elegant shape He's made the cypress." She put her hand on my arm for an instant. "Come, my child, this way. We can sit over there by the fountain, if you like."

Her skirts, as we crossed the lawn, stirred the grass, swift and light as a breeze. My child, she still called me, this country girl with an unsubdued, long-legged stride that matched my own. Outside the convent, walking together in the sunshine, I was far more aware that we were the same height. Her waist, in the neatly turned band of her nursing habit, was smaller than mine, my hips perhaps more slender, her breasts somewhat fuller.

"*Bonjour.*" Old Sister Berthe passed by, raising a whiskered, benevolent little face from her holy book.

"Shall we sit here for a few minutes? It's not too much in the shade? You're quite sure?"

And while we sat on the bench near the marble fountain, Sister Clotilde said reflectively, gently: "Just now when you mentioned your Simon, I thought, If only she knew that two people united in so strong an earthly affection could never be truly separated."

"Ah, well," was my sigh of dissent.

"It's so, Miss Stewart. Remember, I saw your devotion those weeks in the hospital. Indeed, it showed me what it meant for us to stay close to Christ, all the more during a time of trial and suffering."

"We were strongly united, Simon and I, that's true." In her soothing presence, in those sweet, salubrious hours of religious contention, his name came to me with the greatest ease.

"But at its most profound level, this hasn't changed. I think you'll agree that Thomas Aquinas was a most marvelously gifted thinker? He said, 'Faith has to do with things that are not seen, and hope with things that are not in hand.' "

"I sometimes wonder if I've accepted his absence yet."

"Oh, but my dear, He's never absent from His children."

It would have given Simon a fit of cackles to hear the nun and me going on at each other, gabbing about our passions like any two moony women, scarcely noticing when in a plethora of He's and him's we confused our loves.

"Each of us belongs to Him, vowed or not." She sat utterly

still as she spoke, the perfection of immobility. Only now and then did a delicate, impulsive eyebrow arch itself, quiver upward to catch a word or thought. "It says in the Scriptures, 'Do not be afraid, for I have redeemed you; I have called you by your name, you are mine.' "

"Oh, promises," I murmured just as softly. "The world might have been better off with a less articulate god."

But if I never understood what Sister Clotilde saw in Him, I couldn't deny that He made her happy or that I was glad for it. "I learned to love Him when I was a young girl," she once said in the hospital. How very young I didn't discover until that afternoon, at the end of our visit, when we were leaving the garden.

"Do you remember Sister Helena, in the pharmacy?" she asked as we passed a bench where a young nun sat flanked by two dark, sharp-featured women. "This is a very happy occasion for her. Her mother and aunt have arrived today with a church group from Cherbourg, our mutual hometown."

"Does your family ever come to Rome, Sister?"

"My mother died when I was five years old, God rest her soul."

"I'm sorry." It was clear enough she meant to let it end there, but I, alas, could not. "You lived in Cherbourg with your father?"

She remained silent until I began to think not even the exquisite manners of the Holy Rule would prompt her to speak, yet her answer when it came was forthright and lengthy.

"My little brother and I were brought up by the Sisters of the Sacred Heart. It was a difficult situation for my father. He was a poor man, a worker at the docks. What could he know about taking care of two tiny children?" she said with a hearty Norman pragmatism. "So the sisters took us into one of their orphanages, a big old place in the country that had once been a monastery."

"Oh, my dear." Ruder than my questions, I feared, was the sympathy that rushed to embrace her impassive facts. "It must have been very hard."

"For my brother, yes. He was only a baby, not quite two, but naturally he had to go into the boys' wing, and so we weren't together that much. I, also, was too young at first to understand why I couldn't keep him with me."

Only then did her face darken, though so quick a shadow it might have been cast by the tree we were passing beneath. "I can't say one received individual attention, as in a family, of course not. But it was a long time ago, and the sisters, well, the orders in those days were more strict."

She had dropped her gaze for an instant, but when she looked up at me she was smiling. "You'd probably be surprised, Miss Stewart, to know how often I got into trouble. Listen, the bells," she said, her smile broadening at the silvery outburst, and with a farewell no less melodious and urgent, she left me at the convent gate.

"Well, here you are. *Finalmente*," Alex said when I arrived at his apartment. "But why so late? I was beginning to think the reverend mother locked you up by mistake." His expression was waggish, indulgent, and annoying.

"There was a lot of traffic," I replied, following him into a living room that fairly bulged with guests. "Though not so much as this."

As on most workdays lately, the flow of production assistants, actors, and out-of-town friends had been diverted after sundown from the Tiber offices to Alex's apartment. Typewriters were clattering, voices were raised over a soccer match on the television, and telephones were ringing, ringing.

"Let me get that phone," Alex said. "Wait right here."

But where else was there to go? His secretary was rushing in and out of the study. The alcove library was brilliantly lit, and one of the camera crew was testing equipment on—whoever in the world was she—a big blond with a frizzy cap of hair and buttocks that looked like a pair of stolen watermelons.

"*Che carina! Avanti, bella, avanti!*" This directorial lechery came from the midget Milo who was perched, I now saw, at the top of the library ladder.

"*Avanti.*" And the blond, her tight red jersey dress scarcely covering that astonishing behind, began to move, walking with a dainty flip of the wrists, as though such ballast as hers called for a little extra propulsion.

"I read the Paris scene," Alex said, back at my side, "and I think it'll work like a charm. Especially the bit where Cristina's dinner guest has to make his own omelette. Just Antonelli's sort of thing. She'll love it. Very nice, dear girl, very nice indeed."

"Why, thanks." A casual-enough reply had it not been for the grin spreading itself across my face, the involuntary "You really think so? You really like it?"

No, I hadn't taken the job for distraction's sake alone, not simply for the bedlam that Alex so handsomely provided. Go on, "dear girl," admit it was as much for the pleasure of working with him again, for the praise that despite its taint of surprise gave a thrill of filial pride.

"Of course I really like it," he said. "Now tell me, how quickly can you—"

"*Alessi, caro.*" The shrill cry that interrupted him belonged to—to a flamingo. "*Come sta, amore?*" this stranger asked, and with a flap of her pink feather boa, the immensely thin American—or was she German?—dived between us and wrapped Alex in a sharp embrace, while I, backing off, stepped on poor Ugo.

"Anna, *che piacere vederla!* Listen, *cara,* I've been wanting to talk to you. I'm worried about Alex. I think he's going crazy. That Naples scene, the way he wants it, will cost a fortune. It's absolutely out of the question, impossible, forget it. Where is he?"

"Here I am. Why do you worry so much?" Alex said, turning from the flamingo to put an arm around his small, fretful partner. "You're talking about the most important scene in the whole movie. Right, Anna? The princess herself said, 'Ten thousand Neapolitans were ready to follow me to Lombardy.' "

"Any pretty woman who goes to Naples will tell you that. Why do you have to be so literal?"

But Alex, with the deaf smile of a visionary, went right on. "Ten thousand men being led to war by a female crusader whose only weapons were the red, white, and green flag and a passionate cry of *Viva Italia!*"

"Sorry to interrupt." This time it was his secretary.

"Yes, Alice dear?"

"Your call to New York has come through. A dreadful connection. You'll have to take it in the pantry, Alex. That's the only clear line. Don't ask me why."

Transplanted to the sun-baked Mediterranean soil from northern England some years ago, Alice had lost none of her cool, crisp flavor.

"If you're staying," she said to me, "I'd like to show you the corrections I made on those last pages before they're typed over for Alex." Only when she pronounced his name, frequent indeed for one given to such economy of manner, did her tone soften. "Nothing too serious. I caught you out on a few historical facts. And, of course, there's always the spelling, isn't there?"

It was nine-thirty before everyone had gone, and Alex said, reluctantly, "Well, I suppose we can call it a day." His glance traveled over the empty living room, the chairs still balancing glasses on their arms, the thin, disheveled cucumber sandwich lying alone on a plate, and he gave a restless sigh. "Why don't we say hello to your cousin?"

It was his custom at this hour to go upstairs to visit Sofia. Later on, he might leave to meet a certain *marchesa*, or the sulky starlet one only glimpsed with him in the lurid pages of *Oggi* or *Gente*. More often than not, however, he would stay to have supper and a game of backgammon with his former mistress.

"But, Sofia," my perplexed mother once said, "when you're not the hostess of his dining room, he's upstairs in your kitchen. What's so very different, after all?"

"The bedroom" was her succinct reply. "At twelve o'clock I'm free to go home or kick my dearest Alex out. No, not for the sake of a new lover, you innocent Lisi. For the sake of a new pleasure. For the bliss of going to bed alone and reading my magazines uninterrupted by any hunger that a luscious pear or a little bread and chocolate won't satisfy."

"Hello, my darlings." Sofia, greeting us in the dim hallway in a pale-blue robe, thick waves of reddish-gold hair loose to her shoulders, looked remarkably young, scarcely changed from our first family reunion in Paris. "Come into the kitchen. I've got a cozy fire going."

In her passion for country life she had remodeled a baroque apartment to fit some remote, rustic dream. A back terrace, overgrown with herbs, gave its wildly pungent aroma to a huge kitchen that had a brick hearth, wooden rafters, used for hanging sheets of fresh pasta, and a lumpish, uneven red tile floor.

"Oops, dear heart, you have to watch your step on those old tiles. Sit down, both of you, while I get the tea."

Only when she turned on the thoroughly modern fluorescent light near the stove did one perceive an older Sofia, a neck that lately had begun, tallowlike, to droop, to spread, to form a new layer around its base. And, oh, my beautiful cousin, what prankster came in the night to hang those heavy mannish jowls on you?

"Take the rocker by the fireplace," she told me. "Go on, you're a lot safer sitting."

"But, Sofia, that's my chair." Yes, the distinguished, silver-haired maestro was actually pouting, for here in her kitchen he relaxed to a startling degree.

"Such manners," she scolded, throwing him an affectionate glance. "Anyway, I've something better for you. Fresh herb tea."

"And what's it going to cure this time?" He sat down at the

table, loosened his tie, unbuttoned his vest, and with a feminine abandon kicked off his shoes. "Well, I won't say no to a glass."

"Here, Anna. You must try some, too." Sofia said and, having delivered herself of this steaming spicy maternal brew, went to sit beside Alex.

"Now, let's have a look at you, my boy." She studied his face with such an artless tenderness I half expected her to ask him to stick out his tongue. "So? What's new?"

"Not much. It was a quiet day. Except for Ugo. I can't get a sane word out of him anymore. Isn't that so, Anna? He does nothing but rave about costs. I think he really means to stick to the budget this time."

"Scandalous. But knowing you, he'll never get away with it."

They talked on in this vein; she teasing him like a mother cat, giving him playful cuffs with a velvet paw, while he tossed back his head in the rare laughter reserved for her.

I, meanwhile, sat by the fire, glad to be at the end of another day, at ease in the company of this lovingly estranged pair and wholly absorbed in my thoughts.

"I'm going to fix some supper," Sofia said at length. "Why don't you play backgammon with Anna?"

"Heavens, no," Alex replied. "I wouldn't dream of interrupting that pensive mood. It's going to make me money. She's thinking about the screenplay. Aren't you, my girl? I can tell by your frown."

"How clever of you," I said.

Had I really been frowning? I did so now, at any rate, to protect the thoughts that had nothing to do with work, that were exclusively concerned with Sister Clotilde's childhood and mine.

She and her little brother would have been in the orphanage four or maybe five years by the time Lisi took her brood to Flaubert's country. An unusually brief tour it was. Our mother hadn't much liked the stone and flint side of Normandy, the pervasive churches with their squat towers and needle-sharp steeples. "Here's an interesting sample of medieval art, children," she'd say, pointing out a chapel window where prophets nested in a barren tree or a holy-water stoup decorated with a man-faced snail. "Clever work, but one does wonder why men have so often ignored the noblest ideals in favor of such queerly divine ones."

I could picture valleys of heather and bracken, a rough handsome tweed, and a rock pool where my brothers and I stood mesmerized by the tiny silver eels streaking between our legs. And inland hadn't we children discovered another sea, a vast sunny field of flax that moved with the same blue waves. But this wasn't what I wanted to recall. I was searching for another memory—sad, elusive, not my own. In which of the gray, belligerent, flying-buttressed monasteries, viewed from the safety of Lisi's Volkswagen, were those rigorous nuns. Under what Gothic gables a dormitory of iron cots where a small brown-eyed girl lay down to sleep, hands crossed over her chest.

"Are you dozing or what?" Sofia called to me. "Come to the table, dear. It's getting late. I'm going to feed you and Alex your supper and pack you both off."

The days continued in more or less this same pattern until one afternoon, several weeks later, when I was having lunch with Margot. It had been my idea that we go to Giorgio's, a *trattoria* in my neighborhood famous for its bean soup and neither as small nor as unfashionable as one liked to think.

"I always forget how busy it gets here."

"It doesn't matter," Margot said. "I'm not supposed to eat this week anyway."

Work schedules, hers and mine, had kept us from meeting for a time, and because she was now going on location in Turkey, our luncheon was as much a farewell as a reunion.

"What about Cathleen? Will she stay here to mind home and hearth?"

"Don't I wish. No; she insists on coming along to chaperone me. A chaperone, God help me." Margot, in a navy blue blouse with smocking, her curly dark head bent over the crust of bread she was dipping into the saltcellar, looked young enough to need one. "If you ask me, she's doing it to avoid a visit from her papa and his little mistress. Who, by the way, he seems to have succeeded in getting pregnant."

"Poor Cathleen."

"Why poor Cathleen? She's not the one who got caught."

But suspecting that might be what had roused my bemused sympathy, I quickly changed the subject. "You haven't told me a single thing about your movie yet."

"If I say it takes place in Istanbul and my co-star is a dancing bear that tells you everything. The worst of it is I couldn't afford to turn it down. *Me voilà dans de beaux draps!* How I hate money. Oh, yes, I do. I don't know why people think otherwise. If I loved money, wouldn't I take better care of it? Would I ever let it out of my sight? No, really, I assure you, there's nothing to laugh about."

We were sitting at the back of the restaurant in an alcove that separated us from the bustle and allowed me to enjoy Margot's performance. Today she was playing herself to the hilt, a deliciously crude village girl from Burgundy who leaned over her dish of veal in an attitude devout and suspicious, examining the meat with a greedy sniff. Who thrust her broad shoulders forward and demanded to know if I was getting on with my life.

"What are you doing besides all this work?"

"There's not much time for anything else."

"That's what I was afraid of. Have you been going out at all? To the theater, to a concert, even to dinner? No, I didn't think so. And who have you been seeing besides the nun? It's the tall, pretty one you visit, isn't it? Sister—"

"Clotilde."

"That's it. She's the one Alex mentioned."

"Oh, did he?" I tossed it out, a casual cover that didn't quite hide my surprise and annoyance. "How nice you two are talking again."

Margot's pique over *The Revolutionary Princess* was no secret. "I'm honest enough to admit Alex made the right choice," she had said when it was announced. "Antonelli's superb, even now. But he, all the same, what a horse's ass he can be. As though any really good actress doesn't have a range from twelve to sixty-five. And why, I'd like to know, should a Hungarian like him, who's maybe not even that but a Roumanian, care if a French actress plays an Italian princess?"

"But really, darling," she was now telling me, "to keep going back to Monte Sacre, where you're reminded of everything, isn't that bitter medicine? No matter which sister gives it, and, believe me, I know how charming those good creatures can be. There was a certain young nun at my school who taught us music and— Now what? Who are you waving to? Who is that man?"

Before I had time to reply he had risen from the table where he was sitting with two companions and crossed the crowded room to our alcove.

"I never knew you came to Giorgio's," he said, taking my hand.

"Like all the rest of Rome, it seems that I do. Margot, may I present Arturo Massini?"

"I'm greatly honored, Madam Valadier. I have the pleasure of being your devoted fan." It was, in keeping with his general demeanor, a sincere, softly spoken compliment, a grave bow, and clearly a delight to the grinning recipient.

"I'm afraid I have to get right back," he then told me. "It's more business than lunch." He took my hand again, picking it up from the table as though it were something of his he'd left there, and said, "You're not wearing that sweater anymore."

"No."

"I'll call you soon, if I may," and with another bow to Margot, he left us.

"Well," she said, both eyebrows raised. "Who's he?"

"Nobody."

"I see. Nobody." The dark brows climbed higher.

"I met him a few years ago, when I first came back to Rome."

"And what was all that about a sweater?"

"Oh, that. Nothing. He came by to see me once or twice after the accident, and I guess he noticed my sweater." I picked up the menu. "What are you going to have for dessert?"

"An orange," she replied, and out came that chin, threatening me like a small dimpled fist. "What's the use of being a good friend if I can't tell you exactly what I think? It might be worthwhile to have somebody like him around. He seems nice, he's attractive enough. The point is he could be good for you, Anna. Maybe it's time you took a lover."

"Ah, so that's the point?" It wasn't embarrassment that caused me to blush to the roots of my hair. It was anger, indignation and, yes, embarrassment. "You sound like Gina recommending a tonic or a purge."

"Exactly," agreed Margot. "Now tell me, who is he?"

Who indeed? And why had I excluded him from my detailed summary of condolence callers? Surely not because he was nondescript, as I then told myself. On the contrary, Arturo's appearance was so subdued and monochromatic as to give the strongest of impressions, like a section of mellow muted horns. A slight man of medium height, he had brown hair, hazel eyes softened by frequent reverie, an olive complexion, and a wardrobe that remained ever faithful to his coloring. I cannot swear he always dressed in shades of brown, but that was the distinct impression he gave. It was the way I remembered him and, indeed, how I recognized him; for what was he wearing that afternoon at Giorgio's but a tan gabardine suit, a beige shirt, and a fawn-colored suede tie.

Arturo worked for the law firm that handled the affairs of Bella Vista Productions. When I first saw him, over matters to do with *The Blue Room*, I thought I glimpsed in his well-shaped mouth and in the eyes that had the same upward curve, hints of a secretive humor, a tender passion, and I amused myself with the notion that I had met him before, long ago, in a dim dusty office furnished by Gogol or Turgenev. By some queer literary anamnesis I imagined in this shy young man the soul of a Russian clerk, rural and poetic.

A month or two of occasional dinners with him, of spring nights sitting in cafés in one piazza or another, revealed little to change or add to my imaginings. Only a few modest facts made themselves known. Arturo was twenty-seven and the eldest of five children. He had been married for three years, separated for one, and was childless, an admission that brought a hurt, puzzled frown to his brow. He himself was a loving son who spent every warm Sunday with his family at a picnic table in the country. I did not learn this from my reticent friend but from the sharp cool smell of pine clinging to his khaki jacket and the flowers he brought me, scarlet poppies whose brilliant heads drooped, tired from the long drive back.

Did he know me any better? He who was as uncurious as he was unconfiding, who rarely used my name but according to his own sylvan fancies called me Rosa, Peonia, Silfide. Not at all. Yet there was an amiable attraction between us, the kind of uninformed harmony that gives the illusion, or takes the place, of intimacy. No doubt we'd have gone on, drifting into one of those curiously anonymous affairs, had I not then met Simon.

Two years later, on a Sunday evening the week after the funeral, Gina marched into my bedroom. "That young fellow's here," she said. "The one with the poppies."

"With the what? Who on earth? Poppies, you say?"

"I was sorry to hear about your *fidanzato*," Arturo told me, standing in the center of the foyer in his tan mackintosh. He was unchanged but for the addition of a small, rather thrifty-looking brown mustache. "It was a truly awful accident."

I thanked him for his sympathy and for coming by, meaning

that now I wished him to go. But he, failing to understand, simply stood there with the confident expression, the comfortable stance—feet planted apart, hands behind his back—of a patient man who had returned to finish an interrupted dialogue.

"Do you want to take off your coat?" I finally asked.

My reluctant hospitality, the utterly silent hour we spent in the burgundy sitting room, sunk deep in a pair of huge old velvet chairs, did not, apparently, faze him. I can hear even now that awful stillness. On his part it was tentative and sympathetic, but mine was an enduring silence, harsh and bewildered. What kind of conjurer's trick was this? By what diabolical sleight of hand had Simon vanished and this stranger reappeared?

Undaunted by his rude reception, Arturo came back on the next Sunday.

"Would you like to drive out to the country?"

"What, with all the weekend traffic? No, thanks."

"We'll stay here then, *Rosa mia*," replied Arturo who had no idea it was his very refusal to be snubbed, his complaisance, that I resented, for in it I sensed the forbearance of a man who knows he can afford to be patient.

"But it's warm," he said. "Why are you always wearing the same big sweater?"

And I replied with a careless shrug, huddling farther into that cavernous black cardigan, not knowing how else to tell him to go away and leave me alone, a wordless demand that eventually he understood.

Yet at Giorgio's a scarce two months later Margot was asking, "Who are you waving to?" I was surprised by that impulse of mine, too, though, had both my arms started flapping, it couldn't have been a clearer sign of my continuing, accelerating flight. "Maybe it's time you took a lover," she said, and I turned away, shocked. Not by her frank recommendation, but by my own entirely too similar thoughts.

"*Pronto?*"

"May I speak with Signorina Stewart, please?"

"Why, Arturo, hello. It's me. Didn't you recognize my voice?" Did I, for that matter? I was sitting at my desk, absorbed in work, and yet my greeting was as eager as the hand that obviously had been lying in wait, ready to pounce on the telephone at its first ring.

"How nice it was running into you at Giorgio's yesterday. But I didn't get a chance to ask about your parents or your sisters and brothers. They're all quite well, I hope? And you, Arturo, how have you been?"

He could not mistake, anymore than I, the fruity, primitive tone that was signaling my return to society. "Listen, *cara*," he said, "if you're not busy tonight, why don't we have dinner?"

"Dinner tonight? Yes, let's. A jolly good idea. It sounds like fun."

On that same insistent note of gaiety I told Gina I'd be out for the rest of the morning, swept the script into my handbag, and with the too-quick, too-resolute step of one who's getting on with life I paid a visit to Pino, the hairdresser.

His was the simplest of beauty salons—a black enamel sink, a hair dryer that roared like a furnace, and the acrid smell of bleach. That was Pino's, a mere hole in the wall with a bead-curtain entrance, a seductive hint of the oriental Rome who keeps herself half hidden in the alleys. The perfect place, in short, for my curiously sacrificial ablutions.

"I want my hair cut, Pino. Wash, cut, and then, I think, yes, then henna it."

"You really want your hair cut?" He stood behind my chair, a short man whose plump, doe-eyed face was reflected in the looking-glass just above mine. "You're sure?"

"Yes, I'm quite sure."

"*Molto bene, signorina.*" But he changed neither his solemn expression nor the stance that kept him leaning over me. "You never use henna," he told my reflection, his chin grazing her hair and a commiserative hand lingering on her shoulder.

"We'd better get started," I told him, though gently. There was nothing crude or even personal in Pino's looking-glass flirtation. It was his usual consulting pose, a brief image of affection for the female clients he desired, and imitated. How often had I dropped in during the siesta to find his assistant painting her nails, and him this virile, vain little man plucking his heavy black eyebrows, shaping them, coercing them into thin arcs until the surrounding skin was the dusky blue of his close-shaven jaws.

"Okay, cut and henna," Pino said. "But, signorina, are you really sure this is right for you?"

"Positive," my reflection announced herself, while his, more truthful, gave an uncertain nod and a tremulous smile.

That evening Arturo came to pick me up with the sly, expectant look of a man who has arranged a surprise.

"I made dinner reservations at Piazza Santa Maria in Trastevere," he said, naming the delectable golden core of that ancient quarter.

"How splendid."

But when we got there I discovered it was the restaurant Simon and I had habitually visited, the patio we always sat in, and my heart gave a crazy lurch.

"Is anything wrong? I thought you liked to eat outdoors."

"So I do." Staring straight ahead, placing one precise foot in front of the other, I followed him under the arbor and to a table perilously close to what Simon had called our corner.

"What a crowd." Arturo said.

"Isn't it?" I replied.

Having confirmed our arrival, if only to each other, we then sat quietly in the midst of all that clinking, bubble, and chatter, that feverish dining. I kept my nose stuck in the menu while Arturo tried to attract a waiter with his peaceful, benedictory signs.

"Tell me," he said at length, breaking a crisp roll and our silence. "Have they added something very spicy to the menu? You've been reading it like a best seller."

There was no reproach in his observation. It was as full of good-humored patience as the steady brown gaze waiting to meet mine.

"How about the vegetable antipasto?" he said. "The roast peppers are fantastic here. That's what I'm going to start with."

"Are you? And then what?" I asked, still perusing the menu as though choice really was the problem and not my queer sense of infidelity, not this shifty, sad, disoriented eye of mine that refused to focus on the other side of the table.

"Then the taglierini with white truffles." He gave a wolfish smile and undid the middle button of his beige jacket. "A pretty night for dining alfresco, eh?"

"Yes." My reply drew itself out as if sibilance could lend it thought and character. But where had the morning's glibness gone? Hadn't I been able to talk to him easily enough then? Ah, but that was on the telephone, a connection as abstract as my desire for his company. "Yes, it's a lovely night."

Too lovely. April had arrived with the air of a month ripe for folly—mellow, languid, sweetly scented. The piazza itself had a look of ripeness with those sun-baked, apricot-colored façades.

"Some wine, Camelia?"

"Please." I held out a glass to him, but my glance was resting on the church of Santa Maria, my thoughts on Sister Clotilde. She who rarely left her hill, it was very likely she had never seen how the chapel's mosaics gleam at night, the mysterious golden light cast by the wise and foolish virgins, if that's who those ancient figures were.

"They're drug addicts," Arturo said, "purse snatchers."

"What?"

"Those hoodlums near the church. Somebody at the office told me—"

Told him what, I never heard. A wandering minstrel, a full-chested pouter pigeon had landed beside our table. Eyes tearful, smile joyous, he was singing O *Sole Mio* with a passion that drowned out Arturo's words. Embarrassed for this baritone who was so completely at his ease, I glanced away again.

From where we sat I could see beyond the small piazza to the peripheral wash strung across an adjacent alley. White trousers, a green-striped apron, a large square dress, blue as a patch of morning sky.

"Banners," Simon had pronounced them. "There's really something remarkable about Italian clothes hanging out to dry, don't you think? There they are for all the world to see and proud of it. Totally frank, spirited statements of life."

It was the night after Alex's party, and we were dining together in Trastevere for the first time. Simon, with an appetite whetted by our meal, lingered over the coffee, his uncombed, unruly leonine head propped up in elegant hands, those bright-blue voracious eyes sweeping over the piazza, its laundry, me.

"I wonder why English laundry has such a damp, cringing sort of look. Now French things hung up to dry, that's something else again," he said. "Have you ever noticed how they cling together on the line? There's no question about those sly entanglements. As for German wash, what can one say? It's all big, loud empty flaps in the wind. Comes from being so unimaginatively clean, I shouldn't wonder. What's the laundry like in your country?"

"The United States?" I took his question to heart and tried to evade it with my own. "You've given quite a few concerts there, haven't you?"

"I do a tour about once every two years or so. But I still need an authority to tell me what American wash looks like."

"I'm sorry. I don't really know." Sorry? I was overcome by

the sudden angst, the peculiar shame of being unable to describe the laundry of my native land. "When we left New York I was very young. And when I went back to the States to college, well, it was just for a year."

Simon interrupted me with a wild caw of laughter and a kind look. "I was only joking, you know."

I laughed then, too, but a small, grave memory continued to stalk the back halls of the Central Park West apartment, peering anxiously into the linen closets, with their vague smell of lavender, searching for I don't know what. Some parochial detail that would attach me to this eccentric stranger with the savage laugh. Already I feared parting from him, already I wanted to stay close beside him, indivisibly close, mouth on mouth, bodies entwined, and, yes, Lisi, roots mingled.

"Shall we try the roast lamb?" Arturo was saying. "Maybe with some fried zucchini?"

"That sounds good."

"You know, there's something different about you tonight. Is it your hair? I thought so. It looks nice that way. There's been a change in me, too," he added, a shy confession that prompted me to look him directly in the face for the first time that evening.

"Your mustache is gone."

"*Esatto*. So you finally noticed," said those fully exposed, sweetly curving lips. I'd have liked them a lot better for being offended, for a turned-down corner or a curl of displeasure. But no such petty lines interfered with the perfect shape of that mouth. "Now tell me, Silfide, before the waiter comes back, what kind of salad would you like? Mixed or green? Me, I'm going to have the fennel."

There were moments when I doubted we should ever be done with that dinner, with the long, ruminative evening of a couple who have nothing in common but the food in front of them. Why, then, when the end was at last achieved and I was home again, leaning gratefully, protectively against my door, did I declare myself happy to go to the country with Arturo on Sunday? For no better reason than, once suggested, it struck me as being the next logical direction.

"A logical direction?" Alex repeated when I told him this, several nights later. "What, the country, you mean?" my old confidant asked.

"I'm not sure what I mean."

"And no wonder. It's nearly midnight. I've stayed much too long."

What a way Alex had with the truth. One deft phrase and it rolled over into a charming, intimate piece of fiction. He hadn't been with me long at all. If midnight were now upon us, it was only because he had arrived at the apartment so late. I'd been startled, in fact, to find him standing on my doorstep at that hour, his briefcase in one hand and a long black cigar in the other.

"Hel-lo!" he said, no less surprised at the sight of me wrapped up in my old pink chenille robe. "So sorry, darling."

"Come on in. Why sorry?" But a glance in the hall mirror supplied the answer. Strands of hair tucked away and forgotten behind one ear, a remote, rumpled brow, eyes dazed—my reflection had that look of profound disarray with which one wakes not from sleep but deep concentration.

"Don't I recall a young schoolgirl dashing along these halls in a robe almost exactly like that?"

"Almost," I murmured vaguely, while a conscientious flush rose to my cheeks, announcing it the very same old rag. "Let's go to the *salottina*. It's warmer there."

"Poor child, already in bed and fast asleep, weren't you?" His tone of fatherly approval was absurd, and touching.

"Not yet, no. I've been revising the Naples scene."

This earned me another, shrewder glance of approval. "A shame to interrupt you." Nevertheless, Alex followed me to the back parlor and sat down on the sofa, taking his briefcase on his lap as one would a small brown pet.

"I had dinner tonight with Carla di Scalzi," he said. "You know she's already started on Antonelli's wardrobe? Well, so she brought along a few designs. Quite rough, of course, but you might enjoy seeing the first lot."

And out of the inevitable case came sketches of a dozen pre-Raphaelite tea gowns. "Pretty, eh?"

"Very pretty. A bit impractical for the battlefield, maybe."

"Antonelli thought they were smashing."

"She was there, too?"

"Very much so. Have you seen her recently? She looks marvelous. Sober as a judge and positively sylphlike. But she eats hardly anything now. All she had for dinner was a few bread sticks and half a liter of mineral water."

"You didn't order for her by any chance?"

Alex smiled, stretched out his long legs, and with a lover's patience coaxed his cigar back into a smoldering state; in short, admitted to nothing but the utmost complacency.

"Did you know Antonelli's boyfriend has turned up again?" he said. "Back from Morocco or wherever it was he ran off to."

"You don't say."

"Young scoundrel's dead broke, I bet. But she sounds determined to have nothing more to do with him. I gather she went so far as to get a locksmith to put double locks and bolts everywhere."

"Really! Everywhere?" But this silly insinuation sailed right past Alex's ear. Clearly he wasn't paying attention to what either one of us said tonight.

"Antonelli's in the great tradition of Duse, after all, and the Divine Sarah. When it comes right down to it, has she ever really cared for anything but her art? Why, she's even begun to have dreams like Princess Cristina. Strange, prophetic visions, she says."

"Amazing." What could be going on in my dear friend's head? I knew better than to imagine he'd stopped by for idle gossip; his vices were hardly that small.

"She said every night now she prays for a vision of the screenplay." Alex gave a soft chuckle. "What else could I do but assure her she'd have something to read very soon. As a matter of fact, I told her the first draft was finished."

Aha, out at last. Blown at me in a casual puff of smoke from that thin, refined, malodorous cigar.

"Did you? Well, for once you're not a complete liar. It nearly is."

"How nearly, my sweet?"

"I can work through the weekend, all but Sunday afternoon when I've promised to go to the country, and have it done by Wednesday."

"Shall we say Tuesday? Good girl. In that case, you can have your afternoon's outing with my blessings. Paying a visit to the turtledoves, are you?"

"Well, no. Actually, I was planning to drive out to Ostia with Arturo."

"Oh, really?" Alex said, gathering up Signorina di Scalzi's tea gowns with rather more care than they deserved. Could it be disapproval turning his silvery head away from me? But no. "Who's Arturo?" was the afterthought.

"Your lawyer, remember?"

"Oh, Massini, you mean. Of course. He's a nice chap." On went the meticulous business of repacking the sketches. "A dependable sort of friend for just now, hmm? A *galantuomo.*"

"I suppose you could call him that."

"And so he's taking you to the country, to the sea, in fact?"

"Well, depending on the weather. I mean it seemed a pleasant idea for a pretty spring day."

By the time I had done with a few more of these uncertain replies, the briefcase was standing on the floor ready to go. "Mind you don't forget about Tuesday," Alex said.

"Will I have the chance?"

He smiled, dropped a kiss onto my brow, bade me breathe lots of healthy sea air, and off he went, leaving me both relieved and piqued to have his so lightly bestowed "blessings."

It was anything but a pretty spring afternoon when Arturo and I took our drive to Ostia. A sullen Sunday it had turned out to be, with a pale sky and heavy, feverish air.

"At least it isn't raining," Arturo said. We had stopped along the coast for lunch at a restaurant whose windows overlooked a dark, fretful Mediterranean. "I don't think it's going to, either. Those clouds don't look very serious to me."

But what did he know about clouds with that beaming face, that gleaming olive skin still warm and moist from the southern sun of his childhood.

"Did you see the perch on the waiter's tray?" he said. "Some delicious aroma, *vero*? A lot of the tables seem to be getting the fried squid, though."

His features were as mellow as his complexion. The eyes following our neighbor's platter were the softest brown. The nose couldn't have had a gentler slope, a course well known to me. I had more than once sent a finger sliding down its strangely flat ridge. "What are you doing?" he'd ask, not unpleased by this caress, but I would remain silent. How could I tell him I was thinking of the bronze boar in the Florence marketplace and a young girl who used to rub its similarly burnished snout for good luck?

"I'm glad we came here today anyway. Despite the weather, I mean. Aren't you? Hello? Hey, *Lilla. Che mi dice?*"

"Glad? Why, certainly." I cried, rousing myself from a reverie, from an attempt to recall the man who was sitting across the table from me. "Yes, of course I am."

Once let loose there seemed to be no stopping my agreeable, witless responses; even the squid received an approving nod.

And later, when Arturo suggested a walk, I said, "Oh, lovely," leading the way myself through a forsaken row of bathhouses to the dismal windy beach beyond.

"Shall we sit here for a while?" He had already whipped off his jacket and was on his knees, gallantly, victoriously pinning its foolish flapping arms to the ground. *"Va bene?"*

"Va bene."

In another few months these dingy sands would blossom into a gaudy garden of red and yellow parasols, bronze figures, and the thick sweet scent of coconut oil. But now it was a hard, barren ground we sat upon, a crude wind that taunted us, spitting grit into our hair and eyes.

"Comfortable?" Arturo put a hand under my chin and turned my face toward his.

"Oh, yes." My whisper fell into his mouth, right between the firm lips waiting for it. "Yes." So this was what my agreeable, perfidious tongue had been leading up to.

"You're sure?"

"Assolutamente," I said, putting a more nourishing word into the mouth that continued to nibble at mine, reminding it softly, insistently, that they had never been the strangers Arturo and I were.

"Listen, Rosa," he said.

"I am." But memory had made me greedy as well as generous, and I bit the full tender lips I was suckling.

"O Rosa. Listen, next weekend can we leave the city earlier?"

"Perchè no?"

With that pert chirp of a party girl, our staid little past was revived. The regular country drives began again, as did the midweek dinner and the strolls to Piazza Navona or the Pantheon. Those Roman promenades. How supple and resentful I was walking in Arturo's leisurely, seignorial embrace—my flank appended to his; my step measured to fit his brown suede shoe;

my hand clasped around the wrist and tucked safely into the arm he held behind his back.

"I don't understand you anymore. Either you're in the studio or you're running to the office, or you're off somewhere with *him*," Gina was complaining. "But do you have one minute for a healthy swig of orange juice? No."

"Will you please shut up," I murmured into the looking-glass with the blank eyes, the flared nostrils of one whose full attention has been given to a mascara brush. "I'm late enough as it is."

"If you knew how much Sicilian oranges cost these days, you'd drink up fast enough."

Gina's growl followed me around my bedroom as I looked for a certain pair of earrings, put on my shoes, and rushed to the closet, only to stand there transfixed by uncertainty. Was the navy blue shirtwaist dress too sober? Yes, but if I could trust that dim mirror there was nothing sober-minded about the material, a clinging silk that betrayed in flattering detail the slender hips and long legs it so sedately covered.

"The red oranges are the healthiest; everybody knows that."

Now a dash to the chiffonier for the stockings I'd nearly forgotten, and quick to the dressing table again to color my cheeks the same autumnal red of my scarf.

"First my lady won't so much as wiggle a toe, and now she runs like there's a pitchfork at her behind. Here, there, *sempre in giro*, just like the maestro." Gina's small, rosy mouth, pulled down as far as it would go, formed an inverted smile, a merry frown. Such was the complex nature of her tirade, an outburst composed of pride, concern, and rebuke.

"What about the beefsteak I got for your supper?"

"For heaven's sake, I'm only going out for an hour. I'll be back in plenty of time for supper."

"An hour? You're getting all dressed up to meet *him* for an hour?"

"Why are you such a stubborn old mule." I replied, slamming my hairbrush down on the dressing table. "You know his name as well as I do." It was exasperating, Gina's refusal to recognize Arturo; yet how I loved her for it.

"And no, for your information, I'm not. I'm going to the hospital. The little boy's grandmother went home, and I want to take him a toy."

This much was true. Luca's recovery from his second operation had been rapid. "It's a real miracle, thanks be to God. The doctors say he'll be walking before the end of summer," Clotilde told me. "And since the final procedure is minor we've encouraged his grandmother to return to their village."

But I hadn't really deceived myself into thinking that clever young artist needed a toy for his amusement. No, the gift I was so impulsively rushing out to buy was for myself, a *carte d'entrée* to the Villa, a means of stealing a few extra moments from my saintly serene friend.

It puzzled me, I own, that the increasing demands of work and play, as Arturo described our time together, hadn't deflected my thoughts from Clotilde. On the contrary, my need for her had grown apace, though why I should feel most comfortable with a nun whose terrain and language were utterly foreign to me, I couldn't have explained.

It took me an inordinate amount of time to find a present for Luca that afternoon. Indecision led me by the nose—would he enjoy it? would she approve?—to one shop after another, and it was late before I finally got to the Villa, a biography of Leonardo securely in my arm.

I had hoped Clotilde might be at the nurses' station, but the elevator let me out onto a deserted third floor. The big white wall clock whose round, cheerful face bore a queer resemblance to its mistresses, said six-thirty. As though I couldn't have told the hour by that silence alone, that discreet intense hush that preceded the brassy roll of the supper carts.

"Bonsoir." Old Sister Berthe had appeared from nowhere to give me a sad smile. "I hope you've been keeping well, my child," she murmured as she stepped into the elevator and stood there with folded arms, a sorrowful angel waiting to be wafted upward.

"Yes? May I help you?" From the corridor behind me came the impatient accent of Sister Cecile.

"Hello, Sister."

"Oh, it's you, Miss Stewart. What can I do for you, my dear?" she said, cocking her veil at me in altogether too pensive a way.

"I've just stopped in with something for Luca."

"I see."

And what was it those light, wintry blue eyes saw? I turned to go, having no wish to know, but she told me anyway.

"You'll probably find Sister Clotilde there. She was in with a new patient, but I believe she's getting the boy settled for the evening now. It's a very busy time for her."

"I won't stay long," I said, and with a nod as courteous as that speculating, infuriating nun's, I fled down the hall to Luca's room.

"You need a bigger studio," Clotilde was telling him as she tidied the table that fitted over his bed. "A place for your supper tray, anyway," she said, moving sketch pads and paints to a chair. "There, that's better," and then, glancing toward the door, "Why, Anna," she exclaimed. "What a nice surprise. Look who's come to see you, Luca."

"Ciao, Signorina."

I was never quite prepared for his extraordinary yellow eyes, brilliant twin planets flooding that thin dark face with light.

"You've come at just the right time, Anna. Ten minutes ago,

my patient was covered with charcoal. You'd have found a chimney sweep here instead of a young gentleman."

I murmured something appropriate, but the truth is I preferred the chimney sweep. Propped high on a pillow, his narrow frame lost in a pair of overly starched striped pajamas, his wavy blue-black hair slicked back and gleaming like the clipped wings of a bluebird, her young gentleman was too clean, too neat . . . too vulnerable.

"Don't you want to sit down?" Clotilde asked. "Let me put your parcel away for you."

"Actually, this is for Luca."

What a pair they were with their heads bent close together over the package I placed on the bed. "A present. How lovely," she said with childish excitement, while he thanked me with the wry, unsurprised smile of a crippled man.

"The story of Leonardo. Now, isn't that a perfect gift for you." And from you, she added silently, glancing up to praise me as well. "It will be a real inspiration, Luca, to read the life of one to whom God gave the greatest talent."

"But, Sister, did the Pope really ban him from the hospitals?"

"Whatever are you talking about, my child?"

"They say that Leonardo used to go into all the hospitals at night and dissect bodies to study. Yes, Sister, really, thousands of them."

"Oh, Luca. What devil fills your ears with such stories?"

The clatter of an aluminum cart outside the door, the thin aroma of boiled vegetables announced the arrival of Luca's supper, and I got up to leave.

"If you wait a minute," Clotilde said, "I'll see you out, Anna. I have to go down to the lab anyway."

"But you're coming back to say good night, Sister." It was a tyrant's question Luca asked, a demand that elicited only the most loving reprimand.

"Don't I always?"

"Yes, but do you promise?"

"I promise."

"Okay, then. *Addio, Signorina*," he told me, but his fierce golden gaze remained on her, possessive, triumphant, and already a little lost.

We walked down the hall together, my friend and I, as we had done on those winter days and nights.

"This way, my dear." A light, thoughtful hand rested briefly on my arm turning me from the direction of Simon's room. "I thought we could go down by the stairs. Sometimes it's quicker than waiting for a lift."

" Oh, Sister." A nurse I didn't know came up to Clotilde with some charts. "Sister Bernadette said you wanted these." She smiled and hurried on, a hefty nun whose long face and widely spaced brown eyes gave her the look of a bovine creature.

"That was Sister Madeline," Clotilde said as we started down the stairs. "She's only just come to us in Rome, to replace Marie."

"Replace Sister Marie? I didn't know she was gone. That's too bad."

"Yes. We shall all miss her very much."

"Where was she sent? Back to your hospital in Normandy?" Idle questions these were, an excuse to address myself to the profile I admired—a rare piece of classicism, with that straight nose in so pure a line of descent from the smooth white brow. "Or farther abroad?"

"I don't think she herself knows her plans yet. She's left the order, you see."

"Oh, she's left the order." I gave a faithful imitation of Clotilde's matter-of-fact tone, but I was greatly surprised.

Sweet Sister Marie with her ever-present smile, she had seemed the happiest of His children. Was it her defection, then, that had honed Sister Cecile's tongue and put that sorrowful expression in Sister Berthe's rheumy eyes?

"Marie's decision to go out is no longer so unusual or tragic as when I was a girl." Clotilde read my thoughts in one swift glance. "Regrettable, certainly, but it's not her love for Jesus she has questioned, only the best way she can serve Him."

She stopped a moment on the landing to exchange a quiet word with one of the administrative sisters in blue and then turned her serene smile upon me again.

"Marie's an excellent nurse, and she'll continue to do good in His name. We've gone through some dark times in these past years, you know. It hasn't always been easy for us to find the way, but we've come to understand our psychology better. Now we see that we, also, belong to the world and must treat ourselves as women first and then nuns."

This conscientious instruction in the changes of papal policy had taken us down the final flight of stairs and among the potted palms and Near Eastern potentates who filled the lobby.

"May I come to the convent on Thursday?" My weekly visit had long since been a fixed thing, an hour taken for granted between us, and yet I still felt relief at the generous "Why, of course, my dear. Two o'clock as usual," which saw me on my way.

But how slow I was to leave Villa Monte Sacre that evening. Next door, the convent was caught up in the sunset, a tender blaze I had often watched from Simon's room. Oblivious to the traffic, I stood by the road as I used to stand at his window, waiting for the sisters to light their lamps and add the final golden glow to a medieval illumination.

"Alleluia, alleluia." The high, pure voices of the community at vespers brought Sister Marie back to my mind. Was it a recent conflict that caused her to break her vows or had that sunny nun always been concealing some deep inner struggle?

How diligently those sisters practiced their grace. Clotilde couldn't have broken the news to me more serenely, and yet I had glimpsed the tremor in her smile. Brief and shadowy it was, like a ripple that appears from nowhere to cross a tranquil pond.

Only today she herself had named its source. Marie's decision was "no longer so unusual or tragic as when I was a girl," she had said, a clear-enough reference to her cloistered child-hood, to the draconian guardians of that Norman orphanage. But I would have recognized that tremor anyway; for by now I was familiar with the shadows cast by the Sisters of the Sacred Heart. Not just in Clotilde's smile but in her speech. It was their severe, remote, romantic language she uttered most read-ily, as one does a mother tongue, while the liberating phrases of these enlightened days she spoke with the solemn obedience of an old Sister Berthe.

Shadows, bedimmings, penumbras—that lovely nun with her open, radiant face was still a mystery to me. I still puzzled over the warmth that sometimes seemed to come from such a dis-tance; still wondered what emotions escaped their zealous cen-sor only to be detained by a pair of lowered eyes, a thick luxuriant barrier of black lashes.

Yet for all this, I felt I knew her better and that somehow we had grown closer over the last weeks. Perhaps it was simply that our meetings no longer took place in quite so spiritual a realm. The odd antiphony between nun and infidel, that went on, to be sure. Indeed, I was often guilty of questioning certain paradoxes in Catholic doctrine for the sheer pleasure of her response. "Ask the loveliness of the sky, ask the order of the stars," Clotilde would reply, her soft murmur itself an evocation of Saint Augustine's poetry.

But the conversation that used to revolve around the wisdom of her Divine Bridegroom or the empyrean whereabouts of Si-mon now tended to drift on to matters less momentous and more personal. Our talk had, in short, descended to the incon-sequential plane of ordinary friends.

"What a pretty dress." On my last visit Clotilde had come into the reception room without my hearing her, and I spun around from the window.

"I'm sorry," she said, her hand falling from my shoulder. "I startled you."

_157_

"No, not really." Why should I find her appreciation of a summer dress, the gentle touch of her hand on my back so surprising.

"Isn't it a warm day?" she said, leading the way through the marble halls and into the garden. "Soon the hot weather will be here in earnest."

"Do you know what you'll do for your holiday?"

"We don't have our schedules sorted out yet, but maybe I shall make a trip to Germany with Bernadette and Agathe. Then I'll visit as usual with my brother in Honfleur. What about you, Anna?"

"I'm going home to Rosten, just as soon as the script's finished."

"And how is *The Revolutionary Princess* these days? Is she doing battle with pen or sword? Was your cousin happy with the last scene?"

She often brought up Alex, and I'd color a little, thinking how he, for his part, never failed to quiz me about her. "How was your pretty nun today? Did you have a good visit?" His eyes would be amused and frankly curious as he leaned down to greet me with a kiss. "What did you two do on such a nice afternoon?" he'd ask, his head resting an extra moment against mine, that long aristocratic nose pressed next to my hair as though—oh, irritating man—he expected to find some lingering trace of myrrh.

"I wonder if you aren't working too hard, Anna. Did you manage to have any recreation this week?"

"Yes, I spent an afternoon sightseeing in Viterbo," and I described the alleys and archways of that medieval town stone by stone, but about Arturo, who took me there, I said almost nothing.

And if I detected a hint of unmonastic curiosity when she asked about my recreation, what about the impetuous "I wish you had been there to see it!" that slipped into my reply?

Just as impulsive was the "I know you don't have time to

leave the hill, Clotilde, but how nice it would be if one day you came to visit me. The Spanish Steps are covered in azaleas now; you can see them from my terrace. We could have tea. There's a Sicilian bakery in my neighborhood that has the best cake." I stopped, embarrassed that in my secular enthusiasms, my worldly delights, I sounded far more a proselytizer than ever she had.

"How's your new heart patient?" I asked then, setting things squarely back on top of Monte Sacre.

"We expect him to be able to go home next week. And it's all the more remarkable, Anna, when one thinks that a mere five years ago such surgery as his was impossible."

She would often recount for me the medical triumphs of the Villa, sometimes taking a pen and notebook from her pocket and making a quick anatomical sketch to explain her enthusiasm the better.

This same excitement, indeed more, shone from her face when she spoke of the order's bush hospitals in West Africa.

"Oh, Anna, we had the most interesting guest over the weekend. One of our missionary sisters. I thought at the time how much you would have enjoyed hearing Sister Geneviève speak. She is back from Gabon after four years, and, my gracious, what stories she had to tell us. One could almost see the rain forest and the clinic with its thatched roof."

But it was Clotilde's references to her childhood, those casual remarks about the orphanage that I would wait for and listen to most keenly.

What did I hear that made me think I was gaining a deeper knowledge of my friend? Nothing more than the ancient monastery's bell tower, the ringing of the Angelus that woke the children at daybreak, and the low, urgent voice of Sister Ursula shepherding them to the refectory through stone passageways that smelled of cabbage and incense.

"You want to know what we ate for breakfast?" Clotilde's smile broadened as she repeated my question. "You ask me such funny things, Anna. We had simple nourishment. Bread and tea, sometimes bacon. It wasn't a long affair, I can tell you that, and then off we'd march again."

The children marched to meals and baths and twice around the orphanage grounds in the late afternoon, a long line of girls who under the wary, omnipresent eye of Sister Louise took care to remain an arm's length away from each other.

It was only when Clotilde spoke of her brother that she lost her cool tone. "He was such a tiny mite, and I suppose the sisters looked very big and black to him. They did their best, of course, but he was always hiding under his cot and crying."

"Poor boy," I said, wondering if perhaps she still didn't hear echoes of her brother in Luca's room.

"Once, when I was sent down to the basement for apples, I saw the underground passage that connected the cellar of the girls' wing to the boys', and that night I crept over to their dormitory to stay with my little brother."

She paused for a moment. "Dear me, the trouble we got into when they found I was hiding under the cot, too. I never did it again, though for the wrong reason, I'm sorry to say. I was more afraid of that dark terrible passageway, a real twelfth-century donjon, you understand, than disobeying the mother superior.

"Ah, no." That sympathetic murmur, the hand reaching out to comfort came from her. "How you're frowning, Anna. But you mustn't be misled by such a foolish story. My brother and I were very lucky to have the sisters taking care of us, and in time he, too, grew accustomed to the ways of the home. They couldn't have managed so many children without strict rules. But, you know, we had our recreations, too, and our rewards."

Her face took on a glow, became luminous with what? The desire to reassure? A victory recalled? A moment's *verboten* pride? "In the second year I won a prize for my studies, the prettiest blue medal, which I still wear pinned to my vest."

A charming blush followed this revelation, and Clotilde ended on a hasty note of gratitude to "the Holy Virgin who always gave us children encouragement, and above all to Him. It was there, in that sanctuary, I first heard His voice."

Our worlds couldn't have been more antithetical. She raised in the profound calm of faith, my brothers and I in the religious fervor of Lisi's paganism. I sometimes wondered, in fact, if it wasn't this very polarity that gave us our peculiar bond.

Did the same thought occur to her as she sat beside me on the garden bench, listening with so attentive a smile to my childhood itinerary, places as remote, I told her, as those to which our grandmother had once taken Lisi.

"But, my dear," Clotilde said with that earthbound candor that always surprised and disarmed me, "have you never watched certain mother cats with their litters?"

Well, she wasn't far wrong at that. Lisi with her thick mane of honey-colored hair, what a lithe marauder she had been, prowling across the continents, her appetite as innocent and ferocious as the young lioness she resembled.

"Who's ready to see more pyramids?" was a familiar cry in the Egyptian dawn. Or, with a rapturous glance out the window of our blue locomotive, "Annie. Augustus. David. Wake up. We're coming to the Karoo plateau." And at a flower boat in Bangkok, "Look at all those white roses. I must take them back to the pension." No sentiment, no melancholy escaped in her gasp of pleasure. It was inspired by avarice alone, a greed as pure as the flowers she coveted.

"Your mother was still a young woman, wasn't she, when the journeys began?" Clotilde said to me one day. "And in all the years she didn't marry again?"

"No. Sofia says she couldn't stand still long enough." Then, under the compelling warmth of those dark eyes: "We didn't always travel alone, of course. My mother had friends who sometimes joined us."

It had taken me a long time to realize they were her lovers. Not because of any well-practiced discretion on her part, but the utter lack of it. She had treated these occasional men no differently, with no less an inquisitive, amorous enthusiasm than the rest of the scenery.

Lisi, rising exuberantly from the ruins of an ancient palace in Persepolis, adjusting her trousers in the same swift way as her Texan friend. "Oh, there you are, my darlings," she cried out to us, and with eyes shining like the clearest amber in her dusty face, she resumed the day's lesson. "Certain of our laws can be traced all the way back here. Take the influence of the Mithra cult— But really, children, what an astonishing concept theirs was," she said with one of her bemused pauses. "Imagine anyone thinking salvation could be restricted to men."

"It's pleasant when friends share their travels," Clotilde said.

"Yes, although Lisi's friends could never keep up with us for very long."

But hadn't she accelerated her pace at those times. The day the Texan, exhausted by her enthusiasms, finally fell behind, and Lisi sat us down to supper in a cheap, dimly lit café, wasn't there an echo of our relief in her smile and her reckless "Well, children, we're on our own again."

What I learned of Clotilde's past came in random order, odd bits to be taken away and pieced together at leisure. It was another time, a rainy afternoon in the green reception room, when I discovered that the spring Lisi was leading us through Iran, the Sisters of the Sacred Heart graduated Clotilde from the orphanage.

"I was already quite a big girl for my twelve years, and the sisters found me a job on a dairy farm."

She went on to describe, heartily enough, the apple orchards and green pastures of her Normandy: the whitewashed clay farmhouse with a woven thatch and the capricious goats in her care.

"I never knew how hard it was to get milk the year round. Nor the attention one had to give to a goat's private life."

But of the family who owned the dairy—a farmer, his widowed sister, and her two sons—she had almost nothing to say. "They took me to church on Sundays and, just as regularly, the market town on Mondays." She smiled while telling me this, but there was, or so I imagined, a guarded look in her eyes that kept me from asking anything more about them.

"Those market towns," I said instead. "What a mob scene. We went to one once, and I think everybody in Normandy was there, not to mention their livestock."

"So many people, it's true. And the way those animals were bundled in and out of the vans."

Clotilde's discomfited murmur, her air of vague distress told me I'd chosen a subject no safer. We sat in silence then, sharing the memory of a lusty marketplace: the smell of dung and strong cider and sausages broiling over charcoal, and the confusion of a young convent girl caught in the robust crowd, a tall, pretty child who turned away from the sad-eyed cattle standing at the back of their trucks, only to meet the stares of the men gazing over the walls of the *pissotières*.

I learned eventually that it had been an illness, a long bout of rheumatic fever that took her from the dairy farm after a year and delivered her to the Sisters of the Divine Grace.

"They were so kind. I had to stay in their hospital for some months, and they arranged for me to study again. But they were considerate in every way, even to making sure their young patients got treats now and then. I had my first taste of chocolate there."

When it came to this period in her life, to her sisters, Clotilde was positively loquacious, speaking with an animation and a wonder still fresh enough to color her cheeks.

"Once I had recovered, I asked for work, hoping to stay with them. It was my good fortune that they needed help at that time in the mother convent, and so I did their cleaning and some assisting in the kitchen. I was, you know, a *bonne à tout faire*. Later on, when I reached my fifteenth year, I took my first vows."

163

"So young?"

"But even as a small girl I had felt the pull of my vocation" was the glowing reply. "And there with the Sisters of the Divine Grace I heard Him call to me so clearly."

She lowered her eyes for a reflective and secretive moment. How could she know what deep, dreamy lids covered them?

"I can still feel the joy that filled my heart when I first walked into the mother house. Such peace was in that château, and loveliness. The common room and the library still had the original furnishings of the Archbishop de Clemquelle's family. And the chapel, Anna. I could hardly believe my eyes. Angels in the organ loft, yes, with harps and trumpets. And, oh, the beauty of the Gregorian music. It was so glorious, I thought I must already be in heaven.

I had told Clotilde I'd be at the convent on Thursday as usual, but an unexpected location hunt for *The Revolutionary Princess* took me to northern Italy instead, a change in schedule I found upsetting.

"What?" said Alex. "Now that doesn't sound like my gypsy girl, complaining about a quick jaunt." He was at his desk, a handsome teakwood piece fashioned after his own long, trim lines, glancing over the letters Alice had just spread out before him. "The script's finished, at least for the moment, eh? It's time we took a good look at Cristina's country."

"I agree, but you might've given me some warning. This may come as a surprise to you, but I do occasionally have other plans."

"Oh, I see. Arturo?"

"Exactly." I'd forgotten all about him until that moment. It was having to forgo an afternoon at the convent I minded.

"Well, he could always fly up for the weekend," Alex murmured, putting his florid signature on another letter. "Check the schedule with Alice. She has the hotel reservations and your plane ticket."

"My ticket? Already?" How much he took for granted. Entirely too much. "Look here, Alice knows the script as well as I do. Better, I sometimes think. Are you sure you need me along?"

"Need you?" Alex looked up from his desk in surprise. "My dear girl, how can you question it?" He spoke without his teasing smile, without artifice or charm, and how very charming I found him at that moment.

Did I flatter myself in thinking the need he expressed was more for his surrogate daughter than a screenwriter? Perhaps, but that sober glance of his was quite enough to make me forget the autocratic presumption that had booked my flight.

"I'd better get ready if we're going tomorrow," I said, and giving his lean tanned cheek a kiss—Sofia was right; it had grown altogether too lean—I hurried home to pack my bag and leave a regretful message for Clotilde at the Villa.

Alex's quick jaunt expanded to ten days and half the production company. Like a party of Grand Tourists we descended on northern Italy, circling its lakes, climbing the mountains, and stopping wherever possible to refresh ourselves on wild-boar pâté and grilled trout while we searched for our heroine's nineteenth-century homeland.

"The perfect place for Antonelli to do battle with the Austrians," Alex said, claiming a vast Piedmontese field in the name of Bella Vista Productions. "Can't you see our magnificent tigress fighting side by side with her volunteers?"

"It doesn't bother your conscience at all, having a scene that's pure fiction?"

"But what else could it be, child? This is a historical movie."

And at the river Var: "The princess will leave this bank in the night and cross over there to the French side on the back of her fellow revolutionary. You'll admit that's a fact, Anna, and an escapade worthy of *The Scarlet Pimpernel*. So you see."

He was far more youthful and energetic than I, this adopted

father of mine, an inspired and indefatigable traveling companion. The scenery was spectacular, the air exhilarating, the work enduring, and the talk about work unceasing. How then did I find the time to miss Clotilde?

It was a fortnight before I visited the convent again, and I waited in the reception room feeling as breathless as if I'd run all the way back from Lombardy.

"You haven't been waiting too long, I hope. Do please take a seat."

I nearly laughed at Clotilde's formal greeting. No; pleasure, pure pleasure at seeing my friend was the reason for that big irrepressible smile.

"How have you been?" I'd forgotten the way she sat so straight and still on the other side of the table. "You're looking well."

"And you, too, very well." Hers had been the usual professional observation, mine was merely intimate.

"Thank you." Confused by my return appraisal, she dropped her gaze, leaving me free to admire that faint mauve shadow beneath her eyes. Very well, I said, but what I meant was very lovely. There was a pale, remote look about her, a certain tautness to the delicate white skin that heightened her beauty.

"But I haven't had sufficient sleep, I'm afraid," Clotilde said. "Last night I was reading until much too late." She caught the involuntary interest that quickens the eye of a reader and gave an amused smile. "The Bible, Anna," she reminded me. "That's all I've time for. Lately the third floor has been so busy, I haven't had even an hour to study the medical journals."

So this air of formality was due to weariness. I was about to make some sympathetic comment when I recalled once before mistaking a wan, withdrawn mood for fatigue. "We're human, flesh and blood, too. We also have difficulties that we must try to surmount," she had told me that day, a correction that left me feeling as unworldly as it did secular.

"I wish there were more time for the Bible alone. Reading it always has such rewards for me," Clotilde was saying with a soft, rare insistence. "I can't imagine any book that could compare with its beauty and profundity."

She rose then and suggested that her guest might find the garden more enjoyable on so pleasant an afternoon.

"This way, please," she murmured, as though in two weeks' time I could have forgotten the tranquil marble route that led to the convent grounds.

"How's Luca been?"

"Very well," she replied, looking up with eyes that had brightened at his name. "Really splendid. Dr. Ibernesi has scheduled the final operation for the week after next. But it's very simple, this procedure. I tell Luca it doesn't even count. S'il plait a Dieu, his ordeal will soon be over."

"I'm so glad." And glad to see that glow again.

"Would you like to sit in the sun?" she asked when we reached our bench by the fountain. "I must get back to the Villa, but I've a few minutes more."

And, once we were seated, "I gather you, too, have been very busy, Anna?"

"Oh, yes. It was quite a trip."

"Trip?" She turned right around to me, her long white neck in a graceful swivel of interest. "You were away?"

"I've been in Lombardy. But didn't you get my message? I talked to Sister Cecile the night before I left. At least I think that's who it was." Could the sanctimonious Cecile have forgotten on purpose? "Alex decided to look at locations. It was a last-minute sort of thing, and I called the hospital to tell you."

"Did you?" she said softly. "I wondered what happened."

I stared at her in dismay.

"But it's quite all right, my dear. Such messages are easily lost in a busy hospital ward. Now tell me, what was Lombardy like?" she said with that quick warm smile. "Did you find your locations?"

I wasn't sure whether speaking of Luca had restored her spirits or the discovery that I hadn't been the neglectful friend circumstances made me seem. Perhaps it was simply having a rest in the garden, where the air, scented by the convent's lemon trees, was as refreshing as drafts of a cool drink.

Whatever the reason, Clotilde's mood had changed. I felt it was she who had returned from some distance and that our reunion was taking place only now, at the end of the visit, as we walked to the convent gate.

"The garden was so lovely today."

"I'm glad you were able to come to us."

"Please give Luca my love. Is there anything I can get for him? He must find these last days of waiting hard."

"I'm sure of it, though we never hear him complain. He becomes only a bit more mischievous." She hesitated an instant before confiding that she herself was to undertake a shopping trip downtown for Luca.

"Are you really? When?"

"Later this week or early next, whenever time permits. We thought we'd surprise him with some new paints. And a sable brush. I believe he wants a sable brush very much. Sister Bernadette tells me there are some good art shops in the center."

"I can think of several right near my apartment. Perhaps you'll come to tea? You'll be so close. Please do, Clotilde."

She gave, as I expected, a vaguely regretful smile, but this time the words that followed were as impulsive as mine. "That would be very nice. Yes, thank you, Anna. I shall try."

"Whenever time permits" was not much of a clue, and I began to wait for Clotilde's visit with more impatience and nerves than a tea party warranted. But it was only Arturo who called in the next few days, and Margot who appeared at my door. That the latter was back from Turkey I had no idea until the afternoon she stopped at the apartment.

"Why, Margot," I cried, flying out of my studio at the ring of the doorbell. "It's you."

"Certainly it's me," she replied, her husky offended voice muffled by the stack of packages Gina was removing tier by tier from her arms.

"Did the movie go well? Was Istanbul fun?"

"Yes and no. But look here, Anna, what do you mean by letting them wash your *palazzo* stairs at this time of day? I couldn't get through."

Her kisses were a chastisement, one quick sound smack on each of my cheeks. "The minute I started up the stairway your terrible concierge let out one of her yips and came running after me. I thought she was going to bite me in the leg. No, really, darling, she's a bulldog, that one. In the end I was forced to take the lift, five flights up."

"Poor you, and with all those packages to carry."

"It's not funny, Anna. I promised myself I'd never get into another."

"What happened? A bad experience with a Turkish lift?"

"In one," she confessed, rolling those famous big eyes to the ceiling, a sure sign of an hour's diversion.

"Come on into the sitting room. Gina will take care of your loot."

Pleased to see Margot again, I settled down on the sofa with the foolish grin, the incipient titters of one watching a favorite comedienne do the most commonplace things: give a reassuring *moue* of recognition into the mirror, an affectionate ruffle to those short dark curls, step out of high-heeled shoes, sink into the opposite corner of the sofa, and—

"And so?" I prompted. "What happened in the lift?"

"You'll never believe it. When it comes to foreign actresses the Turks have a very peculiar way of showing their homage. But hold on, I'm dying to know what's been going on here. No, wild horses won't drag another word from me until you talk. Did you really finish the screenplay? That's what I heard, and that it's better than *The Blue Room*. I hope not, darling, for my sake. But is it true Alex doesn't have the financing yet?

"By the by, how long has he been carrying on with that South American actress, Fandango or whatever her name is? And what's this about Antonelli going straight? I heard she's given up all her bad habits, even the boy."

"You heard extremely well for somebody in Istanbul." Fandango, indeed. Was the dignified Alex really carrying on with some starlet called Fandango?

"Not a word of gossip about you, though, and that worried me. Still," Margot said, moving closer to give me the benefit of a shrewd scrutiny, "your eyes are brighter. And you've got better color. It's that fellow at the restaurant, isn't it? Come on, tell. You followed my advice about him, didn't you? It's he who's responsible for putting some red in your cheeks, I bet."

"You're as bad as Gina," I said crossly.

"Aha, so you did take him for a lover."

"No, not yet."

"What do you mean not yet?"

"I'm thinking about it."

Margot gave a loud disapproving tch. I had shocked her.

Well, she had a point, after all. Why, when I was eager to get on with life, did I falter over so basic a step, hanging onto Arturo with one hand while the other pushed him away.

"Do you mean nothing happened in all the time I was gone?"

"It hasn't been that long."

His kisses were warming, and more. Yet how quick I was to

plead work, fatigue, Gina, anything to stop that nibbling mouth when it got too hungry. What was the reason for my scandalous behavior? A vague discomfort, an irrational sense of betraying Simon. If I thought I'd chosen a lover, a tonic too mild to matter, I was sadly mistaken. Arturo's blandness didn't mitigate my guilt so much as supply the punishment.

"And are you seeing him while you," gingerly Margot picked the word up and dangled it by its short tail, "think?"

"Of course I am. He's coming over later, as a matter of fact. Listen, I've a good idea. Why don't you stay and have supper with us? We can spend the evening together."

"Oh, Anna. Will I ever understand you? I'm sure it would be interesting, darling, but I can't. I've already invited some of the Istanbul crew to my place."

"Bring them along. Cathleen, too. We'll celebrate your homecoming. I'm going to ring up Alex and Sofia right now. And Ugo. Oh, and Claire."

"*Est-il possible?*" said Margot, listening in amazement, as did I, to the unbridled enthusiasm galloping away with me. "Whatever else the man has or hasn't done, he's certainly made you sociable."

"Good Lord." Arturo, arriving at the apartment several hours later, found a mob in the foyer, the halls filled with smoke, and the air bouncing with the agitated merriment of Scott Joplin. "What happened?"

"Hello, Arturo," I murmured, perversely relieved to see his round face bobbing up in the crowd.

"I don't understand. What's going on? Who's playing the piano?"

Who indeed had trespassed into Simon's sanctum? What stranger was giving his piano that trouncing?

"I can't hear you," he said, and, taking my arm, removed me to the dining room, where Gina, beside herself with delight and suspicion, had conjured up a bar and a cold buffet.

"So many people, my Annabella," she whispered. "But are you sure they're not just coming in from the street?"

"Maybe I'm mistaken," Arturo was saying, "but I thought we made a date to stay home alone tonight. What's this gang doing here?"

"Margot came back from Turkey, and some friends stopped in to say hello. And friends of friends."

Who more hospitable than a guest extending his own invitation, and where more true than in Rome. Capital of pilgrims, haven of transients; even those settled foreigners, who seemed only to be passing through, had but the floating anemonelike attachment one would expect to a Siren city.

"So it's a party, then."

I nodded. "Why don't you have a drink?" I suggested, fearing and hoping he'd turn on his heel and walk out. Surely I deserved it. But, "*Va bene*," he said with that patient, obdurate, maddening little sigh of his. "And you, Rosa? Do you want some wine?"

"Some wine?" I gave it careful thought, the sham deliberation of one who has already had too much. "Yes, why not?" I said, drifting back into the crowd.

"Good evening again, *chère madame!*" This triumphant greeting came from a Russian friend of Ugo's, an ecstatic young émigré who was en route to New York, where an uncle waited for him "on the West Side, in an apartment, *chère madame*, that sounds as big as Central Park itself."

Lisi, Lisi. If you had known what concentric circles we travel, would you still have left Matthew?

"Many's the evening I used to spend in this room, *cara*."

I turned around, but the speaker, a huge, old gentleman covered in sparkling white linen like a mountain with fresh snow, was addressing somebody else.

"Yes, yes, the *duchessa* was a dear friend of mine," he said, his heavy, sad mastiff's eyes drooping, weighed down with memory. "I knew her very well, very well."

"Who lives here now?"

"Some woman writer, an American, I think."

But they weren't all strangers gathered under my roof, and to prove it I waved at Eleonora and Richard, and blew a kiss to Bernard Sheenan. He was Rome's poet-in-residence, a skinny stick of a man who affected a gold pince-nez and looked, with his tangled gray curls, like a superior floor mop.

"Dear Anna," he said.

We had been briefly involved some five years ago, one dark, rainy winter when he was lecturing and I studying at Oxford.

"My, you're a sight for sore eyes." He smiled at me fondly, but kept both hands thrust deep in his jacket pockets, safeguarding the day's collection of café napkins—thin, triangular bits of paper covered with the outpouring of his vital, resonant verse.

"*Ciao, bella!*" That was tiny Milo, sending me a quick wink. He stood on the arm of the burgundy sofa, and in his sly, hopeful voice chatted with Claire Margolis. Talented, romantic, blonde Claire, who in a vast studio filled with sunshine and white dust re-created her lovers out of marble. "You remember Stefano? This is his torso." Or "The hips and legs of my divine Valerie," she'd murmur, introducing one graceful, fluid sculpture after another.

"You should sit down, my girl. You're looking rather tipsy, I must say." And here was Alex, dear Alex, come to give me a surprised, amused glance from under those heavy black eyebrows, such a distinguished, dramatic contrast to his silver hair.

"Wasn't that young Arturo I saw with you?" he asked, but before I could reply he was snatched away by a woman in a long fur, a member of his own pack, one of the potential investors Sofia had been playing hostess to earlier in the evening.

"We've brought you an assortment of cocktail leftovers," she had whispered when they came in the door. Draped in gray mesh from her milky white magnificent shoulders to her sandals, hair plaited and pinned around her head in a wreath, Sofia was *kolossal* tonight, a stunning Wagnerian Valkyrie.

A good thing he hadn't brought along Fandango, even if she were only another of those scandal-sheet acquaintances, as both he and the loyal Alice referred to them. Admittedly, they never were very much or very long in evidence. Still, wouldn't I enjoy giving that philanderer a real piece of my mind one day. But then again, how could I when it was Sofia herself who had left him free to . . . to do the Fandango?

From Simon's room down the hall came a new sound, Puccini, and I guessed it to be the soprano who had arrived with somebody in Margot's crew, a big, handsome, gleaming ebony woman from Kansas who spoke only in Italian. Yes, it was she who had taken over the piano, and now her clear powerful voice, sweetened by heartbreak, was soaring into an aria of Liu's.

That piano. I had arranged for its delivery on the anniversary of our first month together.

"I don't believe this," Simon had said, returning to the apartment one evening to find it installed. "I mean I'm totally nonplussed." His eyes had turned a cloudy blue. "You actually got this beautiful pianoforte moved up here for me? God, woman, you're a wonder."

I gave an embarrassed laugh. "I didn't do it single-handed." Now that he was uttering the astonished, grateful words I had contrived to hear, I felt ashamed. "Anyway, you won't thank me once you're sweating over your concerto again."

"*Buona sera.*" A helpless call from Ugo who had been backed into a corner by two English girls.

"Are you really a producer?" one of them was asking.

"If you are," said the other, "you're the first we've met so far."

"But we've only just arrived. We flew in this morning."

Well, I could believe it. What a pair of cockatoos they were, with their thin, sharp faces and those pointed tufts of blue and orange hair.

I wondered what Clotilde would think of such an assemblage, and of me for calling it. Not much, I should imagine. Nevertheless, I could picture myself describing the evening to her when she came to tea. But, really, I'd become a child where she was concerned, comforting myself with thoughts of her whenever I was uneasy or sad.

"There you are, Camelia."

I dodged Arturo's call, so much more an embarrassment for its low, discreet tone, and slipped away into the burgundy room.

"*Carissima amica*," Eleonora said. "We've been waiting for a chance to talk with our hostess." She was sitting on the arm of Richard's chair, drooping over him with the exquisite languor of the lilacs she had brought in from the country.

"We were just saying what a good party it is," he declared. "Weren't we, *amore*?" How often had I seen him glance at her in that proprietary, helpless way.

"I'm glad you two could come. It's been ages since I've seen you."

"Ages," Eleonora agreed. "But you know what hermits we are. Richard is happy never to leave the country, and I drive into town only when I absolutely must. Two minutes to see my dentist or argue with my translator and, presto, I'm back on the *autostrada* again."

Her gaze kept returning to her husband as she spoke. What a look those dark eyes held—the submissive, proud, exultant expression of a woman well taken in love.

"Peonia."

Was there no escaping that long-stemmed floriferous tongue?

"I think that young man's trying to get your attention," Eleonora said.

But I turned away with a deaf ear, a pinched envious heart, and responded instead to a cry from Margot's nursemaid.

"Oh, shite! I've spilt the wine. I'm sorry, Miss Stewart, I really am," said the lovely Cathleen with one of her fiery blushes. "I don't know why I have to be such a fhucking clumsy cow. Is it true that a drop of white wine will take out the red?"

"Don't give it another thought. You can spill as much red wine as you like in here. Why else did they do the room up in this color?" I was apparently just as tipsy as Alex said. "How was Istanbul?"

"Oh, 'tis a queer old place, but Margot's brilliant in the movie. I've never seen her in better form. I only wish we could've stayed out there."

"You liked it then?"

Her round blue eyes were fixed on mine in the blind pause of one given to imprudent leaps. "It's my dad. He's set on coming to Rome."

"He and Kat?"

"No, just him. Didn't Margot tell you? Oh, he's a right old bastard. He's gone and left Kat just when she's about to pop his brat." Cathleen gave her long yellow hair a flying, dangerous toss. "The man's completely off his rocker. He gives the shaft to my best friend and then expects a big welcome party out here."

The sympathetic murmur I gave resulted only in another of her painful blushes.

"If it's absolution he's after, well, it's not me he should go to now, is it? I tell you, it's enough to make a cat sick to hear him on the fhucking blower. They'll be well taken care of, he says. Neither Kat nor the child will ever want for anything, he says. Oh, sure, only him, the old sod."

A deep flush did not cover but enhanced the pride and scorn on that lovely young face, the sadness; in short, the love.

" 'Twas just one of those things, he says, an affliction of the heart. In a pig's eye. An affliction of the prick is more like it. That's the only heart he's got. You just wait. He'll come out here and go after Margot next. 'Tis inevitable; I know it."

"Rosa." Arturo was approaching again with that everlasting, ever-changing sobriquet, and I hurried away, the steady vibrant hum of his Camelia Peonia Mimosa following me around the room like a good-natured bee.

"It's a famous old *palazzo*, you know."

"Too bad they're always so shabby up close."

"It's certainly big enough for a single person, isn't it?"

Two compatriots of mine, conscientious tourists draped in vivid silks from Piazza di Spagna, were taking in my apartment.

"I heard she had a lover, a composer, who lived here with her."

"They broke up?"

"No, he died."

"Oh, dear . . . how unresolved."

A dreadful giggle burst from me, and I fled down the hall to my bedroom. I meant to wash my overheated face, put on fresh make-up, and rejoin the party. But I hadn't counted on the warm welcome from my blue sanctuary, the lure of the golden bed I threw myself upon as I would the peaceful sunny patch of threshed wheat its grogram cover resembled. Just for a few minutes, I told myself.

"*Cara.*" Arturo's call, his melodic knock on the door woke me. "Are you in there?"

A sober, guilty glance at the bedside clock told me it was after midnight.

"*Permesso?*" He came into my room without waiting for a reply while I stayed curled up on the bed, watchful and unsurprised as a roused cat. Was it possible I had expected him to follow me here?

Clearly he thought so. "*Finalmente,*" he said, removing his clothes with the benevolent smile, the incredible speed of a trysted lover.

"Everybody's gone." His sweater, shirt, and trousers were falling from him, spilling to the rug in rapid shades of brown. "I showed the last bunch out myself. And I told Gina to wait until morning to clean up."

"Did you? That was thoughtful," I murmured, impressed by this masterful intrusion. And, yes, relieved. The decision had been made for me, the moment could be avoided no longer. The time had come to face up. But what thoughts were these to greet a lover?

"Arturo," I said, holding out contrite arms.

"*Ecco mi.*" He had plunged onto the bed and was seeking the buttons of my blouse, the zipper in my long skirt, ferreting out hidden hooks with a dedicated impatience.

"Wait. I'll do it." Shyness was responsible for that eager offer, for the immodest desire to get up and quickly, simply undress myself.

"No, stay still. Let me."

My hands, left free to amuse themselves, wandered slowly down the slope of his back, admiring the smooth olive skin—

"That feels nice."

—burrowed up through his short brown hair, and lifted his head a little so that one finger might caress that appealing nose with its flat bronzed ridge.

"What is it, *Camelia mia*? What are you doing?"

What, indeed? This was no time to be thinking of Florentine pigs, and my finger moved on to trace the molding of those perfectly sculpted lips. But how mobile they had become.

"Put your hand here, *amore*. And your legs like that. There, it's more comfortable with the pillow this way, isn't it? I'll leave the lamp on. It's nice when there's some light. Or do you like it better in the dark?"

The taciturn Arturo was finding altogether too much to say tonight, and I longed for his old secretive, silent ways.

"I can't get this loose. Wait, let me pull it down."

His hands, just as voluble, were in the frankest communication with my legs and the inside of my thighs.

"Turn this way. Doesn't it feel good?"

That anxious mouth was dropping inchoate kisses over my face and on my throat, was darting into my half-opened blouse to graze swiftly, too swiftly in the hollow between my breasts.

"Rosa!"

But I needed no such urging. My kisses were as rash as his, and my body, fearful of being outdistanced, increased its tempo— only why such a hectic race?—clamored, like his, for the final embrace, which now promised our completing the course together.

"Aii!" A promise broken in the next moment by Arturo's startled cry of passion, his no less precipitate leap from the bed.

"It's late. I think I'd better go home," he said, holding the back of his neck in the tentative grasp of a wounded man.

"What is it? What happened to your neck?" Had he suffered a lustful wrench or was it only embarrassment. "Are you all right?'

"*Certo.*" Already in his trousers and shirt, he was rushing around the bedroom gathering the rest of his things so fast, so furtively, he might have been stealing them.

"Don't bother, I'll let myself out."

"Please wait a minute, Arturo. It's no bother," I said, struggling up from the tawdry entanglement of my own clothes. "Are you really all right?"

He turned around then, and in the light of the wall lamp I saw his eloquent answer, the long brown eyes whose startled expression gave them a sudden roundness, the small smile at once apologetic and offended. And so pale a face. That dark complexion was bleached like an almond, had the pure blanched look of a man who has encountered a ghost. As indeed Arturo seemed to think he had.

"To tell you the truth, something strange happened to my neck. *Che dolore!* Just when I was— I had the impression while we were— Well, it felt like somebody came up from behind and gave me a hard whack, a real clout, like this." His fist sailed through the air in a ghostly blow and fell as he saw me smile.

"Oh, *caro*. You're not saying it was Simon. You don't seriously believe that." There was, alas, no way to hide the smile that welcomed this bit of comedy or the gratitude I felt to see our hasty unlovely union turned into a farce, an opera bouffa that would have delighted and flattered its villain.

"Me, seriously believe?" Arturo said. "No, no." But beneath his rational sigh a southern child averted the evil eye with an ancient gesture, gave a swift, reassuring touch to his privities with one hand while the fingers of the other flew into the protective sign of the horns.

"I have to be at the office early tomorrow," he said. "I really should go, Anna." Oh, the dubious triumph of hearing him at last call me by my name.

"Must you go right now? Don't you want to sit down and relax for a few minutes? I'll get you a hot compress for your neck. And a drink. You ought to have something to warm you. What about a glass of brandy?" I said, putting an affectionate arm through his as we walked down the hall together.

"Come to think of it, you hardly had any supper. Why don't I fix you something to eat before you go, an omelette and some toast. You could have it on a tray by the fire." Like the most relentlessly tender of mistresses I babbled on, right up to the front door, such was the giddy, guilty relief of knowing he was about to bid me a final good night, that this curative affair was over.

Few affairs, however, lend themselves to so tidy a break, do not have their own way of unraveling at the end, and this one was no exception. In his flight from my bedroom, Arturo left behind a beige mohair sweater and a creamy ecru silk tie, handsomely and expensively muted items I didn't quite know how to return.

To send them by post to his parents' home might prove awk-

ward for him. The question was whether it would be more discreet, or less, to have a messenger deliver them to his office. In
either case I would have to write him a note, and where was I
to find the phrase obliging enough to sound neither too casual
nor too intimate?

You'll think of something later, I told myself, stashing the
sweater and tie out of sight on the top shelf of the hall closet.
But like most procrastinations, the moment's pleasure was hardly
worth the consequence. At the end of the week, on a quiet
Saturday afternoon, Arturo came to collect them himself, just
as Clotilde and I were sitting down to tea.

My friend had telephoned the evening before to say that the
arrangements had finally been made for her to drive down into
the center with Sisters Agathe and Madeline. Her task being a
simple one, Clotilde said, she would have some free time between going to the art-supply shop and meeting the sisters at
the church of Trinità dei Monti—and this hour we fixed upon
for her visit.

"Sister Clotilde is coming to tea tomorrow." I had rushed to
the kitchen to find Gina, more from a desire to share my news,
really, than prepare for the visit.

"To tea? Oh, Mother of God. There's nothing in the house
for tea."

"What about making a chocolate ricotta pie?" Would Clotilde recall the day I told her the ricotta-tree story? It had been
the first time I heard that slightly startled, very human laugh of
hers.

"A chocolate ricotta pie? No, absolutely not. That's exactly
the wrong thing to serve a *religiosa*. It's too heavy. Maybe some
frappés would do. They're sweet and light enough for an angel."

"Both then, and maybe you should order a quart of ice cream,
too."

"Ice cream? If she's anything like the sisters at home, she
won't say no to a good sniff of brandy. But she's coming tomorrow, and you tell me now at the very last minute? Go look at

the mess in the sitting room. And the floor. Have you given me time to polish more than two tiles? To get fresh flowers? Oh, Annabella."

For once Gina was too taken aback to dissemble, to disguise either her anxiety or her pleasure. Or to look at me with her wise village eyes and perceive my own.

Indeed, our guest appeared to be the only one completely at her ease, who seemed to think there was nothing so very remarkable about the occasion. Or did she? What was Clotilde thinking when she arrived the next afternoon with that breathless smile, holding by its string a brown package of paints and sable brushes for Luca.

"Good afternoon, Anna."

"You're here. Please, come in."

Were the rare descent from her hill and a successful shopping mission the only reasons for the high color in her cheeks?

"I'm afraid I've come early."

"By all of five minutes." It burst from me, that ingenuous confession of an anxious watch.

"*Buon giorno.*" Gina had come trotting out from the pantry and, with a bob of her glossy dark head, was leading the way to the sitting room.

"*Prego, si accomodi.*" Like her, it had acquired a demure tone, a look so orderly and respectable it bordered on the anonymity of a public room.

"*Grazie tante,*" Clotilde said. "Isn't this fine? Nice and cool, too, after the crowded streets. One forgets how busy it is in this part of Rome. Not so very changed, I imagine, from the ancient days." My holy friend sounded astonishingly like anyone else who has dropped in after a round of the shops.

"This is such a pleasant room, Anna. I like the burgundy. It's a welcoming color, isn't it?" She gave me a shy, triumphant look. "You can tell I've spent the last hour looking at paint charts. That boy got wind of our surprise for him. If you could have heard him asking for a shade of blue that's misty, like the sea when it rains," she quoted proudly, "and a shiny beetle brown. Oh, and you also were on his list. A soft gray like a pussy willow, he said, like the eyes of the Signorina."

A flush rising to her cheeks, she glanced away and commented on the practicality of double reception rooms.

"Practical? Yes, I suppose they are," I replied with an irrelevant grin, for I was surprised and pleased. Not by Luca's remark but by the blush that had turned it into a compliment from her.

"The rounded archway and window is so felicitous a design."

"I can show you more of the apartment, if you like."

"That would be nice, thank you."

I found it disconcerting, the sight of Clotilde away from the convent, stepped out of her marble and gliding in those long white skirts through the baroque darkness of my halls.

But she: "There must be so much history here," she said with her easy grace as we walked along the mossy trails of old green velvet.

"This is where you lived when you were a girl?"

"Well, in our fashion. That is, Lisi rented it off and on for a time."

And in the *settecento* gloom of the picture gallery, how attentive she was to the feverish black eyes and long thin noses of my landlord's noble ancestors. "Such interesting faces."

"It was better in those days, don't you think, when people depended more on their God-given talent than a camera," she murmured, viewing now the no less somber pastoral scenes, the dim farmhouses and brooding burnt-umber cows.

"Another hall?"

"This leads to Simon's room."

I had meant to show her the view from the terrace next—a wish I had expressed often enough—yet here I was displaying his room instead, the old *duchessa*'s blue boudoir and the cluttered studio beyond it. An impulse that seemed to be answered by the edge of curiosity in her polite murmurs.

"He composed in here, then. And this is your bedroom. Such an unusual tapestry. So this is where you work. What an agreeable studio."

"We could have our tea here," I said, and the tour ended then, in that shady lair of books and papers, a choice warmly approved by Clotilde's smile.

And deplored by Gina's "*Pazzarella!*"

"What are you thinking of?" she hissed when I went to the kitchen to tell her we'd take the tea in my studio. "You have a clean elegant *salotto*, and you want me to serve tea in that bird's nest? *Ma no!* Where? Tell me. On your desk? On a pile of dirty encyclopedias?"

Irksome woman, how she got on my nerves that afternoon, hovering at the studio door to make sure the tea was strong enough, the frappés light enough. Was Sister comfortable enough in here? Really? Then could she get her more sugar? Another napkin, perhaps? Truly not? In that case, she'd return to the kitchen. But the signorina would ring if they needed anything later, wouldn't she? Gina's face, ambivalent as a clown's, stretched its lower region into a smile while a pair of unhappy eyes flashed me a final reproach.

"It must be encouraging to work in a place where you're surrounded by so many books," Clotilde said.

She was sitting on the sofa by the window, and the sunlight, filtered through shutters and green drapes, fell upon her in the oblique rays of a cool forest corner.

"The truth is, I'm more often encouraged to read than write."

My eye, still adjusting to the sight of her in my territory, marveled at the lighting on that slender sapling of a throat, watched an erratic beam hit upon her gold wedding band, and followed another that fell across her veil, catching out the auburn glints in the narrow rim of hair.

"But how quiet everything is. One forgets we're still in the middle of the city."

"It's siesta time. In any case, there's only an alleyway on this side of the *palazzo*." An absent response that scarcely interfered with my thoughts.

I was deep in speculation about her hair. Was it the rich shade it hinted at being? I wondered how short it was and whether it was neatly cut or shorn by a deliberately careless, pietistic hand. And whether it was as submissive and smooth as that intriguing rim suggested or if at night, freed from the veil, it sprang into a life of its own, into vigorous curls, vainglorious waves.

"The signorina's busy. She has company with her now."

I hadn't heard the doorbell, but that was certainly Gina talking to somebody in the hall.

"She's busy? Well, that's all right. *Non importa.*"

And that somebody, I realized with a plunging heart, was Arturo. It occurred to me afterward that if I hadn't been dreaming about the friend who sat right there with me, I might have heard him sooner. Possibly I could have leaped up and shut the door before Arturo's low voice, distinct as a stage whisper in a hushed theater, penetrated my room.

"There's no reason to disturb the signorina. I only came by to pick up some clothes of mine. Maybe you know what she did with the things I left here the other night?"

Clotilde turned her head away discreetly, but I had already seen the involuntary flight of one delicate eyebrow, a fleeting quiver, an instant's dismay.

"He must be somebody who came here to Margot's party, a guest who forgot something," I said, and bent my head over the teapot, embarrassed, indeed shocked at my swift, foolish remark, at a lie whose mollifying tone sounded not as though it wanted to soothe an offended religious but reassure a lover.

"*Addio!*" The conversation had receded to the rear end of the hall, to the closet, where, thankfully, it became inaudible. And now, "*Addio, signore, addio!*" A clear, hearty farewell from Gina.

185

The front door slammed shut. The heavy bolts were shot—too late, Gina, too late—and Arturo was gone.

"This tea resembles the kind we used to have in Normandy. We made it from the dandelions. One of God's everyday little gifts," a perfectly composed nun was saying. "We used them for soup, too."

The air in the studio had cleared. That uncertain thing between us, that intense fragile moment was over.

"In our profession we often need a reliable stimulant, and so we're apt to become too dependent upon coffee. Yet nothing leaves one quite as invigorated and refreshed as a good tea."

Smiling serenely in the direction of the shuttered window, Clotilde went on to remark upon the small sounds with which the street below was waking up from its siesta.

"That means it must be time to leave," she murmured, but she remained on the sofa and listened with me to the stirrings of my bucolic alley, the roll of carts over cobblestone and the song of a canary whose red cage hung from an ivy-laden window across the way.

"Do you hear the fountain?" I asked. "If we're very quiet, we'll be able to hear the flower girl watering her roses in a few minutes." And "Sssh, can you hear that clatter? I bet it's the peddler with his copper pots."

Clotilde gave a soft laugh. "Whose wagon wheels are those?" she asked, falling in with my game. "Am I right to guess it's the vegetable man?"

We spent the remainder of the visit in this simple way, a childish diversion that led me to breathe easily again, to believe my friend had already forgotten the afternoon's incident and that our hour together had been as tranquil as any other.

Why then didn't we meet the next week? What made her sound cool and unnatural when I telephoned the hospital? It was the day after Luca was scheduled to have his final operation, and I had called to ask whether I might see him when I came to the convent on Thursday and what she thought he might like me to bring him, questions I never got the chance to ask.

Clotilde herself answered the telephone at the nurses' station in a courteous and remote voice. Nor did her tone change when I, thinking perhaps she hadn't recognized me, hurriedly identified myself.

"Yes, Anna, of course. How are you?" she said in exactly the same reserved manner, and without pause went on to tell me that her floor was extremely busy. She regretted it, but she wouldn't be free to have a visitor at the convent this week. A quickly murmured "Excuse me," and before I could say a word in reply or ask after Luca, she had rung off. And I, regretting my interruption, quickly dropped that buzzing, hurtful receiver.

Yet this wasn't the first time my friend had been too busy to speak. I had called before at an inconvenient moment. Such a thing was inevitable and, of course, excusable, she had assured me. As for her not being free to have a visitor, why, nobody knew better than I how much extra duty this dedicated nurse took on.

What on earth then was I fussing about? Our conversation had been neither unusual nor ominous. I'd send Luca some fruit or candy, perhaps a basket of both, and arrange to see him when I went to the convent next Thursday. Meanwhile, heaven knew I had enough work of my own to get done.

So did I assuage my doubts, quiet the suspicion that Clotilde's aloofness was the result of her visit to me. I didn't forget her expression when she heard Arturo in the hall, nor my quick lie. The memory of that uncertain, fragile moment simply retreated, went to the back of my mind where for a brief time it was covered over with thoughts of *The Revolutionary Princess*, with pages of revised script, much as a chrysalis is protected by a scattering of leaves.

Lisi was due to leave for India at the end of June, and in order to free myself for a visit home before this, I had to solve an almost daily outcropping of small problems. Indeed, it seemed to me the screenplay was taking up more time now that it was finished.

"Finished? When the film's been shot, then you know the script is finished," said Alex in the golden voice of honey.

"Now about the salon scene. I think it works better, but there's still one small problem. What's the point in having Liszt come to Christina's if he just sits there with his feet on the table like Musset and doesn't even play one Hungarian rhapsody, for goodness' sake."

"To save money, that's the point" was the inevitable reply from Ugo. "And while we're on the subject, do me a favor, Anna. Tighten up the harem scene. Who needs so many wives?"

The following day it was Antonelli.

"Of course, I'm only an actress, *carissima*, not a writer. But are we showing off the princess's principles to their best advantage by sticking her in a rice field with two hundred angora goats?"

Our leading lady, for all she had begun to betray a real anxiety over the film's delays, was still, as Alex said, a paragon of patience compared to her agent. This tightly wound Signor Donati came daily to the production offices to demand a look at the shooting schedule. Like an acrobat, he had a vibrant spring to his walk, an air of having suddenly landed on his feet, which left one in some doubt as to whether he had arrived by door or window.

"Where is it, Signor Sareuth? The shooting schedule, that's what. You said I could see it today. What do you mean Alice misplaced it? Listen, do you have any idea how much your delays are costing us? Shall I tell you how many theatrical bookings my client's already turned down because of your film?"

At all events, as a conciliatory gesture to "our star and guiding light"—yes, that was the extent of his shameless pandering—Alex had agreed to the three of us meeting at Antonelli's apartment to discuss a small problem.

"If it's small enough, maybe you can figure it out. I'm not going" was my own prima donna's cry. "I'm fed up with your problems."

"Did I say problem?" Alex glanced up from the cigar he was tending. "It was a slip of the tongue. She wants to discuss the motivation in one or two scenes, that's all. Something to help her get into the princess's skin, she said."

"That's all, is it."

"Now, now. Surely my dear child isn't going to let me down?"

"Oh, isn't she!"

But I had the pleasure of fooling myself for only a short time. In the end his dear child did, of course, go along to Antonelli's.

"The signora's upstairs on the telephone. She'll be through in a minute," Renato the butler said. "Please make yourselves comfortable. May I bring you some refreshments?"

Half an hour later he was still wooing us in that charming singsong accent of his. "I'm sure she will be right down. Would you like to try some of her carrot salad? A glass of mineral water?" Fair Renato with his golden hair and blooming cheeks, he might have dropped right out of that heavenly, orgiastic scene on her ceiling.

"Welcome, my friends." At last from the top of the stairs came a greeting—from Princess Cristina!

"*Buona sera*, dearest lady," Alex said, while I simply gawked at the amazing, dismaying degree to which Antonelli had already got into the princess's skin.

"I'm so happy you were both able to come."

But what a pallor. Like Cristina, her face seemed to have no blood to warm it, to rely only on the fire in those huge dark eyes.

"The pleasure is entirely ours," Alex replied, continuing to stand at attention while she drifted slowly down the stairs, pausing now and again as though she were making a descent into his camera.

"I hope Renato took good care of you." She was wearing a turban and a white gown, a diaphanous affair so queerly draped that, as Gautier said of Cristina's, one imagined a dagger hidden in its folds.

"I was very wicked to keep you waiting, but I think you'll forgive me when I explain it was that brat on the telephone again. All the same, I apologize. It shouldn't take so long to tell a little donkey to go screw himself."

Her carriage as she swept down the remaining marble stairs was altogether regal, but that deep gravelly voice and the rueful smile, they belonged to Antonelli.

"Shall we get to work? Thank God for work, eh? It's the only thing in life that really counts."

"How true, signora, how true," Alex said with a lingering smile that continued to praise as she read through her scenes.

But there was something in Antonelli's performance today that troubled me. I could not quite believe in that nonchalant dismissal of the "little donkey." It seemed doubtful to me that her cheeks had achieved such pallor, her eyes their melancholy by method alone. In short, I suspected her of suffering, of pining for the young lover she had renounced. And why, come to it, shouldn't she have her brat if she wanted him?

I dared say as much to Alex later on, when we were driving back to the production offices for a casting session.

"Ah, but she does have him," he replied with a smile as rueful and amused as any of hers. "Oh, yes, she took the scoundrel back."

"What makes you think so?"

"In this case, I don't think, my sweet. I happen to know. Though it would no doubt surprise Antonelli that I do. On the whole, she's kept her foolishness a very successful secret. Some acting that was, hmm?"

"A bravura performance," I agreed. And yet the look on her face when she came downstairs, that smoldering, vulnerable expression, how much acting had it been?

"Wake up, my girl, we're here. You might as well leave your jacket in the car. I'll be driving you right home. This isn't going to last long at all."

So Alex claimed of each casting session that began in the late afternoon and continued until after midnight.

"What, another open call? How can that be?" I kept asking.

"Well, an unofficial call. You know how it is once the word gets around."

"But, Alex, even the minor parts are set. What roles are left to cast?"

"Let's see who turns up."

He could not have given a better illustration of his splendid disregard for the story line of *The Revolutionary Princess*. Nor his enduring affection for the character actors, the picaresque extras who flocked to an office where cigarette smoke rose in a thick blue mist and the spumante flowed like the Tiber below. Patron of performers, of the beautiful, the grotesque, and the unemployed, Alex held casting sessions that were nothing more or less than sentimental reunions.

"*Ciao, Padre!*" Though he was one of the more frequent visitors, Alex always had a surprised, delighted greeting for the seven-foot-tall, spectral ex-priest from Liguria. "Have a cigar, Padre, some *sciampagna*," he said, smiling up at this giant whom no amount of grease paint could have given that chalky white complexion, those dark-ringed eyes.

Patting the chair on his other side, "Come, sit" was the gentle command he gave to the fluffy platinum-haired Scandinavian actress with the flat, short-sighted face of a Pekingese.

And a moment later he was in the embrace of another character actress, a member of *The Blue Room* cast. "Ah, Graziella.

I'm so glad to see you." And, lowering his voice, "Tell me, my dear, how are they doing?"

Was this, as one might suppose, a solicitous reference to the actress's family? No; he was asking after her teats, those mammoth, overwhelming breasts for which she had achieved international fame.

It didn't help, Ugo dragging Alex aside to say in his pale, choked voice: "Why are all these actors here? What is this, a casting call for Garibaldi's army or what?

"And another thing, where does the script call for a bearded lady? That woman needs somebody to give her a razor, not a contract."

"But my dear fellow, consider the bathos of a delicate, adorable nose like hers underlined with a guardsman's mustache. Why, we've signed up nothing less than the human comedy itself."

My protests were just as useless. "Don't fret, Anna. A really good film is, in every sense, like life. The more interesting characters, the more rewarding one's life. Relax. You'll have time to write them in later, on the set if need be. Anyway, look at the backside on her! Does it need dialogue? Take a gander at that tough, pugilist's chin with its dab of pink face powder. Doesn't it speak out loud?"

It was during a lull in one of these evening sessions, the room momentarily empty save for Alex and me, that I tried to get in touch with Clotilde again. An unlikely time and place, to be sure, but a week had gone by since our brief talk, and now, on the eve of another Thursday, I was suddenly seized with the need to hear her confirm our customary meeting.

"I'll be right back. I have to make a call before it gets any later," I told Alex.

"No reason to go." He himself was, as usual, on the telephone, listening idly to I know not whom, his left hand holding the receiver while the right made notes, flipped through pages of the script, and otherwise found gainful employment.

"There's another phone on the desk over there. Just plug it in. But perhaps you want privacy?"

"This is fine." Some misguided instinct, protective and imprudent, caused me to pretend, even to myself, that it wasn't a personal matter. "I'm only ringing up the Villa."

"Hello? Yes, please?" The third-floor phone had been answered by a nurse whose uncertain voice suggested to me the new Sister Madeline.

"You wish to speak to Sister Clotilde? But she's not at the station. Will you give me your name again, please?"

"I don't want to disturb her, but if you could say it's Anna Stewart."

"One moment, Miss Stewart. I'll try to locate her for you."

In the endless moment she was gone, Alex finished his own call and with a discreet nod gave me the "privacy" for mine by retiring behind a trade newspaper.

"I'm sorry, Miss Stewart, Sister can't come to the telephone just now. She asks that I thank you for the very nice gift you sent Luca."

I waited for her to go on, confident that Clotilde had sent some word about tomorrow's visit.

"Is that all, Sister? There was no other message?"

"No, Miss Stewart."

I replaced the phone with a slow hand, too surprised and disappointed to hide either of these feelings.

"The look on your face, my dear girl," Alex said in mock alarm. "What's that saintly creature done? I shouldn't pay it any attention if I were you. They're an enigma unto themselves, those nuns, the quintessence of feminine mystery. What did she do? Break a date?"

"Oh, shut up! You're not funny, you know."

He drew back from my snarl. "No, I suppose not." And after a suitable pause, "But tell this foolish old fellow you forgive him, won't you? The fact is, I've spent too many years teasing my young cousin to know how to stop."

Succumbing to Alex's wistful smile, I leaned over his chair, ready to drop a kiss on the crest of a silvery wave when he added: "Seriously, though, Anna,"

Seriously? I was the one to draw back now, on my guard.

"I think Sister Clotilde has been a good friend to you." His tone was serious, as promised, but those green eyes still had a frivolous light, an inquisitive gleam not at all to my liking.

"Yes, very much so." Reluctantly, I gave the reply he was waiting to hear.

"My dearest girl, I do understand."

"Oh?"

"But surely you didn't imagine otherwise. Of course I understand."

I hardly dared to think where this conversation was leading us. "Good for you," I said lightly, dismissively, and turned away.

"I couldn't approve more of your choice of a friend. She's altogether charming, as beautiful as she is kind."

The persistent Alex went right on, gently addressing my back; indeed, the very hackles rising there.

"Why wouldn't you be drawn to a charm so like your own? It's natural, my darling. Perfectly understandable."

"So you keep saying," I cried, rounding on him. "Though I don't know why the subject fascinates you so much."

In fact, I agreed with him. My thoughts of late had led me to the same conclusion. I could see quite well, perhaps too well, how understandable and natural it was. But Alex's eager discussion, this parental, permissive air of his, they definitely were not.

"Good night."

"Good night? We've got another bunch of actors coming in about five minutes. Where are you going? Whatever's wrong with you?"

"I'm going home. I'm tired."

Sick and tired of your understanding so damned much, I was about to say. But the puzzled and faintly sheepish look on Alex's face silenced me. True, he had teased his young cousin for too many years, but hadn't he also listened patiently to all her girlhood plaints and passions? The fact is, he'd always been an indulgent confidant. Was this generosity, then, so different?

Moreover, reason had come shambling back to tell me that such anger as I let loose upon him was a diversionary thing. The true cause of my upset was Clotilde. It pained me that she said nothing about our meeting again, that her only message had been a gracious, impersonal thank-you-very-much.

What was I to make of it? Busyness alone couldn't account for so deliberate a silence. Didn't the trouble begin, as I first feared, with Arturo? How could she not have been offended by his booming whisper for the clothes he had left behind. And how much more offended by my attempt to reassure her, my quick caressing lie.

It surprised me, the loneliness I felt for my friend in the days that followed. Time and again I found myself looking away from work, hoping to catch a glimpse of her in my mind's eye. But all I ever succeeded in capturing was the odd fragment; an insubstantial impression of a low murmur or a soft step. One night as I was falling asleep I glimpsed her face. For an instant I saw the high pale brow and those dark eyes looking full into mine; then she turned away, her head drooped on its graceful white stalk, and I could see no more.

Despite everything I continued to nurture a lingering hope that she might telephone me, and when by the next week I still hadn't heard from her, I gave in to the impulse to call the hospital one last time.

It was Sister Cecile who replied and in her curt, merciful way got right to the point. "Sister Clotilde hasn't been working this past week. She's in seclusion."

"In seclusion?" I repeated stupidly.

"She hasn't been well, Miss Stewart. She's resting at the convent. We expect her back in a few days."

"Thank you, Sister. Well, thank you very much."

Ashamed at the relief I felt in thinking there was nothing wrong, after all, but my friend's illness, I sat down to write her a letter. It was a rather formal inquiry about her health, but, like the letter she had once sent me, it ended with a postscript, an impetuous scrawl that instructed her to get better quickly so that we might meet again.

Three days later I was alone in the apartment. Gina had gone to the morning market, and I was dressing for an appointment with Alex when the doorbell rang. Since it was too early for him, I thought it must be Gina at the door, burgeoning with flowers and fruits she wished to have admired on the spot.

"*Pazienza!* Keep your shirt on. I'm coming as fast as I can," I shouted in reply to another ring, and opened the door to find Clotilde standing there.

"Good morning," she said. "I hope I'm not disturbing you."

"Disturbing me? Oh, Clotilde. Come in, please." I was astounded and thrilled to see her, and anxious. She looked so unwell. Her very features were weary, drained—lips pale, eyes a lighter and subdued brown.

"Come." I took her by the arm and led her to the sofa in the sitting room. "Is this all right? Is the room cool enough? Will you be comfortable here?"

She smiled faintly at my matron's manner. "I'm sorry to arrive like this, but I received your nice letter and I . . ." She paused an instant. "I took the chance of finding you in," she concluded in the overly casual way of one who has chosen an alternative end for her remark.

"Let me get you something. A cool drink, perhaps."

"No, thank you, Anna." She turned to face me, and my thoughts, more directly. "I'm quite fine now. Although I wasn't really ill, not as you might have imagined. I allowed myself to become overtired, that's all."

I nodded and said nothing, recognizing that distant smile for the signal that closed a too-personal discussion.

But I was wrong. "Sometimes we underestimate the effect of fatigue. It can fool us by providing a false energy that makes us forget that our need is not simply for physical rest but for solitude and contemplation."

Her eyes were cast down, and she was speaking in a voice so low and intimate I wasn't sure it was meant for my ears.

"He is always there talking to us, but sometimes we must stop to listen and hear Him."

"Oh, Clotilde. What happened?" It had taken me that long to understand, to recall her standing in the corner of Simon's room with just such a suffering, beauteous look. "What is it? Tell me.

"Ah, no," I added in the same breath, certain the reply would be "Luca" and instinctively, unthinkingly, I opened my arms and drew her close.

I've no idea how long we sat in the depths of the old burgundy sofa in that silent embrace, her head resting on my shoulder, my cheek lightly pressed against her veil.

"I promised I'd be there when he woke up. It was such a simple operation. There wasn't room for a mistake." She had begun to speak in a barely audible voice, her murmurs falling slow and solitary, like the tears of one unused to crying. "I told him he'd soon be hopping around like a jackrabbit. When you called, I didn't know what to say. From one day to the next we weren't sure if he'd pull through."

What went wrong in the operating room, the exact nature of the "mistake" I never learned. Clotilde didn't explain then, nor did she ever speak of it again. Those hesitant unsequential murmurs told me only that though Luca had recovered enough to be moved to a hospital in Naples, the chances of his ever walking were, once again, negligible.

"The doctor was in no way reprimanded. Worse, we didn't even speak of what happened among ourselves."

"Poor Luca." She might have been the boy himself, so tenderly was I holding her. "It will be all right," I said, trying to remember the seraphic phrases with which she had consoled me. "You told me once it was His real friends He tests most severely."

"Ah, no, Anna, it wasn't Him I doubted in these weeks." Her voice trembled like the heart I could feel through her surprisingly soft habit. "Not Him, but my fellows."

"It's all right," I said. "It's all over now."

Clotilde's reply was a sigh, the prolonged tremor that follows a heavy unburdening.

"It's been a bad patch, but it's done with, and Luca's going to be fine. Why, you know what that boy's like. He's as resilient as they come."

All this I believed, but, lost in the pleasure of comforting her, I spoke in an absent-minded croon. "Everything's going to be all right," I repeated in one way or another until she relaxed in my arms and closed her eyes.

How, when did the benign arms of a friend turn into a slow, stealthy lover's embrace? Too late I was aware of holding her body closer to mine, of leaning over her face so low I could feel the sudden flutter of long lashes as she opened her eyes, the warm breath of the mouth I seemed bent on—

"Anna? I'm here. Anybody home?"

I had completely forgotten about Alex. Startled, roused from that daze, I dropped my arms, hardly daring to look at Clotilde, and yet what a sweet grave smile she gave me.

"Gina? Where is everybody?"

"In here, Alex."

I was on my feet and away from the sofa only seconds before he poked his head into the sitting room, though from his look, the quick shadings of surprise, conjecture, and, yes, understanding, I needn't have bothered.

"Oh, sorry. The front door was open, so I came right in. Don't let me interrupt," he said, backing off again.

"You're not interrupting. Come join us." I spoke softly, but it was a harsh gesture that beckoned him, harsh enough to succeed in wiping that fatherly, discreet, ridiculous smile off his face.

"I believe you remember Sister Clotilde."

"Yes, certainly, I do," Alex said, loping across the room to take her hand. "I'm very glad to see you again, Sister."

And in the same respectful tone to me: "There's really no need to break up your visit. We can easily put off this thing at Cinecittà until tomorrow."

"Please. Don't change your plans on my account," Clotilde told him. "I came quite unexpectedly, for a few moments only, and I must go now."

How quick Alex was to pick up a scent. "Nothing wrong at the Villa, I hope, Sister?"

Startled, she bent her head in confusion. "No. That is, no longer. One of my patients, a young boy Anna knows, has suffered something of a setback."

"I'm sorry to hear it. This wouldn't be the little artist?"

"Luca, yes," she murmured.

"That's too bad. I hope you'll tell me, or Anna, if there's anything I can do to help."

"Thank you, Signor Sareuth. You're very kind."

So he was. And if I hadn't suspected him of some peculiar sort of collusion, I'd have admitted he behaved with all the friendliness, compassion, and generosity I loved him for.

"The cost of medicine being what it is these days, I imagine Luca's funds might need replenishing," Alex said. "But perhaps that's a discussion for another time. If you really must leave now, Sister, then at least let us give you a ride. The convent's right on our way."

"Oh, I don't think so. Thank you very much, but it isn't necessary."

To tell the truth, I didn't much care for the idea either, but Alex's brand of insistence was too gentle not to win out, and in the end the three of us drove up to the convent together in his white Mercedes.

Well, not quite the three of us. I kept leaving the back seat of the car to return to my sitting room, wondering if I had given any real comfort to Clotilde, wishing Alex hadn't arrived at that precise moment, thinking, oh, but what a good thing he did!

"Anna? You're so quiet back there. Did you hear what Sister Clotilde was saying about the Swedish research center? It might be a possibility for Luca later on."

"Yes, it sounds promising."

Loving, tyrannical Luca with that tender and how rightly cynical mouth, what would he do without Clotilde?

And I? What would I do, if it came to that? Had I really been fool enough to put our friendship in such jeopardy? I saw myself holding her again, surprised at the suppleness of that heavily clad body, at the furtive, amorous intentions of my own. Did she realize how close I came to kissing her, my trusting friend whose eyes opened at that moment with a look of such innocent yearning?

But she whose childhood solace had been found on the stiff bibs of the Sisters of the Sacred Heart, she who had never known the embrace of a friend or lover, how could she discern the fine, arbitrary line that separates the two?

"Well, here we are," Alex was saying. "May we take the car right in through the gate, Sister?"

We, indeed. Alert now, I sat on the edge of the back seat as Alex drove up the circular driveway to the convent, wondering what I should say to Clotilde and whether I'd have a chance to say anything at all.

"Thank you so much, Signor Sareuth."

"I'm very pleased we met again. Wait, Sister, let me open the door for you."

But I was already out of the car. "I'll walk her to the entrance," I told Alex, determined to say my good-bye in the privacy of the outdoors.

"I'm glad you came to see me," I told her as we went up the path, "and I hope there's good news from Luca soon."

"Yes, I, too. Until Thursday then, Anna?" she asked, her eyes clinging to mine for a moment.

"Why, of course, my dear. Two o'clock as usual." I in turn gave Clotilde's customary response, her quick, reassuring smile. A reversal of farewells that made me feel proud, and anxious for the long week to pass so that I could make good my promise to her.

"Come in, Miss Stewart," said Sister Bernadette when finally I presented myself at the convent door.

"Sister Clotilde has been detained, but if you wish to wait?"

"Yes, I'll wait."

A month of Thursdays had passed since I last entered that hilltop sanctuary, and I followed Sister Bernadette through the halls, breathing in peace, filling my eyes with tranquillity, marveling at the soothing, sensual look of the marble.

"*Bonsoir, madame.*"

"*Bonsoir,*" I murmured, exchanging nods with the white-robed nuns gliding swiftly by. I might have been returned to the company of angels, so light and high did I feel.

"The reception room, Miss Stewart."

"Thank you, Sister," I said with an enthusiasm that caused my owlish guide to blink.

But I had missed that narrow room, too. More precisely, the pleasure of anticipating Clotilde's entrance, her way of arriving in a sudden swirl of veil and skirts.

"Hello, Anna," she said. "I'm afraid I didn't leave the Villa quite on time today."

This familiar greeting and a single glance at my friend's luminous face told me everything was back to normal.

"How have you been? All has gone well with you, I hope?"

she asked, taking the chair on the other side of the table. "Did you have a good week?"

I replied with a dumb nod. These were the very questions I had been waiting to ask her, and yet I said nothing, worried lest they sound too direct a reference to a visit with me she may have forgotten or repented of. The truth is, I felt shy, thrown slightly off balance to see all that holy equanimity restored.

"I do believe the Villa is having a summer season like the rest of Rome. There were two new patients to admit. That's why I'm late. Both are tourists, and I'm happy to say there's nothing really wrong with either one except too much sightseeing.

"What I'm most anxious to tell you, though, is that we've received an encouraging report about Luca. His progress is slow, of course, but the sisters there say he's in fine spirits, and that is most essential to his recovery."

"I'm so glad."

"I knew you would be. God bless that boy. He has come through his new trial undaunted. What a lesson it teaches us in accepting all that concerns the will of our Lord."

She gave me a thoughtful look, and I waited for her to continue. It was a path strewn with just such homilies that used to lead us right up to the gates of His Kingdom and Simon.

But "It's much too nice a day for the reception room," she murmured. "Shall we go outside?" And, as we walked into the garden: "Such a pretty sight. We are fortunate that so many of the flowers Guido planted are already in bloom."

There was no doubt about it. Clotilde was her serene, radiant, and inscrutable self again.

"This afternoon we have a church group visiting us from Dieppe," she said with a nod toward the palm trees where a dozen women sat meditating over their maps and guidebooks.

"A perfect summer's day for them."

"Perfect." I felt disinclined to talk. It was enough for me to bask in that glow of hers as we crossed the grounds the long way about, walking with slow, well-matched strides alongside the convent wall.

"But where is that lovely fragrance coming from?" And as we stopped to trace a light, sweet scent to a row of yellow blossoms perched like new chicks in the crevices of the stone wall, she said, "I often think His most precious gifts are these small, unexpected ones."

I speak of basking in her serenity, and yet as we sat together on our bench I was aware of a certain undercurrent beneath the calm. Had it always been there, the slight *frisson* that whirled around me, cool and delicious as an eddy in a warm bay? It made me recall what I had promised myself to forget—how near, alarmingly near, I'd been to kissing that tender mouth.

"You're quiet today, Anna."

"Am I?"

And if I were quieter than usual, she, for her part, was downright garrulous. I could hardly keep up with the accounts of community decisions that followed: how the chapel was to be painted, a new cook found to help Sister Andrea, and the vacation schedule for the third-floor nurses changed.

It occurred to me that perhaps this easy sisterly flow was the result of our last meeting, of another grief shared and a bond thereby strengthened. Why, then, did I feel a moment's sadness, a loneliness, as though in being closer I was more conscious of . . . of exactly what? A gulf still unbridged and unbridgeable, an imprecise yearning, an unknown desideratum. But what was she saying? I had missed it completely.

"So, because we three are no longer going to Germany, I shall take my holiday sooner. That way, I'll be back before Sister Cecile leaves, and we won't risk being short of staff."

"You're not traveling in Germany at all then?"

"No, but it doesn't matter. Now I shall have more time to spend with my brother and his wife in Honfleur. What about your plans, Anna? Are they settled?"

"Pretty much. I leave for Switzerland in about three weeks, just in time to help Lisi pack up her knapsack for India."

"Will she be there long?"

"If Augustus decides to stay into the fall, I expect she will, too. David's travel book seems to have started the family caravan rolling again."

"And you?" Clotilde glanced up, her head at an angle that displayed to perfection a clean, broad sweep of jaw, an elegant precision, a line as delicate as it was strong. "Are you planning to join the caravan?"

"Not this time. I've more or less promised Alex not to wander away until the filming's over."

"Yes, of course," she murmured. "And how's the work going? You haven't mentioned the *Princess* once today."

"Probably because I have a whole new scene to write. Alex decided to show Christina nursing Garibaldi's men during the siege of Rome."

"Oh? I didn't know she was also a nurse."

"Indeed she was. 'Nothing is more pleasant than to attend the sick, for in the sickroom one is sure of doing good.' "

"She said that? Well, yes, it's certainly true."

"In this scene she's been working without sleep for three days. Her only respite is when some friends make their way through a street battle—Garibaldi has just encountered a French regiment—to a confectionary shop on Via Condotti and take her an ice cream."

"An ice cream?"

"It was summer."

"I see. Of course."

Her thoughts were no more on this conversation than mine, and I'd have given a lot to know what she was thinking then. How deeply I gazed into her eyes, trying to find their meaning, not realizing it was implicit in their steadfastness, in their willing acceptance of my search.

I carried that image away from the convent with me, and,

reluctant to lose it in the back of a jolting taxi, decided to walk along the hilly streets for a while. It was late afternoon by then, and the sun reflecting on the domes of the city below created a multiplicity of sunsets.

So absorbed was I in the view and in my thoughts that I nearly walked right by Eleonora without noticing her. But it was too unlikely a sight to register. What reason had I to suppose that the woman who was emerging from a shabby apartment house, who was being so affectionately escorted to a taxi by a dark, heavyset young man was Eleonora?

If she hadn't seen me, hadn't attracted my attention with the despairing flurry that sent him back into the building, I'd have gone right by, never realizing that the woman whose head had been thrown back in laughter, whose hand so heartily clutched her companion's behind was the sensitive, languid poet I knew. Or thought I knew.

So he was her "translator," that big, good-natured-looking fellow stuffed into a tight jersey; he was the "dentist" she hated leaving her country nest for.

"Anna!"

I walked over to the curb where she was standing with one hand on the taxi door. "Why, Eleonora!" I cried in the same pleased tone.

"But what on earth are you doing here?" she demanded. A healthy instinct made that quick offensive move; for she, poor woman, looked too rattled to have thought of it herself.

"I was visiting a friend." And if I hadn't noticed Eleonora leaving her unlikely rendezvous, wasn't it because I'd just come from an even unlikelier one?

"Let me give you a lift."

"Thanks, but it's such a nice day I thought I'd walk back," I said, anxious to get away for both our sakes.

"Walk back? That's ridiculous. It's miles. Come on, I'll take you home." She got into the cab, holding the door open for me, and, when I still hesitated, "I must talk to you, Anna," she said in a lower, more urgent voice. "I know you saw him with me."

"Please, Eleonora, there's no need for another word," said I, begging to be spared the confidences of that—that mock turtle-dove.

But my surprising friend grabbed my arm and with an iron grip pulled me into the back seat.

"*Avanti!*" she told the driver, and when the taxi had leaped forward, "There," she said, turning her face to me slowly, defiantly, as though it, too, were a secret to be bared. "Now we can talk."

The trace of powder remaining on her cheeks was not nearly enough to cover their high excitement. A loosened chignon had allowed two dark curls to fall into slender, wistful sideburns, and the mascara streaked beneath her eyes only made them seem larger, darker. In other words, I was gazing upon a face whose artful beauty love-making had at once ruined and improved.

"For heaven's sake, Anna, don't just sit there staring. Go on, say something."

"We're friends. Why bother saying anything at all?"

"There's no use pretending you didn't see him. I want to explain."

"You don't owe me any explanation."

"Pah, I know that," she said with the impatient gesture my prim little protest deserved. "But if you're my friend, don't you owe me the courtesy of listening? He's got nothing to do with Richard and me. That's what I want to tell you."

"I understand."

"There's more than that to understand," said the determined confessor. "He's simply a convenience. Why, I hardly know him. He may have been my lover these two years but, I assure you, I'm as ignorant of him as Richard is."

"You don't have to say another word. I'm convinced."

And I did believe that fierce, touching exaggeration. But I

had heard enough, and I turned away to look out the window, wanting to learn nothing more about the devoted couple I had so envied.

"I hope you haven't got the wrong idea. He isn't a gigolo."

"No, I didn't think he was." As if that robust farm boy could be mistaken for anybody's fancy man.

"In fact, even though he can't afford it, he insists on acting the perfect gentleman. *Che bella figura!* He never lets me pay for my cabs, and each time I go to his room I find flowers and a bottle of champagne."

There was no stopping her. "Oh, so you drink champagne," I murmured absently, scarcely expecting a reminiscent cat to look at me with that slow, satisfied smile.

"Well, no, we don't exactly drink it."

"Oh, Eleonora! At least spare me the details."

My outburst brought no more than a moment's silence and a reproachful: "But, Anna, without details a picture can only be seen, not felt. Richard always says that. It's the painter speaking, of course, but doesn't it make sense for us all?"

I gave her the compunctious nod she had counted on. "Of course it does."

" 'I have been faithful to thee, Cynara! in my fashion.' There's the truth. We adore each other, Richard and I, but for a long time now he hasn't been able to— We haven't had a real marriage in that sense for years. And so I maintain myself"—it's exactly how she expressed it, that wise, practical poet—"I make sure that I remain in bloom, a desired and desirable woman who perfectly satisfies the eye of the man she loves."

This time my compunction, the warmth of the hand that reached out to take hold of hers, was genuine.

"Funny our meeting today, isn't it, *cara?*" she said with a regretful, resigned smile, "I never thought I'd see anybody I knew up there. I've always been so very discreet. Richard knows nothing, you understand, absolutely nothing."

What I understood was that proud, helpless, loving way he

looked at her, loving enough to allow her, to encourage her, to believe in his ignorance.

"But what a fast drive. Here's your corner already, Anna."

And there on my corner is where the trouble began, for I carried away a souvenir of my ride with Eleonora. Doubt left the taxi with me, an ugly flaccid frog squatting in the palm of my hand, breathing in and breathing out uncertainty. Although inspired by Richard and Eleonora, it no longer had anything to do with them. What did the latter reveal about her marriage, after all, but a devotion more profound than I had imagined?

No, this doubt of mine was, or pretended to be, a more general thing. The sort of flouncing rhetorical apprehension that wags its head and wrings its hands over the Bal Masque.

How deceptive appearances are, it sighs, how little do we ever know of one another. What do we see or hear except what the other wishes or what we ourselves wish? Having got through that set piece very nicely, it then turned on me and plunged like a dagger to the heart of the matter, showing itself for the intensely personal misgiving it really was.

"Unresolved" was the epitaph my unknown party guest had put on Simon and me, and how right she was, and how it rankled. Would we still be together if he had lived? For that matter, were we ever together in the way I thought? Or were we, too, not quite what we seemed, not altogether true to appearances?

Those recollections of Simon that came barging, self-confident and devastating, into my mind, was it safe to believe them? How true were they? If the moment's perception was questionable, what dissimulation was memory not capable of?

"We'll have to come back to Cornwall every year, Anna," he said. "We'll celebrate our anniversary right here in this same frumpy room. What do you think?"

I thought, I hoped, Simon was referring to a wedding anniversary. But had that free-spirited, unfettered man whose eyes were as blue and then again as green, as evasive a color as the Cornish sea, ever made a serious reference to marriage?

"Tickets for the theater? What, tonight? Oh, bother! I completely forgot. Sorry, my love, but I promise once the concerto's finished you shall have your choice of amusements. We could even get married if you like.

"Provided I've got enough money to buy a new pair of shoes. Have you ever noticed what incredibly shiny new shoes people get married in? I must say I've never understood why," Simon had said, spinning around on his piano stool to give me a quick leer. "I should have thought shoes were the very last thing one wanted on a honeymoon. But then, if it turned into a real issue, I mean if spanking new shoes are totally *de rigueur*, you'd treat me to a pair, wouldn't you, my beautiful, bountiful lady?"

Like most of Simon's jests, it was half in earnest. Nor did I ever know whether it was caring so little about money, or too much, that enabled him to accept it from others—his parents, his manager, me—with what he, frank and unperturbed, called a lavish hand.

This uncertainty led the way to a more disturbing one: my own attitude about money. What about the pricks of discomfort that bounty of mine caused? The suspicion that it was what Simon most liked about me; the worry that once the money from *The Blue Room* was gone, the small income Matthew had left me might be endangered. Oh, far better to be a generous taker than a secretly begrudging giver.

One hour, two hours, I lost track of how long I sat in Simon's room entertaining doubt, circling around the structure of our life together, tapping it here and there for a weakness, a hollow sound.

"*Eccola!* I've been looking everywhere for you," Gina said, bursting into the room. "*Ma che fai?* It's pitch-black in here. You can't even see the delicious *aperitivo* I brought you."

"I don't have to."

"You'd better drink it. Dinner's going to be late. I'm still waiting for the butcher's boy to bring the veal."

"It doesn't matter, Gina. I'm not hungry tonight. I think I'll skip dinner."

"Oh, and what am I supposed to do? Send the veal back to the butcher? Do you know what's wrong with you? You're overworked. Here, drink up," she said, handing me the inevitable Sicilian orange juice. "Go on, drink it," she ordered and stood with arms akimbo, watching until I raised the glass of red pulpy juice to my lips.

Simon used to loathe this maternal offering. "No, none for me. Wouldn't you think Gina could remember that by now?" Offended, he sat hunched over his piano, making irritable notations on a sheet of music. "Tell her I'm allergic. I probably am. And why, Anna, must she make such a ceremony of it? You'd think she was serving up Christ's blood with a bit of ice.

"Now do you want to hear this or not? First we have the oboes, the clarinets, and then." Those graceful hands spread their fingers and flew along the keyboard in an ardent, a lyrical—

"A really quite brilliant passage," Simon said.

"I'd have said it for you, you know, if you could have waited a second longer."

"Now was that one of your ladylike digs by any chance? Well, it's no use, my darling. You'll never convert me to anything as self-indulgent as modesty. There isn't an instinct more unnatural to mankind than modesty. Or to the animal kingdom, come to think of it," Simon said, showing me his crooked smile with its crooked teeth. So boyish and puckish a smile. Or was it simply feral?

And who but an irresponsible, fickle man, a tergiversator of the first order would have such mobile features, so many swift expressions, so many shades of blue to the eye. Inconstant Simon, I watched you leaving me to follow the pipers. I saw you from the window, walking away with that sturdy solid grace, the toes of your canvas shoes pointed outward and your head tilted, listening, listening. Oh, what cruel idiotic thing did you do, you foolish dreamy savage!

He turned the corner and vanished, again, and I called a halt to my wild thoughts. Surely the memories springing from a survivor's outrage could be trusted least of all? Exhausted, shaken, I answered Gina's summons to dinner, sat down obediently, wordlessly, to a plate of veal, and went to bed directly afterward.

Sleep came quickly, but it brought neither peace nor oblivion. My mind had no intention of being got rid of so easily, and hardly stopping to bother with the niceties of distortion, it took me right back to a perfectly recognizable Cornwall, to a high windy cliff above the sea.

Simon, wearing a cape that flapped like great wings, was some distance ahead of me, walking close, much too close, to the edge of the cliff.

"Wait, Simon," I called, running after him, but on he went, never turning around to me, his head now lowered against the wind, now facing out to the sea.

"Simon," I called, "Simon!" When at last he stopped and turned around, it wasn't Simon at all, but a pale, beautiful Clotilde in her nurse's cape who stood on the cliff's edge smiling at me. I hurried toward those outstretched arms, but before I was halfway there I realized it was I, ubiquitary dreamer, who stood on the precipice holding out my arms to her.

I woke in the morning with a dull headache and a decision to go to Switzerland at once, without seeing my friend again. Gina must be right. I was overworked, overwrought. I would finish the work on my desk and catch a plane on Tuesday.

Fearful of Alex's questions and, worse, his knowing smiles, I marched into his office and gave my notice in a firm, flat voice.

"I'll have the new scene done before I go. After that, Alex, even you will have to admit the script is finished." I walked over to the window and looked down on the green leafy trees along the Tiber, the better to lie. "I've already got my ticket, so there's no point in trying to talk me out of leaving."

He came to the window. "Anna." With a gentle hand he turned my head around and gave me a searching gaze I was hard put to meet. Yet all that unpredictable man said was: "I wouldn't dream of trying. It's quite a good idea, in fact."

Saturday evening I delivered the last revision and spent an hour drinking tea with Alex and Sofia at the latter's kitchen table. Sunday I said good-bye to Margot who was herself getting ready for a tour in Australia. Monday morning I discussed household matters with Gina. In the afternoon I packed my suitcase for Switzerland, a methodical job that included a careful selection of the books I meant to read while sitting on the sunny green slope at the back of the chalet. In other words, this was no slapdash flight. For the first time in many months I knew what I was doing and proceeded about my business in an orderly, reasonable fashion.

Even where Clotilde was concerned. Monday night, according to schedule, I sat at the pretty white ecritoire in my bedroom—why, when I'd never penned a letter there before?—to write her. But what, now that I came down to it, was I to say? I could tell her I was leaving sooner because I needed a rest, but could I confess my hope that the mountain air would clear my head of its confused dreams? And how to explain this cowardly note, the fact that I daren't see her before I leave for fear that I wouldn't then go?

In the end I tore up a half-written letter, decided there was no harm in saying an ordinary good-bye on the telephone, and rehearsed it so thoroughly that when Clotilde came on the line I rattled off my speech without a pause for breath.

"A nice long holiday will do you good," she murmured when I had done.

"Yes, I'm sure of it."

"Well, Anna. Thank you for calling. I shall say good-bye now and Godspeed."

"Wait, Clotilde. Since your holiday plans have changed, too—If you'd like to, before you go on to Honfleur, well, Lisi and I would be very happy if you came to stay with us."

There was a silence on the other end of the line. Did that awkward outburst surprise her as much as it did me? Was she smiling or was her look contemplative? All I knew for certain was the relief I felt when quietly and simply she said yes, accepting the invitation with far more ease and grace than it had been given.

A fortnight later Clotilde and my mother and I were sitting in the kitchen at the back of the chalet. Lisi's parlor, my brothers had dubbed it, and, true enough, one could hardly find the sink for all the bookcases and plants, the Etruscan vases and bark-cloth drawings from Colombia.

"Look at those alps," Lisi said. "It's extraordinary how they seem to change shape in the evening."

Supper had been a simple meal of sausages and *rostli* provided by the hasty, part-time Thea, and now we three sat around the huge window, watching the mountains that had turned indigo yet still lingered one shade beyond the dusk.

"Wouldn't you like a pillow for your chair, Sister?"

Clotilde, sitting in the rocker next to me, wore a blue serge habit that made her look like a schoolgirl in long skirts. "But she's so young and pretty," my mother had whispered the night she arrived.

"This is fine, thank you. I was just thinking how much I'm reminded of our convent in Normandy."

"Are you?" said the startled Lisi.

"It's the smell of the herbs." My friend glanced up from her sewing with a gracious smile that reached out to include me in the conversation.

She couldn't have been more at ease in our home circle. "Why don't you let me hem that for you, Mrs. Stewart?" she had said. "My hands have been idle too long." And there she sat chatting and stitching away at my mother's new khaki-colored traveling skirt, while I, overcome with the camaraderie she inspired in me, had never felt so unsociable.

"Oh, the herbs. My cousin Sofia brought those plants from her garden in Rome. Did you ever see such a giant rosemary? Thea says the air's gone quite sharp with it."

"For me it's a sweet fragrance. When I worked in our community as a young girl, it was one of my chores to help gather herbs. Thyme and hyssop and angelica and, oh, many more, for the medicines the sisters made."

"Imagine being taught an art like that in our age. What a fascinating education for a child," Lisi said, appraising, absorbing Clotilde with her wide, eager smile.

She was remarkably unchanged, my mother, as though in rushing around the world she had only brushed against time, accidental encounters that did no more than scatter white hairs through that tawny mane and soften a contour of cheek.

"Anna dear, do you remember the Benedictine monastery we visited in Normandy? It was still famous for a medicine the monks had brewed in the sixteenth century."

"I remember you told us it was famous for getting the patients drunk."

Clotilde gave her soft laugh. "I'm sure our remedies were never so potent as theirs."

The alpine air could be congratulated for the color in that white translucent skin, as delicate a pink as gleamed through marble. And the blue habit I wasn't yet accustomed to, mightn't it also be responsible for a difference in tone?

I dared not look at her long enough to decide and turned once again to appeal to the old cuckoo clock above the kitchen table, urging it on to the hour when I would be alone with my friend.

"Then your interest in medicine started when you were very young?"

"Oh, indeed yes."

Lisi the wayfarer, explorer of unknown landscapes, with what pleasure did she sniff at the rare blossom I had invited into her own backyard.

And did it discomfort Clotilde? Why, not in the least. She sat there serene as ever, her amazing needle darting and leaping through Lisi's hem like a tiny minnow.

"The women in active orders have always taken such a lot upon themselves." Wherever was it going now, my mother's musing? "One does wonder why, having in all likelihood turned from a similar role in society, they were then content to accept so domestic a position in the hierarchy of the church."

"Our desire and our purpose has always been to love and serve God."

How many such simple, sturdy, glowing explanations had I myself earned.

"But isn't it easier to accomplish your goals now that the church is more lenient toward its women?"

"It's a good thing, yes, that we're no longer too isolated from the world." Clotilde's response came in a slow, pensive voice. "Having greater freedom has naturally given us more ways to do His work. And I believe it has shown us," she added more slowly yet, "that walls do not necessarily fortify our faith, or keep those who wish to from following their religious path outside the community."

Certain she was thinking of Sister Marie, I half expected to hear that name murmured. But "How wonderful to lift one's eyes to such enduring beauty," she said, looking up at the window again.

"I knew this was the house for us the moment I saw that vista," Lisi told her. "There's really something quite magical about it, especially on a summer's evening."

And I, who used to think the same, who only the week before had called the gradual disappearance of alps into black velvet a stunning entertainment, now yawned with impatience, as though at the work of an inept conjurer.

"Tired, dear? I shouldn't wonder with all the hiking you two did today. Well, it's nearly nine o'clock."

"That late already? Is it really?" said I, feigning surprise, a stretch of arms, a reluctance to get up from the armchair, everything but my smile of relief.

This announcement was what I'd been waiting for. In another minute that rambunctious, profoundly silly cuckoo clock would, to my infinite gratitude, verify the curfew, the hour when

Lisi turned to her journal writing and Clotilde and I, following the custom set long ago by the children of the house, would go upstairs to drink hot chocolate by the fire in my bedroom. Clotilde's bedroom, I should say, for she was staying in it that week.

A maze of wooden rafters, abruptly pitched corners and windows at jaunty angles, my bedroom had that air of haphazard invention peculiar to some dormer rooms. As for the furnishings, the lumpish bed and the thick slab of a desk, they were more rustic yet.

Why, then, did I insist on our guest staying there while I moved to Augustus's room on the floor below? At the time I thought it was simply to provide her with a kind of retreat. My room was at the very top of the chalet and to crown its privacy had an ornamented balcony, a wooden diadem that sat in the air as purely aloof as the white peaks in the distance.

"It gets so cool at night" Clotilde said at the end of the cuckoo's ninth call.

"Chilly enough for a fire, I'd say, wouldn't you?"

An expression as wistful as it was reserved crossed her face, such a funny, endearing look. "I think so, yes," she murmured, returning needle, thread, and thimble to their basket. "Why don't I light it when I go up?"

"Good idea, and I'll make us something hot to drink."

This exchange, like our nightly chores, had already put its tender roots in the nine o'clock tradition. So, too, the way she waited for me in the bedroom, sitting on the bench by the hearth with a large white shawl over her habit.

"Oh, Anna, you're here. Please, come in." Her casual tone did not conceal a certain shyness, a momentary confusion. "Let me help with the tray."

And when we had settled by the fire with our heavy sweet chocolate and the plate of biscuits neither of us ever touched:

"I still feel bad," she said, "taking your room from you."

"But you mustn't. I wanted you to have it."

It gave me a peculiar feeling, though, I admit, to glimpse the medical journal on my desk, the plain sky-blue slippers by the closet, her small white Bible and thin spiritual book on the bedside table. Not because her imprint on my room was alien but because it seemed so light, so evanescent.

"I tried to describe the view from the balcony when I wrote to Luca yesterday. But one really needs his brush to do justice to this magnificent scenery."

"I'm betting on that boy. Someday he'll come here and paint it."

She herself was an exquisite black-and-white drawing in the firelight, her brow and long slender throat a pale ivory, those thickly lashed dark eyes and the border of hair beneath her veil drawn in with the softest charcoal.

"I pray for the day he can enjoy such a walk as we had this afternoon."

We had gone to fetch the cheese Lisi regularly bought from one of Thea's uncles. An isolated farm it was, high in the green hills where the only sound was an occasional cowbell.

"I've never seen anything so beautiful." Clotilde had stopped in the middle of a sunny meadow, arms outstretched to the hills and the mountains beyond them. "Just look, Anna."

I was looking, all right, but at her. At lips that were the fresh pink of the alpine rose, at small even teeth that gleamed, white and moist, in the sunlight.

Such moments stayed with me, discrete and enduring, while the days of the week dissolved one into another like rings of water. Twice Clotilde went to mass with Thea in Zellen, an hour's drive away. The other mornings she would return to her room after breakfast for several hours of meditation and study. And I, jumping up from the table, would announce to Lisi:

"This would be the perfect time to straighten out David's closet." Or "Don't you want to clean the attic before your trip?" I suggested one day.

"Not really, dear," replied my mother, giving me a baffled look.

As well she might. Before Clotilde came to stay with us I had done nothing more energetic of a morning than carry Chateaubriand's memoirs out into the garden. Now I performed the most trumped-up task to make waiting for her less acute, and was overjoyed should any legitimate business happen to come along. I even welcomed an hour's conversation with Alice, who telephoned one day from the Bella Vista offices to read me the list of historical inaccuracies she had culled from the last revisions.

"What do you think of that?" Alex said when at last she put him on the phone. "We're going to end up with an annotated screenplay no less. Very classy. So, my sweet, having a good holiday?"

"Except for the last hour, it's been marvelous."

"I hear Rosten's a popular place this summer. Sofia tells me the sister is planning a visit there."

"News travels slowly." My tone, like his, was excessively light. Had we ever engaged in a more curious badinage? "Clotilde arrived several days ago."

I could picture my lanky friend pacing across the office as we spoke, his silver head bent over the telephone receiver in a way that prevented me, thank heavens, from seeing his expression as he said:

"Did she? She's actually there now? Well, well. Be sure to give her my regards."

With an admirable, indeed palpable, restraint, Alex then changed the subject. Was Lisi packed up yet? Had Alice told me the shooting would definitely begin in mid-September? Did I know a prestigious American magazine was doing an interview with La Antonelli, and would I speak to the journalist when I got back next week?

Fine and, you know her, she never packs until the last minute, and, oh, good, and good again, and certainly I would. For my part I made the proper responses and even came up with a few pertinent questions of my own, but all the while I was listening for the sound of Clotilde's soft step.

"Hello. Here you are. Ready to go?" I said as soon as she came downstairs. "Where shall it be? Would you like to visit the abbey in Wurstenburg today?"

"Very much," was the reply that lit her face. "And could we then go to the lake your mother mentioned?"

"There might be just enough time," I said, glancing at the clock, the sun, the calendar. I was always measuring and weighing time now, so precious had it become to me, while she scarcely ever consulted that large nurse's watch of hers.

"We could take along the cheese sandwiches Thea left us and eat them on the way to the lake."

"Is it very far? Shall we go up in the *funiculaire?*" Clotilde asked, her eyes shining.

"No, it's not that high. Still, it's a pretty good climb." I hesitated, as I had each day before we set out, then finally took the awkward plunge. "There's a lot of climbing gear in my closet that you're welcome to. That is, if—"

Gently she finished my stammering thought. "Yes, we're permitted holiday clothes. But I'm quite comfortable like this." Giving me one of those quick broad smiles, she put a sandwich and apple into the pocket of her habit. Rosary, Bible, jackknife, pen, notebook—what a collection it held. "Today we shall eat like the shepherds. Like I used to do on the dairy farm."

She had never been more appealing, this long-legged country girl I had first glimpsed striding down the hospital corridor, and, thinking it was safe to be with her under Lisi's roof, vague as to my actual meaning, I took full pleasure in her company again.

"I know the ideal place for our picnic," I told her. "Augustus found it one summer. There's a waterfall and sometimes a family of deer will come along."

Shall we go here or there, see this or that? We talked to each other like a pair of daily trippers, and yet our kinship—what else to call so sisterly a bond?—deepened each day. Blessed with perfect weather, as she said, we were always out of doors. If we didn't take long walks in the mountains, then we traveled around one of the larger lakes in a paddle steamer or spent the afternoon in a nearby market town sitting in the sun and sharing a basket of wild strawberries as we listened to the village band.

But all this pastoral simplicity is deceptive. Determined to capture one truth, I let escape another. Our homespun activity was, in fact, anything but plain and straightforward. Beneath that calm was the uncertain expectation of passionate friends, a light-headed, giddy tension apt to break loose at the slightest provocation.

One evening, when my mother was showing Clotilde photographs of her young nomads, the latter gave a surprising giggle at the sight of a tall, skinny girl whose gawkiness was topped by, flourished into, a black Cossack's cap. "Oh, Anna, is that really you?" she said with the tender incredulity one expresses on meeting an intimate's younger self.

Another night, when the three of us were sitting in the kitchen over an informal fondue of cheese and white wine, Clotilde's bread fell from its long fork into the communal pot. Trying to retrieve that crust, my own fork encountered hers. "*Pardon!*" I cried, drawing back with a nervous laugh, oddly thrilled, as if it had been our limbs touching in that warm bed of molten cheese.

Saturday caught me unawares. Despite my careful, indeed penurious, spending of the hours, we had come to the end of the week. What muddled feelings I had that afternoon as we walked in the mountains. Stricken at the thought of parting with Clotilde on Monday, I was at the same time beginning to look forward to having the visit safely over. Relieved that I wasn't alone with her on those secluded alpine trails, I resented the group of grinning French schoolboys who kept stopping to pass the time of day with the pretty sister in blue.

"Shall we take back some flowers?" I don't recall whether it was Clotilde or I who first saw the yellow iris growing in such profusion, with such graceful abandon by a stream, but it was that discovery which led us off our track and into a small dim forest.

"I love this smell," I said, quickly picking up a handful of pine needles, as though seeking in their piquancy an antidote to those sensitive, trusting irises.

"A strong, clean scent, isn't it?" Clotilde's head was bent over the needles I held in my palm, but her brown eyes, warm and enigmatic, were gazing up into mine.

"It's very quiet here," she said.

It was altogether too quiet, too clandestine, this shelter of tall pines that housed only the two of us.

"We seem to have lost the others."

"Or ourselves."

Her murmur was as vague and inattentive as mine. But those dark eyes, what were they saying as we stood together, so still, separated by only a handful of pungent needles? Was she, too, recalling the time I held her in my arms, our faces close together, my mouth drawn to hers as it would be again if I moved my head a fraction . . . a single, subtle centimeter . . .

"Do you hear that?"

I gave a guilty start at the rustling behind us. "One of our fellow climbers, probably."

"Yes, one who goes right up the tree," Clotilde said, laughing as she pointed to a stocky, red-coated squirrel with an impertinent stare.

Was it the hushed atmosphere in that high-domed, green-lit cathedral of a forest that made our laughter sound so intemperate, so very giddy?

"We should start back. It's getting late." I turned away from her and with a virtuous, regretful sigh led the way out of the woods. "Augustus and David raced home from here once."

"My gracious, did they?" Clotilde's tone was polite and submissive as she followed the change of direction, of conversation.

But when we came in sight of the steep green slopes: "Why don't we have a race," she said.

"What, all the way home?" I was taken aback, not so much at the suggestion as by her challenging smile.

"It isn't very far." She was already gathering up her long skirt; quickly, deftly folding and pinning it—pins, too, in that infinite pocket?—around a white petticoat.

"Well? Are you ready?" she said, and plunged down the hill, running swiftly ahead of me, her veil flying, her legs in their white lisle stockings as long and shapely as I had imagined.

What did Lisi think when we arrived home panting, flushed, exhilarated, and laughing again?

"You both must have really needed this holiday. You're blooming in the mountain air, just blooming, the pair of you."

"We raced home." Never in my girlhood had I felt as tentative, jubilant, coltish in front of my mother as I did now, a woman grown.

"You know, the fact that I'm leaving on Monday is no reason you two should," she said. "Alex can certainly spare you another week, don't you think, dear? And perhaps Clotilde won't have to hurry on to Honfleur.

"Stay another week?"

"Oh, that's very kind."

"A marvelous idea, in fact."

"Such a long holiday in the mountains. It's a wonderful gift."

"One does feel so healthy here."

We were speaking at the same time—reprieved, grateful, reckless remarks addressed not to Lisi but to each other.

Late Monday afternoon I drove my mother to the Zurich airport, and while we waited for her flight to be announced we had a nostalgic terminus tea, an overcooked, elated meal. My high spirits I judged to be vicarious, reflecting nothing more than Lisi's joy of departure. Why then, after she left, did my heart continue to soar, to reach new heights as I started homeward? Because that elation came, it seemed, from quite another source: from a realization that I was soon to be alone in the chalet with Clotilde.

Rosten was a two-hour drive from Zurich, but thoughts of my friend—the way her eyes held mine when I left, such an embracive look, as though I were the one setting out for Calcutta—took me over the alpine roads at so abstracted, parlous a speed that I got back earlier than I expected.

The downstairs was quiet and dimly lit, though it wasn't yet nine-thirty. Well, Thea would have long since given our guest her supper and gone dashing down into the valley. As for Clotilde, I had seen her lights on from the driveway. Perhaps it was still early enough for the fireside ritual.

"Hello, I'm home," I called upstairs, and going straight to the kitchen I prepared our nightly tray and rushed up to the third floor with it.

"Hot chocolate time." It was an intrusion worthy of the headlong Thea, the way I barged into the bedroom, still in my jacket, both hands steadying the tray while an expeditious hip pushed open the door.

"Oh!" Clotilde cried.

She was not, as I had unreasonably supposed, sitting on the usual bench at the usual hour. No, that flustered cry came from the hearth, from a molting swan. Downy white shawl, habit, petticoat already shed, she stood in front of the fire clad only in her black tennis shoes, those lisle stockings, a pair of white knee-length drawers, and a long-sleeved vest. And pinned to it, a tender blue glimmer in the firelight, wasn't that the childhood medal she had won from the Sisters of the Sacred Heart?

"Why, Anna." Swiftly she raised her shawl. "You're back so early. I didn't hear you come home."

"I'm sorry." I was just as embarrassed as Clotilde, and yet I neither left the room nor averted my gaze.

"Did your mother get off all right?" Her voice, discomposed and muffled, came from under the large nightgown she was pulling on while still holding the shawl—a magical feat of propriety—in front of her vest and knickers.

But I hadn't been staring at those provocatively stern underclothes. No, my gaze was riveted to her unveiled head, to that naked undulating auburn hair. Shorn in uneven layers that accented the waves, it was darker than I had thought and not quite as short.

"Oh," she said again, a dismayed hand reaching up to her hair to shield it from my eyes.

That gesture of modesty, chagrin and vanity, that single movement, it alone defeated me.

"My darling," I murmured, depositing the tray of chocolate and oat cakes—had I really been foolishly holding it aloft all this time?—on the table.

Wait, Anna, think, I warned myself. What's folly for you is far worse for her. Think what you're doing. But this desire was no more capable of reasoning than any other, and I took off my jacket and put it on the bench.

Clotilde, standing with such grace in that white flannel tent of a nightgown, said nothing; simply watched me coming toward her with eyes that were huge and black in the firelight.

It's not too late to stop, to turn around, to leave the room. Take care, that prudent voice spoke out a final time. But we shared the same pounding, agitated heart, my censorious self and I. Furthermore, as well she knew, her cautionary cries were by their very nature too late, for they were nothing more, those thrilling alarms, than a slightly disguised expression of the same yearning, the same amorous excitement.

Clotilde's mouth, softer than I had imagined, was waiting for mine. Gently, briefly, we kissed, and I removed my lips to her cheek—skin that looked pale and cool but was warm to the touch—only for the pleasure of returning to that soft clinging mouth again.

She sighed and closed her eyes while her body, trembling beneath its protective layers of flannel and jersey, moved closer, revealing to me the slope of a high breast, a firm thigh I recognized as the twin of my own.

But what was she thinking, she with her warm breath quickening into gasps of oh and ah while those profound brown eyes remained silent, shut away behind heavy lids.

With the furtive hand of one whose hostess has absented herself, I reached out to touch the arch of a delicate eyebrow, a loose wave of hair, and returned to her lips again, to a kiss that suddenly turned willful, intractable, went its own way with an intensity that left me as surprised and shaken as Clotilde.

"Anna," she said, pronouncing my name slowly, as though for the first time. Her eyes were open now and, like her voice, held a comprehension, a pained joy that weakened me the more.

"Shall we go down to my room?" I could hardly hear myself.

"This is your room," she murmured with a faint smile. "Stay."

What a lesson I learned that night in love and desire and possession. It amazed me, in fact shocked me, to find that lissom body so familiar, our embrace so natural. But then, wasn't this the refuge, the real sanctuary I'd been running to since Simon's death? Hadn't Clotilde's world and mine, such forceful opposites, been moving steadily toward just this collision, I gravitating to her ethereal calm, she pulled earthward.

I don't know the words chaste enough, potent enough to describe the intoxicating mixture of her purity and passion. The soft, tremulous kisses fluttering down on my face like a deluge of petals, the frank haste with which she lay her naked body next to mine, adjusted those satin-covered curves to my own, and yet contrived to stay hidden beneath the bedclothes.

Shadowy, vague blue veins leading to the center of a perfect breast, the slow smooth inclination of a marble hip, a cache of that auburn hair curling lightly between her thighs—only this much beauty did I glimpse as my hands and mouth sought the rest.

"No . . . wait . . . ah . . . yes."

"My darling, my heart, my own." Such were the covetous replies I made to her uncertain moans, to a sudden frenzy of anxious, demanding, grateful kisses.

"Anna!" Her long white neck was flung back, abandoned in pleasure, and I, how proud I was to hear that exultant call.

"I love you."

She, resting her head on my breast, repeated the phrase after me with an easy ardor. "I love you."

Too easy, as if it were a liturgical refrain, and like any new lover I regretted its familiarity, wished for a different, worthier set of words, an exclusive phrase better suited to this tender passion.

"Comfortable?' I shifted my limbs under Clotilde's weight but not in search of comfort. No; I moved for the sly pleasure of feeling her body move with mine, the sensation of being covered with this other luxurious skin, the subtle realignment of her cheek to my breast.

"Your hair is the richest color." I smoothed the shingled hair on her nape, and winding one strand around my finger briefly wore a gleaming auburn ringlet.

"No treasure would shine more in the firelight," I murmured, and doting on her shy beauty waited to see those long feathery eyelashes brush my skin in a bashful, delicious response.

"Thea certainly knows how to build a roaring-good fire."

Out they popped, one remark after another, and yet it was no desire to converse that prompted them. Involuntary sighs, that's all they were, irrepressible expressions of the contentment that filled me; filled, by the look of it, my rustic bedroom. It had never seemed so charming a haven; the squat stone fireplace and the bedside lamp had never combined to give the walls such a peaceful, rosy glow.

"We forgot the chocolate," I said, glancing across the room to the tray I had left on the table so long ago.

"Are you thirsty?"

"No." I had, in fact, a terrible thirst, but I was far too content and lazy to get up, too unwilling to relinquish the warm, supple body in my arms.

"You're sure?" Clotilde spoke without moving from her resting place.

She didn't stir, no, but her murmurs, her breath moving lightly across my breast was as provocative as any caress and left in its wake a trail of surprised, stippled skin. How addictive this passion was, an appetite that increased with appeasement.

"The chocolate must be cold by now." Propped on one elbow, Clotilde was whispering over the nipple she had roused like a curious, wondering child attempting to coax a bud into flower. A maternal child, who, glancing up then with a serious mien, took me into her arms.

"My dear," I recognized that gentle term but not the husky intonation or the luscious mouth ready to quench the thirst that appeared, after all, to be only for her.

"Oh, Anna." Those strong hands whose roughened skin smelled faintly of carbolic soap were making the same loving promises. Soothing, inflammable caresses they were, given with the generous candor of the innocent. Caresses that brought me a sensual pleasure so exalted and pure it seemed somehow— dare I tell her?—sanctified.

"Clotilde," I began as we rested side by side.

"Dearest?"

But not knowing how to express that grateful blasphemy I merely said: "I think I'll go and fetch the tray."

We might have been stopping for one of our mountain picnics, the ravenous way we sat in the middle of my old bed with the tray between us.

"Isn't this refreshing," she said, spooning up the dense chocolate from the bottom of her cup.

"Delectable."

It was true. Nothing could have tasted better than that sickeningly sweet, disgustingly cold drink and those harsh, grainy oat cakes.

"I was hungrier than I knew." Clotilde's shawl slid down the graceful slope of one shoulder as she leaned over to put her cup on the tray.

Auburn waves falling over a high white brow, a warm gleam on the nose that descended in so straight, classical a line below it, flushed cheeks—how disarray improved a statue's perfection.

"Oh, my goodness, quarter past two!" She had picked up her nurse's watch from the bedside table and was giving me such a shocked look that I burst out laughing.

"I remember the first time I heard you laugh." Eyes cast down, she readjusted her white shawl, spreading it wider with arms raised like downy wings. "I thought it was the prettiest sound," she murmured, and only then at this confession, this intimacy, did the bold, timorous angel give way to a deep blush.

To say we fell asleep in each other's arms is too simple, too austere a description, for ours was the entwined, meandering repose of a pair of vines. The exquisite ledge of her jaw gave shelter to my forehead, and my hair covered her shoulder. While my leg draped itself across her thigh, her slender foot curved around my ankle, and her arm encircled my waist as mine curled around her neck.

It was the absence of this tendrillike embrace, an awareness of a chilly space between us that woke me early in the morning. So early I could see nothing through the dormer window but a leaden dawn, an unappetizing wedge of leftover night. I shivered, missing midnight's warm glow, and Clotilde.

At some point in our sleep she had left my arms to revert to a more familiar position, to return to Him. Lying on her back, arms crossed over her chest, she might have been in her own chaste bed or in that first narrow orphanage cot. It made my heart wince to see that beautifully composed, lonely figure in the pale light. Or was it my own sudden loneliness that prompted me to lean over and kiss those pious, passionate hands?

"It's twenty-five minutes after nine," Thea said, coming out to the porch several hours later.

"I'm sure it is."

"The sister still hasn't come down for breakfast."

"So I gather," I replied, refusing to glance up from the newspaper I held as my shield. This was the third time Thea had come dashing out to me with her fat ginger curls bobbing all over her head.

"But she will want her breakfast this morning?"

"Of course. Why wouldn't she?"

"There's no reason to snap at me, *Fräulein.*"

Oh, wasn't there? Let her poke her head over my newspaper again and I'd bite off one of those sausage curls.

"It's the wash. I have to leave early today, and I want to start the wash."

"Start whatever you like. I'll see to the sister's breakfast."

"*Danke, Fräulein.*"

"*Bitte sehr.*"

But where on earth was Clotilde? What was keeping her? I was getting so anxious I'd read the same paragraph twice over without making head or tail of it.

"The sister's usually at the table eight o'clock prompt. I hope she's feeling all right. Should I go upstairs and give her a call?"

"No. I'm sure she's fine. Well? I thought you were dying to start the wash? Go ahead. Don't worry. She'll be down soon."

And if she wasn't, what would I do then? But why such a bother over someone sleeping late. That's probably all there was to it. She fell asleep again after I left. Ah, but what would she feel when she woke in the clear light of day? What would she think this morning of the tumbled eiderdown, the crushed pillow that still held my scent? What would she say when we met each other face to face today?

"Good morning, Anna! Isn't it a beautiful day? I'm sorry to be so late for breakfast." Clotilde had come out to the porch swiftly, softly and with a bright smile, just as always.

Well, not quite as always. Instead of her habit she was wearing my old green corduroy trousers with a yellow sweater and a kerchief to cover her hair.

"As you see, I've accepted your kind offer of mountain garb."

"I'm glad."

I was flabbergasted, in fact. I felt touched, culpable, vaguely narcissistic, and proud. In short, it threw me into the happiest of confusions to see her wearing my clothes.

"They're a good fit."

"Yes? Do you think so? Thank you. It's a generous loan. Sister Agnes bought an outfit like this for her holiday in the Dolomite country last summer."

Clotilde's murmurs were shy, her manner as polite as ever. "Today's trek sounded like such a long one, I thought it wise to be more appropriately dressed."

"Very wise for that climb, yes."

She continued to stand near the door, coming no closer to me, nor did I move toward her. But just as my eyes were embracing the figure revealed clearly for the first time, the gently rounded hips and the long tapering line of legs, so did her gaze caress my face, linger on my mouth.

Our encounter had been far briefer than I expected. An ascetic breakfast of tea and dry toast, a smiling nod, and, like any other morning, Clotilde was gone again, returned to the solitude of the third floor while I sat on behind my newspaper, dreaming of the night before and the afternoon ahead.

We went high into the mountains that day, taking a *Luftseilbahn* that delighted Clotilde, to a remote lake town. A medieval Christmas card, Lisi called this wooden village whose extravagantly carved and richly colored houses circled a deep blue lake.

"It's very lovely."

"Yes, but wait" was my smug counsel. "Wait until we've climbed higher," I said, and led Clotilde by the hand along the rocky track, through the woods, and up into the alpine pastures above it.

"There!" With a triumphant gesture I spread out before her a vast meadow of wild flowers, an inundation of violets, ane- mones, and roses, a carpet of scarlet poppies, yellow lilies, and gentians that were a stunning blue.

"They're extraordinary," she sighed. "Breath-taking. All the brighter and more glorious for being up here, closer to Him. What gifts of beauty He gives."

And I, hearing those rapturous murmurs, felt a prick of dis- appointment. With a lover's generosity, a lover's vanity, I thought it was I who had given her that brilliant tapestry.

"Anna, look." Was it because she saw my discreditable pang that she reached out then for my hand? "Up there, look," she said, directing my gaze to the stout-legged goat in a shaggy white coat standing apart from its fellows on the slope above us.

"Do you see her?" she asked, smiling broadly. "That goat is the image of Dominique, who was my special charge at the farm. It was to keep her company, you know, that they hired me from the orphanage."

"Surely not."

"Oh, yes. They bought her because she was a prize goat who gave over four quarts of milk a day. But not, it transpired, when she was left alone. She had got used to being with people, you see. So, that was my job. I would sit beside Dominique while she grazed and talk to her until the milk came."

"That was your job? Sitting all day with a goat?" I was ap- palled and yet, like Clotilde, I had begun to laugh. "And what did you talk about, you and Dominique?"

"Oh, my goodness, anything I could think of. I told her the clover she ate was the symbol of the Blessed Trinity and that the donkey in the next field was the animal who carried our Lord into Jerusalem. Then, there were the stories Sister Agnes told us at the home. About the saints and angels, and the conversion of atheists."

Clotilde swept me a look with her long dark lashes, a look of rare mischief, and laughed again. She was utterly charming, the young shepherdess I glimpsed that afternoon, as vivid in those green trousers and yellow sweater as the lilies we walked among.

"I also told her how often the goat is mentioned in the Bible. It's true, my dear Anna. Why, Job's goats were so strong they could carry bears on their horns."

"And was Dominique impressed by the brawn of her ancestors?"

"Ah, no. That sort of thing didn't much impress my she-goat."

Such a laughing spell took us then, such a giddiness seized us that we laughed ourselves into tears, a sweet senseless sound I now recognized as the laughter of Aphrodite.

Was it love, that inarticulate joy, that tender bond, I asked myself, and replied with the dreamy reflections of any lover, answers as commonplace as the question.

Clotilde's arms kept me safe as a child, and had she been my daughter I couldn't have felt more protective of her. Looking at my friend, watching for a certain turn of profile, a flash of those dark ardent eyes gave me the greatest pleasure, and should she happen to lower the full voluptuous lids that were more naked, more revealing than any glance, I went quite weak with desire.

My one wish was that we could linger on in Rosten exactly as we were. The idea of separating from her shocked me as much as our becoming lovers once had. What would happen to us after this week? What were we going to do next? I had no idea. If the promises we exchanged in a glance or embrace were mute, no less so were those in our conversation.

"Perhaps Luca can come here for a visit next summer."

"Oh, Anna, wouldn't that be wonderful?"

Or "There's such a great need for nurses in West Africa, especially in the bush country. Have you ever been there, Anna?"

"No, but I would like to go, very much."

And "What is New York like?"

"Very tall and busy."

"Sister Bernadette has a cousin who lives on the Hudson River, I believe. It sounded pretty."

That was as far as our elliptic wishes, our hesitant little forages into the future ever went. But it hardly mattered. The net of serenity Clotilde cast about me was so secure I felt we had more than enough days ahead to sort things out. Time, in a generous mood for once, wasn't rushing us at all. While she stayed upstairs in those morning hours reserved for study and reflection, I sat in Lisi's kitchen armchair and dreamed up our day's outing.

A net of serenity I said she cast, but a spell is more like it. I had never seen her so radiant as those afternoons when she emerged from her third-floor retreat to wander over the countryside with me, a quaint worldling in an ancient lavender chiffon dress she had found in the back of my closet.

"Everything sparkles so here, Anna. The water as much as the sun." We had stopped to sit beside a mountain stream that day. "If you watch for the fish, you'll see how they, too, are sparkling." But I was watching eyes that were far more lustrous than anything they beheld. And on another afternoon, when we had gone into the hills to pick berries and discovered instead a wood filled with honeysuckle: "Shall we have our picnic here, Anna?" she asked with a smile that lit up the small dim wood. "I've never smelled anything so sweet in my life."

We took to going farther afield, staying out longer each day for the delight of returning to an empty house, a cold supper of beef and cheese tarts left by Thea, and a bed sweetened with the scent of the honeysuckle that still clung to us.

"A healthy outdoor life certainly tires one out."

"I, too, am tired this evening."

"I suppose it comes from all the walking."

"And the mountain air, also."

"Shall we go to bed, then?"

Upstairs in our bedroom, for so I now thought of it, my methodical undressing couldn't have seemed slower, or clumsier, compared to the swift, amazing modesty that moved Clotilde out of her clothes and into a tent of bedcovers without exposing as much as a small rounded knee.

Yes, I knew exactly the shape of that unseen knee. My hands traveling nightly over a beloved landscape of gentle curves and plateaus saw it all with an avid clarity; the tender hollow at the base of a long elegant back, the smooth, firm buttocks, tapering upward to form an inverted heart of alabaster.

"Ah, no," she whispered in my ear, scandalized, when I told her so.

And not having the audacity to praise her further, I gave myself up to a silent joyful passion that brought a contentment too deep, in fact, for words. Side by side, her leg and mine joined at the hip as though to their rightful mate, we rested on the brink of sleep.

"Me, in my glass, I call thee—" Drowsing off, I tried to collect the lines of Donne's poem that were straying through my mind. "Hand to strange hand, lip to lip none denies / Why should they breast to breast or thigh to thighs." Half asleep I reached for the elusive stanzas but what I heard was a harsh loving caw from Simon.

"How can I kiss you when you've got a mouth full of poesy?" he said to me from the tumbled depths of another bed.

Oh, Simon, so mirthful, so princely and impatient, what are you doing here?

"A pretty bedtime recitation, love," he said, bending over me again. "And now that you have the sanction of the poets, can we get on with it?"

Time did pass, however kindly its intentions seemed. The end of the week came and with it a battery of disturbed thoughts that forced their way up through my sleep and attacked just before dawn.

Wishing to protect Clotilde from my unrest I left the bed, settled a log on the fire and myself close to it. How soundly she slept, how peacefully, she who regularly left me in the small hours to return to her Bridegroom. Like that other dawn, the sight of her reverential sleep, those well-shaped hands with their blunt nails crossed over her chest, made me vaguely sad. Or was jealous closer to the truth?

What would happen to us when we left Rosten? Surely we could no longer content ourselves with gazing at each other across the convent's reception-room table. What then? A room in one of those shabby villas near Monte Sacre where in the rush of dusk we would bump into Eleonora and her young man? Or would we travel together on Clotilde's summer holiday—the Nun and the Nomad. And where on earth would so Chaucerian a pair go. . . .

These were the questions that continued to come, the doubts that chased themselves around in my head. And what was going on in her head? What reflections did she have here in the room we shared? That she adored Him I knew, but did she still consider herself His bride now that she was my mistress? Was it herself she was thinking of and not just Marie when she spoke of those who followed their religious paths outside the community? But a divorce from Christ. Could she ever be content with the love of a mere human after that? Adoring the God who invented vice and virtue, how long would she tolerate the love of a heathen, a woman who couldn't always distinguish between the two?

Grown chilly with these thoughts, I moved closer to the fire. It now seemed extraordinary to me that the end of the week was upon us and we hadn't yet discussed our situation. Enigmatic Clotilde, what had she been thinking? Was it her politesse, her sensitivity that kept her from speaking of our future until I spoke? Had I been waiting for the same reason, or had I unconsciously been avoiding a discussion? I couldn't picture us apart, true, but was I any more imaginative when it came to our being together? Too cowardly to look at what was behind me, did I also lack the courage to look ahead? Tomorrow we must talk.

"Anna."

How long had she been awake, watching me? "Couldn't you sleep? Come." She sat up, holding her arms out to me with the most compassionate expression, the sweetest of smiles. "Come back to bed, darling."

She had never been so tender. My darling, my own—those loving phrases she spoke for the first time were the ones I had whispered to her each night.

"It's all right, go to sleep now," she murmured, soothing away my frenzied thoughts and doubts with leisurely caresses, with languorous kisses that grew heated and wild, and which I, never so passionate, proudly tamed.

In the morning I drove Thea to the marketplace in the next village, and we returned about noon. I had thought Clotilde would be downstairs by then, and when she still hadn't appeared by one, I went up to the third floor.

The letter she left me was on the desk. No, it wasn't a letter. It was hardly a note, only a few uneven lines on a single sheet of notepaper, words fallen to the page like incoherent sighs.

"It's time now for me to go. I am sure this is how it's meant to be. Forgive me for leaving like this, but it is for the best. Never doubt my love for you. I am not going to Honfleur but to the home convent for now. May God bless you and keep you."

Well, I didn't believe a word of it. I ran through the house like a crazy thing looking for her. And when it was clear that she was really gone, I searched all the harder, though I scarcely knew what for. Another note, perhaps, a memento, a keepsake she had left behind, an amulet. How eagerly, foolishly I examined every table, dashed back upstairs on absurdly feeble legs to search my desk again and the bedside table for the gleam of a blue religious medal.

"Did you lose something, *Fräulein?*"

Thea, in her apron and hat, was following me from room to room, picking up after my unhinged limbs, my shattered heart.

"Is there something you want before I go?"

"No, thanks. It's nothing. You go ahead. Oh, and by the way, Sister Clotilde had to leave rather unexpectedly. You might as well take a few days off, since it's only me here now."

With Thea safely out of the way, I felt I would be able to— to what? I was, in fact, able to do nothing but sit and stare at the floor or out the window. It didn't matter where, because what I saw, in an agony of regrets, was myself getting out of bed to sit by the hearth and Clotilde, awake and watchful, reading each uncertainty that crossed my mind in the firelight.

It was the only explanation for her going off like this. Her generosity, the grace that always placed others first would have kept her from saying a word. Only that infinitely tender, fervently silent good-bye. Where was she now, how far had she got, and what would I do without her. Did the sight of those doubts marching across my face incite her own. Is that what sent her so quickly back to the convent. What would happen when she got there. And what must she be feeling now, my pale beauty in her blue habit, alone, lost somewhere between heaven and earth. But I wasn't going to sit here and let her go. How could I? I'd catch a train, a plane.

The telephone rang then, and, certain it was Clotilde, I raced to it with a wild heart. "Well, well. You're all out of breath," a cheerful, curious Alex told me. He had thought I'd be back by now, he said, and what about Clotilde? When were we leaving Rosten? I gave him the minimum amount of truth. I said she had gone on to Normandy and, as for me, I'd be back in Rome sometime soon. He could hardly hear me, he complained, and cunningly I said nothing. I allowed him to think the connection was broken and went to sit again in my chair, for by now I realized there could be another explanation. Perhaps Clotilde had always meant to leave me at the end of this week. Perhaps she hadn't spoken about the future because, wiser in the ways of the world than I imagined, wiser than I, she knew that our separation was as inevitable as the love that had brought us together. Or was this version only a balm for my guilt, something to ease the pain and make me feel worse.

I stayed on in Rosten another ten days, still hoping to hear from Clotilde, unable in any case to pull myself together and leave. She had, quite simply, become essential to me, and I missed her in a total, desperate way, was haunted by the sight and sound of her. When I walked in the hills I'd see her, a graceful country girl kneeling to pick wild flowers, her hair gleaming, a rich dark red in the sun. And at night when I lay in bed I would hear her sighs, her sweet moans. Envisioning her shut away in an unknown convent, alone, holy and contrite in an austere room, her veiled head bent in sorrow and repentence, I yearned all the more, with love's irrationality, to hold and comfort her.

It might have been an illness, a long–lasting fever I suffered from, so aimless and weak did I feel, so slow was I to stir myself. Surprised at such debility, I tried to take myself in hand and like an obedient convalescent sat in the garden with the glasses of *Alpenmilch* I advised myself to drink. Eat that sauerkraut with sausages; it's good, it will pep you up, I told myself. Try to read. And, that's better, I said, feeling that considerable progress had been made when I could concentrate on a printed page.

One afternoon, toward dusk, I came home from a lonely walk in the hills to find Alex waiting in the kitchen.

"You're just in time for tea," he greeted me, and I flew into his arms as thankfully as ever I had done in my childhood.

"How did you get here?" I said. "When did you get here?"

"Just an hour ago." It was he who withdrew from the embrace first, and, giving me a paternal, tobacco-flavored peck on the cheek, he led me over to the sofa.

"So? How are you, my girl?"

"Fine, perfectly fine."

His response was a long, doubtful, kind look; a look that invited me to tell him what he already knew.

"How's Sofia? She didn't come along?" I asked, changing the subject I feared he might begin.

"No, I'm on my own. Just passing through."

"Passing through Rosten? Where to, the Splugen Pass?"

He smiled. "In fact, Paris. As soon as Ugo found out Antonelli had a television show to do there, he said let's shoot what we can while somebody else is paying her expenses."

"Considerate as ever."

"He and Alice found a nice squalid flat for the beginning of the Princess's exile. We've only to do what Cristina did, paint *La Princesse Malheureuse* over the door, and move in."

"I thought we had decided to leave the sign out. You're as bad as Lisi. You believe every bit of nineteenth-century gossip you hear."

"Come along then and keep an eye on me. I do need you, you know."

Did that beguiling smile belong to my seductive producer or my dear silver-haired old friend? But what did it matter? I wasn't ready to leave Rosten, not yet.

"Well?"

"I can't, Alex."

"Why not?"

I said the first thing that came to mind. "I only have country things with me. I don't have clothes for Paris."

"Oh, yes, clothes. I thought that might be the case, and so I took the liberty of asking Gina to pack some for you."

"You didn't! That's too much of a liberty, even for you." I said, outraged, and grateful.

11

Alex and I were married four months later, on a clear, sunny November day. A day I remember as being extremely bright, without a cloud to soften or disguise a remorseless brilliance. The wedding, conducted by a Roman magistrate on Capitoline Hill, took place in an office that had the gold and crimson trappings of a throne room. Two sentinels in dress uniform stood at the door, the usher wore a black frock coat that was so distinguished, so venerable it looked quite capable of performing the duties on its own, and the official who married us was girded by a sash of his country's colors. In short, that legendary little hill, that theatrical "golden capitol" gave our simple civil ceremony all the pomp and splendor we had thought to avoid.

"A very slap-up office," remarked Sofia.

She and Ugo were our witnesses, and they were standing with us at the back of the chamber while we waited our turn to go before the magistrate.

"Let's hope they don't drag things out," Ugo said. "If we miss the afternoon flight it will be Friday before we're back on location."

It was his anxiety to rejoin the production company in the lake district, his rabid thoughtfulness that had got us to Campidoglio with corsages and boutonnieres, a bottle of champagne, the rings, the documents bearing an incredible number of ministerial stamps . . . and an hour to spare.

"What, we're too early? But how can that be?" cried Ugo when we arrived to find the majestic desk unoccupied, the guards still in their shirt sleeves, and the telephone on the clerk's table ignored, drowned out by a recording from *La Traviata.*

"We have different music for the wedding. This is just for us," a kindly guard explained.

"You can sit down and wait for the other couple to get here," the usher said, "or return later, whichever you prefer."

Our party had come rushing up Michelangelo's glorious ramp not only too early for our own wedding, it appeared, but the one scheduled to precede it.

"Aren't they a little young for marriage?" Alex was saying as now, finally, we watched that first ceremony from behind a row of potted azaleas.

Pink cheeks, long black hair, a filmy white dress and new satin slippers—she looked like a picture book bride. He, too, was all in white save for a red bow tie and the matching carnation in his lapel.

"She could hardly have waited any longer," Sofia observed, her misty blue eyes betraying a cynic's sentimentality as the pregnant bride rose from her gilded chair, the nosegay she held in front of that billowy dress a decoration, a medallion, a sweet badge of springtime for her swollen belly.

"*Per favore*," the usher whispered to the wedding guests and they, too, stood up to hear the magistrate speak; the bride's family on one side of the room and the groom's on the other. Two complete sets of parents, grandparents, aunts and uncles, sisters and brothers. All of them dressed to the nines, in Sofia's phrase, from the crowns of their extravagant, exultant hats to the gleaming tips of their brand-new shoes.

Those shoes . . . Simon, not even you could have imagined so many shining, sparkling, spousal shoes . . . pair after radiant pair lined up against those crimson walls . . .

"Listen, darling, are you sure my suit looks all right?" asked Alex who far outshone his bride in her simple, schoolgirl's organdy. "The jacket feels too tight."

I gave a proprietory and self-conscious caress to his well tailored shoulder. "It's a perfect fit."

But, "Tell me the truth, Sofia," my nervous, resplendent bridegroom said, turning to his former mistress. "How do I look?"

"How do you look?" Her glance started at the peak of a silver wave, traveled the full length of a lean, youthful frame impeccably draped in a cream-colored suit of raw silk, and ended with the usual amused and proud smile. *"Bello, molto bello!"*

The evening Alex first spoke of marriage I had said: "And—and what about Sofia?"

"Sofia?" His eyes had registered surprise at my shy, pained query. "Why, she'll be pleased as punch. Oh, come now. You know perfectly well it's been years since—" and his words had trailed off, leaving behind the small secretive smile her name always evoked.

"Bravo, the wedding march!" cried Ugo darting in front of me for a better view of the proceedings. "They can't be at it too much longer now."

"Don't you want to sit down, Anna? Maybe come outside for a breath of air?" Alex asked.

"You go," I told him. "I'm fine."

"She's so calm," he said to Sofia.

It's true. I was in the intensely relieved, nearly impassive state of one who has found her destiny written on the most homey, familiar face of all.

"Too calm," Sofia remarked with a look as searching as those I had given her in the past weeks.

Yet no matter how deeply, timorously and, yes, somewhat defiantly—she had chosen to "retire" after all—I searched for signs of regret, I never uncovered more, or less, than the affectionate smile she was giving me now, a smile not unlike the one with which she favored her "other child."

"Look, the witnesses are signing," Alex said. "It will be our turn in a minute."

"You and Alex! What? Can you speak louder?" my mother had exclaimed, her waves of astonishment coming at me across heaven knew how many waterways. "Getting married!"

Well, I too had been astonished when Alex proposed, had sat staring at him, struck quite dumb. "Is it really so shocking a suggestion?" he had said with a wry, tender look that turned my astonishment inward. How blind I was not to have recognized so obvious and logical a fate, not to have realized that my surrogate father had been, as he said, the most patient of lovers.

"Oh, Annie," Lisi sighed, and there followed such a long tactful pause I feared that our connection was broken, that she had gone on drifting down the Punjab.

"Alex is a dear, of course. But the difference in your ages."

"Is there so much of a difference anymore? You forget I'm thirty-one."

"Alex is still nearly twice that, dearest," my mother pointed out after another of those pauses. "Don't you want to take some time to think it through?"

Think? It was the last thing I wanted to do. I was utterly wearied, defeated by thought.

"Hello? Annie? Can you hear me? Why not wait a while, at least until your brothers and I come back. Surely there's no need for this rush."

"Rush?" I repeated on the same note of perplexity, for it now seemed to me that I had been waiting to be with Alex, safe and secure, since my girlhood.

"Ready, Anna?" he asked.

The relatives of the bride and groom—what a sea of happy, bobbing faces—broke into applause as the couple left the chamber; she cradling the municipality's gift of pale, peach-colored gladioli, he looking dazed, his smile, like his red bow tie, just slightly askew.

Ugo turned to us. "Come on, you two."

With the suspended belief, the sense of total unreality that attends our most profound moments I took the royal chair next to Alex, agreed to the marital conditions set forth by the magistrate in his green, red and white cummerbund, and signed my name away at the clerk's desk, suppressing a horrified giggle when the telephone rang and Alex started to reach for it. Golden rings exchanged, I then received my own armload of anemic gladioli.

"And the deed is done," Ugo said, expressing his relief in so oddly Thespian a phrase that we all burst into laughter.

Our honeymoon, for thus did Alex refer to the filming of *The Revolutionary Princess*, began at Lake Maggiore. Cast, crew, friends and relations of both, visiting investors, the "fascinating faces" Alex couldn't resist collecting—we traveled from location to location with an army as dedicated and chaotic as Cristina's own. How my husband thrived on that pandemonium, what a talent he had for turning each daily crisis to an advantage.

"Trouble with the sound recorder? What trouble? The van broke down in the middle of Varese? Oh, Lord. Well, we'll have to dub the lines later.

"No, wait. The whole scene might play better if Cristina doesn't speak at all. If she vents her fury at the errant prince by—wait a second, yes, I've got it!—by methodically undoing his place at the dinner table. By slowly, regally, taking up each knife, spoon and fork. Why, just one of Antonelli's gestures— so grand, so ladylike, so very nearly obscene—will be worth a thousand words. No offense, Anna darling, but you do agree?"

"Completely."

Whether inspired by the affection or defection of her "little donkey"—who could keep track?—Antonelli's performance was never anything short of superb. Such was her involvement with the Risorgimento heroine, so intent was she on the quirks and quiddity of her character, that even when she lost her balance during a boating scene one cold dawn and fell into the lake, she managed to surface with that tragicomic smile of hers intact and a *"Viva Italia!"* that stirred and delighted the crew.

"Stupendo!" cried the director, and turning to his scenarist: "I think we should leave that in, Anna, don't you agree?"

"Absolutely."

Since my job was now pretty much limited to these endorse- ments, I had no qualms about leaving my canvas chair for the more familiar comfort of a green bench. But was Lake Maggiore any more real than the movie set I had left it for?

Palm trees that wave a skittish frond at the white-domed, sober-sided alps . . . tiny islands flowering in mid-lake . . . habit had put a notebook back in my hand. Like a conscientious art student I studied the shores and hinterland; went from one island to another, sketching that ten-layered horticultural confection called Isola Bella or the charming, rather feminine disarray of Isola dei Pescatori whose little esplanade of lime trees still wore last night's fishing nets.

"So you played hookey again this afternoon?" Alex said when I returned to the mainland at the end of one such day. "I hope my child bride isn't getting bored with life on location."

"As though I could ever get bored when you're around."

We were sitting at a lakeside cafe under a sky shot through with pinks and reds, a bravura display put on by a loitering twilight, a youthful evening that refused to sober up and grow dark.

"I wish we had more time, you and I." Alex sighed and leaned back against his chair in a moment of unusual weariness.

"We will once the movie's finished," I said, reaching across the table to put my hand on his.

"Dearest girl." That supple lower lip paused to give me a wistful smile. "It's my age I'm thinking of. Someday in the not too distant future you're going to look across the table and wonder who that old fellow with the rattling teacup is." Alex's voice was teasing, but those green eyes, how solemn they were.

"You an old man? Never," I cried, startled by this rare mood of uncertainty. And pleased, for at such times I could believe that I had married Alex not only for his strength but for the weakness he showed in needing me.

"Why, you, you'll be like a northern twilight. Like this sky, the pink that gradually grows into a deep rose but nothing more serious. The blue that changes only to take on the richness of purple."

I broke off, embarrassed by my lyrical outburst, but not so Alex. With the restored animation, the gratified, flirtatious smile of a vain woman, my husband jumped up from the table.

"Shall we get back to the hotel, darling? What a shame it's only to work. But later on . . . well, you'll see what I've been thinking about all day."

The hotel in question was the Grand Royale which served as headquarters for the production company. It was an elegant old place with formal gardens and a long line of plane trees whose trim expectant air suggested the momentary arrival of the nineteenth-century *beau monde*.

Here, in one of the public rooms, under the remote glitter of a Venetian chandelier, business continued as usual. The next day's scenes were discussed, yesterday's rushes awaited in vain, the forecast of rain agonized over, and blows between the assistant director and the dialogue coach barely averted.

At about ten o'clock when Alex had soothed the last ruffled feather of his crew and cast, when he had escorted Antonelli into an elevator lined in gold moire, when Alice had given him his briefcase and me a baleful "Good night, Mrs. Sareuth," why, then, we left the hotel and drove up into the hills to the second-class *pensione* I called our home.

"My darling girl, are you serious?" Alex had said when I first took him to that Piedmontese farmhouse. "You really prefer this to the Grand Royale?"

"Definitely!"

"What a little snob you are," he murmured, his tone amused and lenient while a dubious eye took in our room—the *letto matrimoniale* that was covered by a thin pink cotton spread, the bare green tile floor, the tall narrow wardrobe with its mirrored door.

"But the view, Alex. Look, you can see all of Lake Maggiore from our window."

"And does this mansion of yours boast a telephone?"

"Why, naturally there's a telephone. Right out here in the

hall. Well, it's a bit dark at the moment. Wait until I find the light switch. There, see, there's the phone, right by the W.C. Oh, look, that dear old dog's come to say hello to us. Hello, old boy! Would you believe he still goes out hunting truffles with *Signore* Abbesi? He said if they find enough tomorrow, he'll stuff a pheasant with them for dinner."

"Clever dog."

"You know what I mean. And on Wednesday they go after hare. *Signore* Abbesi makes the most divine hare stew with pine nuts and raisins. You can't imagine how delicious it is served up with slices of fried polenta and a salad of crisp fennel. Well, the fact is, nothing's really changed since the old days."

"Now I understand. This was one of Lisi's gypsy camps, was it?"

"One of the best. You'll see. Just wait until Friday when you taste a salmon baked in paper so that not one drop of juice gets away. Oh, and there's black rice, too, made with the freshest of squid. And then on Sunday they have a roasted wild boar with chestnuts and red-current jelly."

Unaccustomed to our new intimacy, I praised the elaborate meals of this simple pension, extolled the grapes in the arbor, the shade of the pear trees—too shy to confess that the real virtue of the place was its distance from the rest of the company, that only here could we be alone.

"Well? What do you think? Do you like it? Can we stay?"

"Anna, Anna. Sometimes you really are such a child." This was not, alas, a criticism. Far from it. "Come over here, then, and give your very fond, very foolish husband a proper thanks."

I don't know why it should have surprised me to discover that Alex was as much a director in his home as on the set, bringing to our nuptial bed the same exuberent, devious, inventive skill, the same eye for detail.

"With your hair tumbled over the pillow and your eyes so big, you're like a little girl suddenly waked," he was apt to pause in his lovemaking to say. "You could be twelve years old again."

Or, "My goodness, such a flushed, shy, wild thing. That's the way you looked the first time we met, as though you were half ready to run away. Do you remember that day, when Lisi brought you and the boys to tea?"

And how many times did I hear: "Ah, this is how I love to see you. The picture of a young girl I used to know, a greedy creature who when she had her fill of sweets used to curl up just like that, contented and sleepy."

Flattered at being so thoroughly recalled, I was at the same time embarrassed by such a lascivious memory, jealous of the young girl who had so completely captured the imagination of my lover, and proud and relieved when at last with a sated sigh he'd call me his 'own darling wife.'

"But you're not getting up now?" I invariably asked. "It's so late."

"A quick glance at next week, that's all," he replied one night, reaching to the bedside table for Alice's newest schedule. "Well, well. I see we're going to be in Lake Como on Thursday."

"Are we?"

"Perhaps you and I can sneak away to have dinner alone, just the two of us."

"That would be nice."

"We'll go to Villa d'Este. Did you know the scandalous Queen Caroline once owned it? I wonder if Cristina was ever a guest there."

"Not in this movie," was my drowsy reply. Would my wakeful, untiring husband never turn off the light and let me curl up next to him again?

"Before the queen there was some sultan who took his entire retinue, all his slaves and horses and monkeys and elephants, to Villa d'Este."

"I see what you mean. It sounds just the place for an intimate dinner."

"And before that they say the villa was a nunnery," Alex added in a voice so low and casual it jolted me awake.

"A nunnery?" I sat up, giving him a swift sidelong look as I fussed with the pillows. Was his exceedingly offhand manner due to the schedule he was still reading, or did it mean that my silver fox had seen the envelope with the Sisters of the Divine Grace imprint? "That's what they say about all the villas around here."

Alex glanced up at my own preoccupied murmur. "Why are you frowning?"

"Am I? It must be the light."

That letter, forwarded to me by Gina, was the first word I had had of Clotilde since she left my mother's house. I had been distressed, no, devastated by the silence that was now our only connection, that stretched, taut and painful, between us. Was she all right? Was she safe in her serene world? Would she remember our days in Rosten? These hopeful, sad thoughts had gone unanswered for many weeks.

"I bet it's your nun who's responsible for that faraway look, isn't it?" Alex asked, and ignoring my rude shrug, "You still think about the beautiful Clotilde, hmn, darling?"

It wasn't until the eve of my marriage that I dared break the long silence. Not knowing whether she had returned to Villa Monte Sacre or remained at the convent in Normandy, I wrote to her at both places. But the answer, when it came, was from England.

"Well, there's no reason why you shouldn't think about her. It's perfectly understandable."

What a sense of relief and joy, and loss, I felt at the sight of that envelope with its London postmark. Clotilde's reply was as warm and platitudinous as the letter of condolence she had once written to me, and I was surprised to find myself just as comforted by it. Generously concerned with blessings and good wishes, she mentioned only briefly the news that told me her own hope had been fulfilled. "I remained for some time at the mother house in Normandy. From there I was sent to London to resume my studies in tropical diseases. Perhaps someday soon, if it be God's will, I shall put this knowledge to good use in Africa."

"How strangely quiet my girl is."

Clotilde's precise, flowery script ended as it began, with a phrase of pious warmth. But at the bottom of the page an impulsive hand had once again added a hasty scrawl: "I haven't forgotten you, Anna. I never shall."

I was as quick to respond to this letter as I had been to the first, telling her about our new location, about the morning wind, the *tramontana* that comes down from the mountain, and the *inverna* that blows in later from the plains; filling two pages with chit-chat, with utter trivia—all for the sake of adding my own identical postscript.

"I can only imagine you're thinking about her now."

"I was, yes."

"But it's all right." Alex put his hand beneath my chin, a gentle hand that nonetheless insisted I turn and look at him. "You know I don't mind."

If only he did. I'd prefer his disapproval by far, even his anger to this kindly prurience.

"My darling Anna, the expression in your eyes. Why, I would be quite jealous except—"

"Except?"

He smiled. "I simply mean the love that exists between two women is such a different thing, after all."

"Ah, well, yes."

And lest he detect a similar chauvinism in my answering smile, a certain rue, I put my head down on his shoulder and found at last the slightly hollowed place that was my nightly refuge.

From Lombardy the Bella Vista company moved south to Naples, from there to the rice fields of Princess Cristina's "ciftlik" in Turkey, and then on to the Paris location. In all, it was late March before the filming was done and we were back in Rome.

"*Finalmente!* So you decided to come home, *signora.* It's about time."

Despite the severe pose Gina had struck on greeting me—fists on hips and those short, sturdy legs widespread as a wrestler's—she was grinning from ear to ear.

"You a married woman! *Che bellezza, signora mia!*"

We were in my studio packing up the books I had left behind, a task my old friend seemed scarcely able to keep her mind on.

"And the maestro? How does married life agree with him, *signora?*"

It was appalling, the flush of pleasure my marital status brought to those plump cheeks, the melodious and trimphant *signoras* that rolled off her tongue.

"And what about you? Can't you stand still for one minute and let me have a look at you? Santa Maria, how pale and thin my *signora* is! It must have been a good honeymoon, *e vero?*"

"Shut up, you old busybody, and give me a hand with these books."

"*Si, signora.* Where do the cartons go? To the maestro's apartment? Or have you found a new place to start your married life?"

Her question took me by surprise. "A new place? Why would we want—" and here I stopped, halted by the reedy music of the pipers in the street below.

"*Eh, gia.* You see how long you've been away?" Gina said. "The shepherds are back for Easter."

"Anna, quick, come to the window. Those fantastic pipers are here again," Simon had cried, bursting into my studio. "Bring some coins, will you? I say, what luck. But you never told me they came back at Easter."

"If you ask me, *signora,* we're going to need another six cartons just for the books alone."

"Listen to them," Simon said. "You'd think they were wandering through an enchanted forest. Well, not down Via Corso anyhow."

"Be careful." He had leaned out the window to throw a handful of lire into the street, and I couldn't keep myself from grabbing him around the waist as one might a precipitate child. "Do watch out."

"I shouldn't wonder if there's some real thematic material here," he said, turning round to give me a warm, vague embrace. "But those fellows, they're jolly clever. Imagine getting that haunting tune out of an old stick and a scrappy bagpipe."

"*Signora!* Where are you going?" Gina cried as I rushed from the room.

"To the maestro's."

"But your things," she said, following me down the hall. "We haven't even started the packing."

"I have to leave, Gina. It's late."

"Are you crazy? It's early. You just got here. Oh, look at her go. *Pazzarella!* Don't tell me your're still running like a headless chicken."

Was I? I hadn't thought so, yet I can't deny that I startled myself as well as Gina rushing off like that, dashing anxiously through the narrow back streets that led to Alex's apartment. Not that there was any hope of his being there. Involved now in the editing of *The Revolutionary Princess*, he rarely came home before nine or ten o'clock.

Still, I was content enough to be waiting for him in the familiar disorder of his study. Settled with a book in the corner of a tattered leather couch that reeked of stale cigars, I grew calm again, even amused as I recalled other long-ago afternoons when, with Augustus and David, I had flung myself into this hideaway just as breathlessly.

Fancy Gina thinking I'd want to move to a new flat. Such a notion had never entered my head. Nor had I any desire to "do over" this one, a suggestion of Sofia's which I had declined with a heartiness matched only by my husband's relief. The truth is, this cluttered old place suited us both admirably.

"I thought I might find you tucked away in here," Alex said, waking me with a kiss when he came home that night. "Sorry I'm so late but Ugo had arranged a dinner with some "potential money" as he calls her. In fact, I'm not sure she has any other name."

The night air was still clinging to his coat as indeed was I, sniffing beneath that freshness for a more satisfying breath of his cloying scent.

"My precious girl. You missed me a little, did you? Come, give your faithful, adoring husband another kiss—he deserves it, I assure you—and then we'll go say good night to Sofia."

No, it was not our living quarters alone that remained unchanged. My "faithful, adoring husband" had kept all the habits of his bachelorhood. He was as likely to stay out discussing the next project with this or that actress, or to bring home a hungry flock of sound technicians as to dine with Mrs. Moneybags. And then there were the nightly visits to the apartment upstairs.

"Hullo, what's this?" Sofia opened the door to us, regal and gemutlich with her thick braid hanging down the back of a purple velvet robe.

"Well, I never! Have you two really come to pay a call at this time of night?" she asked, her smile as cheerful and expectant as the kitchen fire she was leading us to, as the whistling tea kettle.

"It's Ugo's fault I'm so late," Alex told her.

"Naturally. What's the brute done now?"

"Don't ask. He dragged me out of the editing room and insisted on my sitting through one of those seven course dinners at Alfredo's."

"The man's unconscionable," Sofia said. "Go make yourself comfortable. I'll get the tea."

"Not another of your terrible brews?" Alex asked with an eager glance at the stove.

"It can only help after a seven course dinner, believe me. Now go and sit by the fire with your wife."

Tie loosened, vest unbuttoned, he fell into the rocker, an obedient silver-haired boy whose rare laughter would soon fill Sofia's kitchen.

"A penny for your thoughts, little cousin," she said.

"Me, I'll have to pay much more, just wait," Alex told her. "I'm sure Anna's hatching another screenplay."

I looked up from the fire in surprise. "Well, you're dead wrong."

"Am I, darling? But you are writing again."

"Yes, a journal of sorts. Though it's none of your business."

His answer to that was a coy, calculating look. "And you don't think it might be at some future time? You don't see a film in it?"

"Not on your life!"

"Alex, behave yourself. Stop teasing the child," Sofia said, and turning that same indulgent smile on me, "Tell me about the plans for the fete, dear heart. Who's coming?"

"It would be much simpler to tell you who isn't," I replied, listing for her the guests she knew all too well. They were interchangeable, the business people Alex entertained on a serious scale once a month. American bankers, Swedish entrepreneurs, German distributors, they approached our ancient Roman corner with the same quick Northern gait, the same apprehensive eye, and a game smile that seemed to say: "We've nothing against the habit of drinking melted pearls, nor will it inconvenience us to find the couches occupied by circus elephants."

"Better add Madame Potential Money to the list," Alex said. "And Ugo is bringing along some embassy people, too."

But a submissive nod and a soft "The more the merrier" was my only response. Anxious to prove myself in the role of Alex's wife, desirous that he should regard me more helpmeet than child, I childishly gritted my teeth, draped myself in hostess gowns not unlike Sofia's, and presided over his Sunday "fetes" with an alarming conviviality.

It was this same wish to make an impression upon my husband's bachelorhood that led me to buy an extensive, indeed unremitting set of flowered baking dishes, frivolous bouquets of pink roses that belied an earnest, prolific state of earthenware.

"Why not leave work early for once," I'd suggest to Alex every so often. "Couldn't you lock your disciples up in the studio tonight and come home alone? If you do, I'll make a special dinner."

"Will you, my darling? A candlelit dinner for the two of us," he would sigh. "If you knew what an appetite the mere thought arouses in me."

At mid-morning I would set out for the market, a red string shopping bag in each hand. Mammoth cheeses, tubs of fish, stalls hung with lambs far too tender for their own good, I browsed among them all. I wandered along banks of chicory, rugula, spinach—an acre of greens brightened by the orange blossoms of the zucchini—and deliberated over the display of olives; light green and dark green olives, pitted and pimien-toed.

"Oh, Anna, really! I've seen women choose emeralds at Bulgari's more quickly." That observation came from Sofia who sometimes accompanied me to the marketplace for "a breath of the real country," and who nearly always ended up sharing the candlelit dinners Alex forgot about.

"Dear little girl, can you forgive me?" he'd say, coming home late with half of Cinecitta behind him. "I forgot. That's the simple truth," he'd say, never more irritating or more appealing than at these moments of public confession. "Shall we get some sandwiches from the bar, or is there enough here to feed our friends?"

Friends? I could see Ugo and Alice in the crowd, and I thought

I recognized a long-haired young gaffer. But did I know the big redhead swathed in harem pants and the very short, bald man who stood at her side like an ivory-headed cane?

"Anna, *chere amie*. So it's really true about you and Alex."

I turned around gratefully at Margot's husky cry. "You're back! How was Australia? When did you get home?"

"Two minutes ago. I simply couldn't believe what I heard. Don't bother unpacking, I told Cathleen. We must go straight over to Alex's and see for ourselves."

"I wish you lots of happiness. He's a handsome devil, your old man. I always thought so," said Cathleen whose flaming cheeks clearly confessed to thoughts of her own old man.

"You could have knocked me over with a feather," Margot was saying. "Really, it's possible to do things a little too *en douce*, you know. When I think how you never let on a thing."

I gave her a welcoming and apologetic embrace. "But there was nothing to let on."

"Do you expect me to believe that? In fact, you never open your mouth wide enough to spit, as they say in my village. All the same, I'm glad for you, darling. And for me, too." Up went that short, impudent chin, on came the urchin's grin. "You've only moved two blocks away from the shops, after all. Now, what about lunch at Giorgio's on Tuesday?"

And so it went. Mornings spent at the desk in the spare room, weekly lunches with Margot, an occasional visit from Eleonora and Richard whose enduring passion for each other still gave me an envious, shameful pang—my life was as unchanged as Alex's. Light and easy Roman days, they drifted along until just before our first anniversary when they came to a sudden, abrupt end.

Sudden I write, abrupt . . . but it was no such thing. Those vigorous words express only the conceit of a memory that wishes for its momentous occasions the dignity and grace of resolution. But the decisions that affect us most profoundly, that cut to our very core, that alter our lives most dramatically, hardly ever present themselves with a great fanfaronade, stand clearly, ceremoniously, illuminated in a moment's revelation. No, rarely do the mind and heart give us so spontaneous and brilliant a collaboration. Instead we discover one day, quite by accident, that reason and emotion have been wandering along the same byways, louche and awkward, out of step, unaware of their consanguinity until their exhausted, surprised embrace at the end of the path.

So it was, more or less, with me. Nor can I say how long that "sudden, abrupt" end was in coming, though I know it was already on its slow, uncertain way the September afternoon I paid a visit to Gina.

"It's cold enough to freeze the balls off a bear," she said. "What's wrong with you, walking around without even a jacket on."

"I haven't been walking around. I was in the park, sunning myself."

"You need more than sunshine in weather like this."

"Don't you ever stop arguing, you old mule?"

I was sitting at the kitchen table, watching, jealously, as she prepared dinner for the new tenants. There was a tantalizing hiss and sputter, an explosive little dialogue, taking place in the iron skillet. I could identify the onions and the less distinctive tomatoes, but what was that elusive spiciness? And the faint sizzling, the aromatic crackling when Gina opened the oven door, did it come from a roasting lamb?

"I see you left your head home today, too. I asked you, do you want to take some cake back for the maestro?"

"Of course I do. He'll love it."

"He's done all right for a man his age, eh?"

"What do you mean?"

Gina glanced up from the bowl of cream she was beating so mercilessly, the corners of her small pink mouth pulled down in a smile. "What do you think I mean? The baby, of course!"

She couldn't have startled me more, and I gaped at her, speechless. I had only found out for certain I was pregnant a few weeks before. "How did you know?"

"What questions you ask, Annabella mia," she said, throwing me a look of loving contempt. "And don't keep your mouth open. It's bad for the baby. Think of it, a *bambino*! I bet the maestro's as puffed up as a rooster."

"Well, you can imagine."

My reply was more than vague, it was downright evasive. Alex had no idea about the baby. Why was I waiting so long to tell him? My initial reason had been sensible enough. I wanted to be sure, but then as soon as I was sure about my pregnancy I began to feel uncertain of Alex. How would he react to the news of his fatherhood? We had never discussed the possibility of our having children. Was it because—oh, here lay the tangled roots of uncertainty—because we were family enough, my paternal husband and I? Troubled by this thought and others that it led me to, I kept silent.

Protective of my secret, savoring it, I stayed very much to myself at this time. Twice a day, I walked up to the Villa Borghese. Not for reasons of health and exercise, but to sit alone in the sun with my hands on a still flat abdomen, amazed to feel the same content, the same sense of fulfillment I had known with Simon.

And now wasn't I getting nearer the truth? An embarrassing truth, even a bizarre one. If I hadn't yet told my husband I was pregnant, it was in part because his child had brought me close to Simon again. Slowed, steadied, indeed grounded by the wonder of the baby, by the intrinsic weight of it, I was no longer in flight from him. And had I not been too cowardly to love a dead man, I'd have understood sooner what Clotilde had so often tried to explain—that the haven I searched for was the very memories I fled. Memories of a gentle blue-eyed savage that I now invited, embraced, freely took pleasure from, and pain.

260

I could see the joy lighting Clotilde's face, the dark glow of her eyes as she read the letter that told her all this. Oh, my beautiful friend, it's with a similar pleasure and pain that I think of you surrounded by your mountains and rain forest, imagine you in your bush clinic, dispensing medicines and, far more healing, the radiant smile that warmed me more than any sun.

Is there no flight long enough, then, no distance great enough; in other words, no cure for love at all? No, though perhaps that realization is the first, not entirely welcome, sign of recovery . . .

Such were my thoughts as I sat in the park. Thoughts that were still only too willing to be distracted by the solemn children gathered around a Punch and Judy show, by the bells on a horse carriage, or a glimpse through the cypress trees of a dusty orange city below. And in this way another two weeks passed before I told Alex about the baby.

But by now I had other things to confide in him as well, such difficult things. How to tell the man I had loved since I was a girl that I had confused my childhood refuge with marriage, my surrogate father with a husband? Could I expect him to understand so seeming a paradox as: now that my flight is over, I must leave, must go forward. On the night of our talk I still hadn't found the right words. Aware now that there could be none, I lingered at the window, opened the shutters wide, and wider yet, straining to see across the red tile roofs, beyond the domes and spires, to the very hills enclosing Rome.

"Hey, it's cold with all that air blowing in here," Alex said.

His last guest had finally gone, and he was sitting on the sofa in a welter of scripts and espresso cups and stale apricot tarts.

"You should put on a shawl if you're going to stay hanging out that window."

"This place can use some fresh air, and no mistake about it," I told him. Yet it was with a kind of nostalgia that I wandered around the sitting room, emptying ashtrays and rescuing wineglasses that had been left high and dry on the bookcase.

"Whew, that was some mob you had tonight. Who was the skinny brunette with all the poodles? Did you get a whiff of the cigar she was smoking? Honestly, it made yours smell like a rose."

"A rose? Really? Well, I'm grateful to her, whoever she was," he murmured. And then, glancing up from the *London Times* somebody had left behind: "What a restless mood my girl's in. Shall we leave the mess and nip upstairs to see your cousin?"

"I'd rather not. Actually, I've been waiting for a chance to— to talk to you."

"Oh?" That long intelligent nose of Alex's twitched with interest. "It's as serious as that, is it? Come sit down, then. Here, beside me. Now, what's it all about?

"Well, my sweet?" He gave me an encouraging smile. "Could this have something to do with a new screenplay, with the so-called journal, maybe?"

And in the end, after days of composing my speech, I blurted out the words of any other pregnant woman. "I'm going to have a baby."

"No—a baby!" Bewilderment, fastidious alarm, uncertain pride—they might have blown in from the window, those expressions crossing his face so swiftly.

"When?"

"March."

"Good lord." He took my hand and put a small awed kiss in the palm of it. "March. Well, *The Revolutionary Princess* should be released by then."

It was, as I had feared, hardly the reaction of a "puffed up rooster."

"When in March?"

"Early, but—"

"Well, that gives us time to get organized. The best maternity clinics are probably in London. I'll get Alice to start checking around."

"Alex, wait—"

"Obviously we'll need more room now, but don't you worry, dearest girl. Just leave everything to me."

"I can't, not anymore."

He didn't hear that, either. But why would he? He had always known it was a father I had run to, a father who had no intention of letting his "dearest girl" grow up. If I had only needed him less, or if he had needed me more . . .

"I'd hate to leave this old flat. Maybe we can turn the guest room into a nursery and the laundry into a room for the nanny. No, I don't think a child will change our life too much."

"But it already has changed things," I said sadly, gratefully, and stopped; fearful of thanking him for this most generous gift of all; this sweet ballast that had enabled me, finally, to slow down, to take a good long look around. "It's the familiar landscape, children, that we need to look at the hardest," Lisi used to tell us.

"You're quite sure about the date? My word, wait until Sofia hears this."

Sofia. How many nights had I watched Alex sprawling in her kitchen rocker, laughing over a game of backgammon, before I came to understand that it was she who was the wife and I the mistress.

"Come along, darling." He was already up from the sofa and on his way to the hall. "Let's go surprise her."

"You surprise her. I have to start packing," I said, flinching at so blunt, so sharp an announcement.

"What?" he asked, but the back of his head and the sudden set of those silvery waves told me this time he had heard.

"I didn't hear you," he said, retracing his steps across the sitting room. "What did you say?"

"It's my fault. I made a mistake." But this wasn't the way I meant to tell him, and my voice quavered, reluctant to continue, yet unable to stop. "I'm leaving. It will be better for all of us this way."

"Have you lost your mind? A minute ago you told me you're pregnant. Now you say you're leaving?"

"Try to understand. You always have before."

"I wasn't married to you before."

"We'll still belong to each other. That can never change."

"And where the devil do you think you're going?"

"To New York. I'll find a place, somewhere near Central Park. That will be best for the baby. I'll go on with my writing, of course. If I run out of money, perhaps I can do some free-lance editing. Oh, Alex darling, don't you see? I've got to start being responsible for myself now, and for the baby . . ."

Accustomed to the wide screen, to the deep, persuasive throbbings of an Antonelli, the perfect shimmering tear of a Margot, Alex listened to my faltering, inexperienced truths with an unconvinced, impatient ear.

"What's wrong with you? Can you hear yourself, Anna? Do you realize what you're saying?"

"I'll bring the baby to visit you and Sofia often. I want him—I feel sure it's a boy—to know you and love you as I do."

"Stop it! That's enough." Alex shouted. "Did you imagine you were playing house and now the game's over? Well, you're wrong, do you hear me!"

Me, hear him? The whole palazzo, the cafe on the corner must have heard this red-faced, explosive Alex I had never seen before.

"You're not leaving. Forget about it. You're not going anywhere."

How I welcomed the stamping foot, the masterful command that reduced my confused emotions to a simple rebellion.

"Oh, yes, I am!" I shouted back, and waited, trembling.

But the hand he raised, the flat, rigid palm was only a brush for his hair.

"Dearest girl, it's only natural that your condition has upset you. And me, too, it seems." With no warning at all, my silver fox had turned tail, was retreating, slinking into charm. "Serious thoughts should never be let into the house at night. They have a way of looming over one. All out of shape and proportion, like shadows.

"Come, darling," he said, holding out his hand to me. "Come to bed. I promise you everything will look different in the morning."

"Will it?" With difficulty I ignored the impulse, the habit of taking that neatly manicured, sweet-scented hand and pressing it against my cheek. "Will everything look different to you in the daylight?"

Alex gave a sigh. "No, I don't suppose it will," he said, and sat down on the sofa next to me, gazing at me for such a long time, so silently, that I scarcely knew what to expect next. Certainly not the familiar:

"How well I remember a young girl with big scared eyes like those and a stubborn mouth that wouldn't give an inch. I do want what's best for her," he said, putting his arm around me, and though I recognized the wiliness behind his liberating embrace, it came closer to keeping me captive than he ever knew.

"Why go so far away, though, why New York?"

I smiled, thinking of that first dinner with Simon. "What's the laundry like in your country?" he asked me.

"You smile, but it's a serious question, New York."

"I suppose I want to go there because it was the starting point," I said, meaning that I wanted to take my son for Sunday afternoon strolls in Central Park as Matthew had once taken me.

"And how long do you think New York will last?" Alex asked. "You do recognize, dearest Anna, certain similarities here? To go off like this, bolting with the child, well, it's just what Lisi and your grandmother did, isn't it?"

I had known that sooner or later we would come to this obvious and troubling question, and I had my explanation ready. I wasn't so much repeating the pattern of those vagabonds, I

265

meant to say, as looking for a way to break it. Why then didn't I speak up and reassure us both? Because I was distracted by a faint breath of excitement, a sudden lift in my spirits.

"Surely they're reason enough to consider this move very carefully."

Was the cool leafy green trail in Central Park only a traveler's mirage? That woman and little boy in a hotel restaurant, he drawing a map on his napkin, she studying a train schedule, was that lonely excited couple my son and I? Possibly. But who can know? Which of us can be certain of his destination before he arrives?

"Chances are, if you leave now, you'll end by following right in Lisi's footsteps."

Dormant for so long, it took me a moment to recognize my vague exhilaration as the curiosity with which I had once watched the turn in the road give way to a new landscape.

"Maybe," I said, ready to claim again the restlessness, the seeking that wanderers call hope.